EAGLETON

CONFIRMED BACHELORS BOOK 6

JENNY HAMBLY

For my dad,
I am so glad you lived to see my success. You will always be in
my thoughts and heart.

CHAPTER 1

Alexander Wraxall, the 6th Marquess of Eagleton, lay with his arms behind his head, staring into the inky darkness. His eyes stung with tiredness, but he refused to allow sleep to claim him. He preferred to contemplate the nothingness surrounding him than suffer the tortuous nightmares that awaited him on the other side of consciousness. There were only two ways to avoid them. One was to drink himself into oblivion, but although he had done this countless times before, that panacea was no longer an option.

A faint, unhappy wail penetrated the thickness of his door. It gradually gathered momentum, becoming increasingly agitated. His lips twisted in a bittersweet smile. His daughter had arrived a month early and had been sickly for weeks after her birth. Any doubt he may have had to her paternity had soon been put to flight. Her green eyes mirrored his own. She had clung to life with tenacity even as her mama had faded. Now, at just five months old, she was motherless and seemed to find nights as difficult as he.

Her wailing did not annoy him; it reassured him. Such lusty cries might proclaim Lady Francesca's dissatisfaction, but they also affirmed her strength of character and healthy lungs. Knowing that her nurse would be unable to pacify her, he threw back the covers and strode to the door. A young woman with a plain face and calm demeanour smiled ruefully as he entered the room opposite his own. She passed him the tightly swaddled bundle in her arms.

"She's been fed and changed, my lord. There's nothing wrong with her but a strong desire to have her own way. You're spoiling her. You'd not hear her cries if you'd only allow me to take her back to the nursery wing. She'd soon wear herself out."

Alexander's sudden frown was not aimed at the nursemaid but at the distant memory of the many occasions he had been left to cry himself to sleep as a small child. It alarmed her no more than his sudden appearance clad only in his nightshirt. She was used to both.

"It costs me nothing, Jane."

The baby's desperate sobs ceased abruptly, and a contented gurgle issued from her tiny mouth.

The maid sighed. "You'll have to break the habit sooner or later, my lord, and the longer you leave it, the harder it will be."

Her eyes grew moist, and she turned away.

"It must be difficult for you to care for my daughter after losing your husband and babe, Jane," he said softly. "Perhaps I should not have asked it of you."

Her shoulders straightened, and she turned back to him. "Nonsense," she said brusquely. "My family owes you a debt."

"There is no debt," he said sharply. "Your grand-mother lost her employment here only because she tried to protect me. It was years before I found her and could make amends."

"There's many as wouldn't have gone to the trou-ble, my lord. Besides, debt or no debt, I needed a purpose, and I have come to love Lady Francesca."

He nodded and carried the baby back to his room. He lay on the bed, removed the tightly wrapped blanket that swaddled her small form, and laid the infant on his chest. She turned her head and wriggled until her cheek found a gap in his nightshirt and rested against his skin. He pulled the cover over them, laid his hand gently on her back and slipped into a dream-less sleep.

He awoke with the dawn. It was not the soft click of his door closing that roused him. Jane always took the baby before she could disturb him. Her considera-tion was misguided, however. The leaden weight that surrounded his heart always returned the moment she lifted Francesca from him. His valet knew it if she did not and had laid out his riding dress. He slipped from the bed and washed, the cold water dispelling any lingering strands of drowsiness. He dressed quickly and carelessly, made his way around the galleried landing, down the impressive sweeping staircase and traversed several rooms and corridors to reach the side door that led to the stables.

Eagleton Priory lay a few miles from Okehamp-ton. Little evidence of the original priory remained, the house having been remodelled several times over the centuries. The result was fractured. The entrance hall and principal rooms were spacious and grand, but in other wings, they were older, smaller, and neglected. There was no heart to the house, no central focus. Alexander had no happy memories that might have instilled in him a fondness for it or a desire to make it a comfortable home.

He had been granted full possession of his estates when he turned twenty-five, thirteen years previously, but until he had married, his visits to his main seat had been infrequent. He preferred Pengelly, a smaller manor that overlooked the River Lynher in Cornwall. His bride had not understood his desire to install her elsewhere, however, and had felt slighted at the suggestion. Unwilling to explain his reasons and not wishing to begin their marriage under a blanket of resentment, he had given his marchioness what she desired.

Lady Eliza Eagleton had found no fault with her new home. To his surprise, once installed at Eagleton Priory, she had found no fault with anything, least of all him. If anything, she had been over-eager to please him. His lips twisted, and his footsteps quickened as the desire to flee almost overwhelmed him.

His spirited stallion awaited him. He mounted swiftly, nodded at his groom, and kicked his heels against the horse's flanks. They flew across the park and made their way along a rough track that led up to the northern edge of Dartmoor. It was the beginning of August, but low, heavy clouds blanketed the sky. The wild, windswept landscape looked particularly barren today. Stunted trees and large grey rocks jutted between gorse, heather and fern, and a kestrel hovered above a swathe of rough grassland. Alexander reined in, his eyes fixed upon the predator. It suddenly plunged downwards, rising moments later with a small mammal clutched in its claws.

It was a thing of beauty and grace, yet a deadly killer. Alexander's lips twisted in bitter derision, and he knew a stab of envy that the bird would suffer no pangs of conscience. He turned his horse, leant over its neck and returned the way he had come. He reined in as he reached the head of the track, his eyes roaming over his house before coming to rest on the chapel, a relic of the old priory, standing half hidden by a stand of trees. Generations of Wraxalls were buried there, including his mother, father, uncle and wife. He was, in part, responsible for their deaths.

He grimaced. Why did he stay here? Francesca was healthy enough to travel now. They would go to Pengelly today. He would not have his daughter brought up in this harsh, desolate place where misery polluted the atmosphere. His decision made, he returned swiftly to the house, strode purposefully into the hall, and was about to fling orders at the two footmen who waited there when his butler appeared.

"You have a visitor, my lord. I have put Mr Winters in the library."

Alexander glanced at the long-case clock. It was not yet eight o'clock. He frowned. What could have brought his man of business at so early an hour?"

"Thank you, Manton. Have you offered him breakfast?"

"Of course, my lord. He wanted only coffee."

Alexander nodded and made his way through several adjoining apartments before reaching the corridor to the east wing. The library was a long, low room, rather shabby but comfortable. The air was cool and a little damp, but a fire had been lit in the grate. A slender, elderly man sat in a wing chair beside it, his walking cane propped against its arm.

As he reached for it, Alexander said quickly, "Do not get up, Mr Winters."

The visitor's stern countenance relaxed. "Thank you for your consideration, my lord. My knees are rather sore today."

"I can well believe it. It was foolhardy of you to come all this way again so soon. You should have written to me or sent your son."

Mr Winters' clear, grey eyes warmed a little. "Perhaps, but although Phillip has been helping me with aspects of your affairs for some years and will take them over completely when I retire, he is not as fully conversant with your family's history as I."

Alexander sat opposite his visitor and glanced at the bundle of letters tied with a black ribbon that lay on the rosewood table next to his chair. A prickle of unease disturbed the hairs on the back of his neck.

"It is a matter of some importance, I presume?"

Mr Winters observed him gravely. "It will be to you, I believe. When your uncle died almost to the day you came into your full inheritance, you were adamant that you wished every last article that belonged to Lord Peter removed from this house, that his things be sold, and the money raised given to The Foundling Hospital. His personal correspondence, you instructed us to burn."

"What of it?" Alexander said, his eyes returning to the letters.

"My son, Phillip, not understanding the relationship between you and your uncle, could not bring himself to do it. He had some sentimental notion that you might regret your decision, which in his eyes appeared overly hasty."

A bitter laugh escaped the marquess. "Hasty? I had known for years that I wanted none of my uncle."

"Indeed," Mr Winters agreed. "But Phillip was not to know it. Nobody but I knew of it, and I only became aware of the reason for your hatred when you needed to persuade me to increase your allowance so that you had enough funds to live away from him after you finished university."

The hint of a smile touched the marquess's lips. "My father was wise to put you in control of my trust rather than my uncle. You were always very generous, Mr Winters, and he would not have been."

Mr Winters sighed. "Your uncle was always meant for the church and was not a worldly man. Your father thought him prosy, yet your uncle adored his brother, even though he considered him a profligate. Until he met your mother, he was. He could not know how fanatical and unbalanced Lord Peter would become. I wish you had confided in me far earlier; there are ways to dispose of an unwanted guardian if there is enough cause, you know."

Alexander grimaced. "Not without letting the whole world know why."

"That is true," Mr Winters agreed. "Your pride would, of course, have baulked at that. But we digress. I have been going through old files so that I may leave everything in order before I retire. I came across the folder with your uncle's correspondence." He smiled a little grimly. "Phillip explained why he had kept it but agreed there was no point in keeping it any longer. I took it home and burned everything." He picked up the bundle of letters. "Apart from these."

Alexander's face became a haughty mask. "I don't want anything that passed through my uncle's hands."

He stood and snatched the letters. He would have thrown them into the fire, but the old gentleman, divining his attention, rose hastily to his feet, saying in an imperative tone, "Wait!"

Alexander had little choice but to obey this command, for he had to steady the attorney to prevent him from falling.

"Thank you," Mr Winters murmured, straightening, and reaching for his cane. "Do you still hate him so much? Your estates may not have come under your full control until you were five and twenty, but Lord Peter's guardianship ended on your twenty-first birthday, and yet you allowed him to reside here for a further four years."

"How could I move him? He was clearly unhinged. I would not have wished that to become common knowledge. Besides, he had not dared touch me for years. Instead of trying to drive the devil from me, he began to flog himself for his failure." He gave a bitter laugh. "When he died from the infection his self-inflicted injuries caused, I thought I would rejoice, yet I did not. I felt relief, certainly, but also pity." He shook his head as if bemused.

"That will be your salvation. You spent many years trying to prove yourself as black as he painted you—"

Alexander laughed dryly. "Trying?"

"Come, my lord," Mr Winters said, smiling gently. "I have known you too long for you to pull the wool over my eyes. I will allow that you have fought many duels, sometimes on the flimsiest of pretexts, but you never killed or even seriously injured your opponent. It is a wonder that you were not killed." His smile evaporated. "I have sometimes thought that you were courting death."

Alexander did not reply. His eyes fell to the crumpled letters in his hand.

"Some of them are addressed to you and all concern you. I would not have come if I had not thought you would want them. I arrived late last night. As usual, I put up at The New Inn in Okehampton." He put a hand into his coat and withdrew another letter. "Fate sometimes works in strange ways, my lord. The post was being sorted as I left, and knowing me well, the landlord asked me to bring this letter to you." He held out his hand. "You may imagine my surprise when I realised the direction was written in the same hand as the other letters in my possession."

"Who are they from?" Alexander asked.

"Read them and find out. I shall go upstairs and pay Lady Francesca a visit, if I may?"

Frowning, Alexander waved him away and sat down. He stared at the direction on the latest letter and then slowly untied the black ribbon that bound the others. He compared the handwriting. It was undoubtedly the same, although it was not quite as uniform as it had once been. Taking a deep breath, he opened the most recent missive.

Villa Montovani, Malcesine, Lago di Garda, 3rd July 1816

Dearest Grandson,

Does it offend you that I address you thus? Is that why you have never answered any of my letters? I knew, of course, that your father wished to bury his wife's connection to trade. How could I not when he made it a condition of the marriage that my husband and I should never travel to England? We did not agree lightly, but he promised that once every five years, Livia would come to us. When she died, we begged that he relent so we could at least visit her resting place and meet our only grandchild. Unfortunately, he did not relent, and neither did your uncle. I had hoped that you, who have Montovani blood running through your veins, would not be so cold, but as you never once acknowledged our existence, I must presume I was mistaken.

I have been a widow for many years now and am old and tired. I do not fear death; I look forward to the day I will be reunited with my husband and daughter. And yet I resist it. Perhaps it is because I am uneasy about you. Until fourteen years ago, a distant cousin in England forwarded me such news as she could glean of you. As she did not move in the first circles, it was mere rumour, of course, but it seemed to me that you were rather wild and restless. I would like to know that you have found some happiness before I leave this earth.

If you can find it in your heart to write to me, I will, perhaps, be able to face my last sleep more peacefully.

Angelica Montovani

Alexander's eyes remained fixed on the words, blank astonishment in their frozen depths. Several minutes passed before he blinked rapidly, dropped the letter on the floor and reached for the next.

Villa Montovani, Malcesine, Lago di Garda, 10th March 1778

My Lord Marquess,

I have received word from a connection of my family that my beloved daughter died in childbirth. As we received this blow from so distant a relation, I must assume that you are so sunk in grief that you were unable to inform us. That, I can understand. My husband suffered a mild stroke when we were made aware of the loss of our only child which is why I have taken it upon myself to write to you.

The doctor is confident that Eduardo will be fit enough to travel in a few weeks. I beg that you grant us permission to break the terms of the marriage settlement so that we may come to Eagleton Priory and visit Livia's resting place. We would also very much like to meet our grandson and offer our support. Surely your son's needs must outweigh the pride which prompted you to force the separation between us? We may not be of the aristocracy as you know it, but the Montovani family moved in the first circles in Venice for centuries. There, a successful merchant was granted the respect he deserved. If that had not been the case, you would never have met Livia. That our glass business failed was no fault of ours but due to the new markets in Bohemia and France, as you know.

As I believe you have no close female relation who might provide the love and care that the poor infant deserves, I would be prepared to take on that role. If you cannot countenance us living with you, we could bring the child to Malcesine for his early years. The town is difficult to reach and almost unknown to foreign travellers, and the mild climate and beauty of Lago di Garda must benefit the child.

Please, have mercy on us, and at the very least, allow us to come to you for a brief visit.

Angelica Montovani

Many of the other letters to his father and uncle

were in the same vein, each more desperate than the last. The final three were to himself.

Villa Montovani, Malcesine, Lago di Garda, 28th January 1799

Dearest Grandson,

Today is your twenty-first birthday, and I congratulate you on reaching your majority. It has broken my heart that you have grown up without ever knowing my or your grandfather's love. I have written to you many times over the years, and all but one of the letters remain unread in a box by my bedside. Your uncle, you see, wrote to inform me that he had burned the first as he would any others that followed. He claimed that you had no wish to know us, that you were as ashamed of the connection as your father.

You are now your own master, and he no longer holds any power over you. It is my dearest wish that you read them all and know that you were never forgotten but always in our thoughts. If you only write to me once, I shall send them to you. I shall await your response with hope, Alexander. I am sure my faith in you cannot be misplaced.

Do you know why you were so named? We lost a child, Alessandro, and Livia always said she would name her firstborn son after her brother. Your mother was not ashamed of her heritage. I wonder if you resemble her in looks, at least?

With much love,

Angelica Montovani

The last question he could not answer with any certainty. His mother had died before his father had commissioned a portrait of her. His old nurse had said he did, but then she had always tried to comfort him in any way she could.

The other letters did not hold the same hope yet were still filled with longing and love. The last one, informing him of the death of his grandfather, had been written a month before his twenty-fifth birthday. He gathered the letters strewn across his lap and tied the black ribbon around them.

"Your life might have been very different if your grandmother had been allowed to come to you."

Alexander had not heard Mr Winters come into the room. He glanced up, his jaw tightening. "Perhaps, perhaps not. What use are might-have-beens? They change nothing."

"To know one is loved must change something," Mr Winters said gently, approaching his chair. He prodded the letter Alexander had dropped to the carpet with his walking stick. "May I?"

Alexander reached down a hand and picked it up. "As you have read all the others, you may as well."

"I never burn anything before I have read it," Mr Winters said, taking it from him. "Otherwise, these letters would not have survived the flames." He scanned the lines quickly before glancing at the marquess.

"You may not be able to change the past, but you can certainly ease your grandmother's mind."

Alexander looked at him broodingly. "How is it that you did not know she was still alive?"

Mr Winters looked grave. "I knew of the marriage settlement, of course, although I did not draw it up. I would have tried to steer your father away from so harsh a decree. He met your mother in Venice and married her there. If she had lived, I would no doubt have had to make the arrangements for her to travel to her parents when the time came and might have had some correspondence with your grandfather, but the occasion never arose.

"Your grandparents moved to Malcesine after the marriage, and I had no reason to doubt your father when he informed me that they had drowned on the lake in a boating accident a few months before you were born." He sighed heavily. "I think it was his jealousy as much as his pride which prompted him to behave thus. It is said that if a rake falls in love, he falls hard and that was certainly the case for him. He did not like another man to so much as look at her." He sent the marquess a penetrating look. "Will you write to your grandmother?"

Alexander rose swiftly to his feet. "No, I will not write to her. You are right. I cannot change the past, but the future is what I make it." The ghost of a smile touched his lips. "Someone I once admired told me that. My grandmother shall see both her grandson and her great-granddaughter. Make all the necessary arrangements, will you?"

A slow smile lightened the attorney's countenance. "Certainly. I shall discover the best route and obtain passports and letters of credit. When may I expect you?"

"By the end of next week," Alexander said decisively.

"You will make your grandmother very happy," Mr Winters said softly. "You resemble your mother, as Lady Francesca will resemble you, I think."

Alexander's eyes went to a large parcel that leant against his desk. A portrait of his wife hung in the main hall. Francesca would, at least, be able to envisage her mother. But Eliza had borne another child from her first marriage to an aged earl. Henry Brandforth was seven years of age and the ward of the current Earl of Ormsley. He had only his memories to remember her by, but memories faded, and so he had had a copy made.

"Do you begin your return journey today, Mr Winters?"

"That is my intention," Mr Winters confirmed. "I have a great deal to do, after all."

Alexander nodded and strode over to the desk, his hand resting lightly on the parcel for a moment. "Will you take this portrait of Lady Eagleton with a letter I am about to write and ensure they are delivered to Master Henry Brandforth at Leighfield Park as soon as possible?"

"Certainly, my lord. However, it would be more proper for you to address your letter to Lord Ormsley."

"I shall write to Henry, although Ormsley will undoubtedly read it."

Mr Winters smiled. "Do I take it that your turbulent relationship with the earl will not preclude you from fostering a relationship between the siblings?"

"I shall put no obstacle in the way of their knowing each other," Alexander said tersely. "What Ormsley will do, is another matter entirely. He has no reason to love me."

"That is true," Mr Winters acknowledged. "But then he doesn't really know you, does he? I wonder if anyone does?"

Alexander sat behind the desk, his lips twisting. "I think it is not only your son who has sentimental tendencies. Rid yourself of the notion that I am more honourable than I appear. I married because my hand was forced, I remained here because I was tired of the sycophants that surrounded me, and I am going to my grandmother because I wish to spite my father and uncle."

A glimmer of wry humour sparked in the old gentleman's eyes. "If you say so, my lord."

CHAPTER 2

"Addio, Sirenetta!"

Nell waved to the boatman as he pulled away from the small quay. "Addio, Antonio."

It was late afternoon and the wind had dropped, leaving Lake Garda still and calm, forcing the boatman to ply his oars for the crossing to Limone. It was there the lemons thrived. Monte Baldo cast its shadow over Malcesine in the morning, and although this did not discourage the vines or olive trees, the citrus fruit preferred the conditions on the other side of the water.

Nell bent to pick up the basket of fruit he had delivered, her eyes straying to the dark clouds bubbling behind the mountains beyond Riva del Garda at the northern edge of the lake. They might come to nothing, on the other hand, they might develop. None knew better than Nell how quickly things could change.

She had been caught in a storm as she made her way from the south end of the lake towards Torbole from whence she could begin her climb into the Alps via the Brenner Pass. The wind had suddenly veered, confused waves had tossed the boat about and she had been thrown from it. She had washed up near Malcesine, on the shingle beach next to the small quay in front of Villa Montovani, exhausted but very much alive. That is why the boatman had called her little mermaid.

Had it only been a year ago? The gentle rhythm of her life, welcome after the chaos that had gone before, made time seem insignificant, as did the sublime magnificence of the mountains that lined each side of the lake. It was not insignificant to Angelica Montovani, however.

Nell turned towards the old villa, glancing up at a first-floor balcony. A white-haired old lady garbed in black sat there, her eyes fixed on the water. Nell sighed. It was nearing the end of September and although the daytime temperature remained mild, the air cooled in the evening. Angelica should have gone in half an hour ago.

As she moved closer, she saw the old woman's lips moving and knew a fierce spurt of anger. She would be praying that a letter from her good-for-nothing grandson would soon arrive. Nell doubted very much that her prayers would be answered. Even taking into consideration bad weather at sea and the poor state of the roads, more than enough time had elapsed for his missive to arrive.

A pang of guilt drove out the anger. She had borne her part in Angelica's latest disappointment. The stoic lady had grown increasingly weak over the last months and there was nothing that could be done.

Old age was not a malady that could be cured. Unable to bear any longer the sadness too often present in her green eyes, it was Nell who had encouraged her to write one last time to the Marquess of Eagleton. She had clung to the hope that age might have brought the marquess wisdom and softened the edges of his careless cruelty. Her experience argued against it, but she could not allow her cynicism to stand in the way of the one thing that might bring Angelica peace and happiness. She owed her so much, after all.

As she reached the house, a distant rumble of thunder confirmed the storm that was to come. Pausing only to deliver the lemons to the kitchen, she made her way upstairs and out to the balcony. The clouds had now tumbled over the mountains and were advancing across the lake, bringing with them a chill breeze.

"Come inside, Angelica," Nell said urgently. "There is a storm brewing."

As if in reply, a loud boom of thunder sounded, and a streak of lightning flickered briefly in the rapidly darkening sky.

"I hope Antonio reaches Limone before the storm worsens."

Angelica drew her shawl closer around her and rose slowly to her feet, accepting the arm Nell offered her. "Bless you, my child. He has been sailing these waters all his life and will use the conditions to his best advantage."

Nell glanced over the lake and saw the truth of these words. He had hoisted his sails and the boat skimmed across the water, already halfway to Limone.

"You, my dear, were unfortunate to have been in

the hands of an inexperienced boatman when you suffered your accident, but I cannot regret it for it brought you to me. This storm will be just as furious and pass as quickly." She sighed and spoke so softly that Nell had to stoop to hear her. "And perhaps the night boat will bring me something almost as precious."

They stepped through the door into Angelica's private sitting room. Nell closed it before easing Angelica into an armchair. She pressed her lips firmly together as she shook out a blanket and laid it over the old woman's legs. She would not voice her thoughts but allow her employer and friend a few more days of hope.

"You doubt it, I see," Angelica said with a faint smile.

"No—"

The old woman chuckled. "You are a terrible liar, my dear. You have one of the most expressive faces I have ever seen. Your eyes speak volumes. Do you know how changeable they are? They shift between green, gold and brown, depending on the light and your mood. They remind me of autumn in England as does your hair."

"Do you miss it?" Nell asked, grasping the opportunity to change the subject.

"No. I was only seventeen when my father brought me with him to Venice on a business trip, and I never returned. His ship sank in a storm on the return journey." Her expression sobered and her eyes glimmered with unshed tears. "And my daughter went to England when she was seventeen and never returned."

"I am sorry," Nell said softly, the words seeming

woefully inadequate. She bent down and took her friend's hand.

Angelica's thin fingers clasped it. "Ignore the ramblings of an old woman. One should try never to look back on any but fond memories. I have told you that before."

"Yes, and it becomes easier to do so with every day that passes."

"Good girl," Angelica said gently. "You are feeling a little guilty, Nell, because you think you have raised false hope in my breast. Don't. I should never have stopped hoping or writing. Whether or not I receive a reply, I will at least know that I never gave up on my grandson and so will he. That knowledge alone brings me a little peace."

As rain slashed against the windows, cheerful whistling floated up the stairs. Nell stiffened and straightened.

"Try to like Bernardo for my sake," Angelica said softly. "I am happy that the rift between his grandfather and Eduardo has been forgotten. It was not of my husband's making, but it was a terrible thing for two brothers to be so estranged. Eduardo was greatly saddened by Donato's greed." She shook her head. "We publicly blamed our business's demise on the burgeoning markets in Bohemia and France, which was largely true, but you may imagine the shock Eduardo felt when he discovered his brother had been falsifying the accounts and stealing from the business for several years."

Shadows darkened her eyes. "Livia's marriage to the marquess did not restore our fortunes to anything near their former state but allowed us to buy this property and the vineyard. Not that we would have agreed to the match if she had not desired it. It was through sheer hard work and some astute investments that we rebuilt our wealth, and if only Donato had made a small gesture of goodwill, Eduardo would have accepted the olive branch offered." She sighed. "He never did, of course, nor did he ever admit what he had done. He claimed that Eduardo had manufactured the evidence to conceal his mismanagement of the business. Donato had made a good marriage to a silk merchant's daughter from Verona and was given a position in that business when ours failed, and he eventually inherited it.

"It is a shame that Donato's son assumed his father's prejudice and Bernardo did not feel he could attempt a rapprochement until he died." She waved a hand as if dismissing the past. "But this is old history. It was Bernardo suddenly visiting me as much as your words that gave me hope that another rift might be healed."

Bernardo had made the journey from Verona to Malcesine shortly after his father's funeral a little over a month before and stayed for a week. He had arrived again earlier that day, and Nell had been grateful when he had disappeared for most of the afternoon to observe the harvesting of this year's crop of grapes. He was handsome, charming, and attentive to his great-aunt and to Nell, yet she did not trust him. She forced a smile to her lips.

"I do not dislike him. It is just that he sometimes looks at me in a way that makes me feel uncomfortable. I cannot explain it."

Angelica chuckled. "The Italians are a passionate

race, and you are very beautiful although you do not seem to be aware of it."

Nell was fully aware of it, but her beauty had brought her only misery and she had come to despise it.

"I must change before dinner. Shall I send Beatrice to you?"

Before Angelica could answer, a woman of middling years entered the room, her rapid words incomprehensible to Nell.

"Yes, I will go down to dinner tonight," Angelica replied.

They always spoke to each other thus, the maid in her own tongue, Angelica in English, comprehending each other perfectly. It was fortunate for Nell that all Angelica's servants understood English. She had a smattering of Italian, but the Venetian dialect that the servants spoke in Malcesine was more difficult to understand.

She left Angelica to her maid's ministrations and went to her room. It was far grander than a companion's ought to be. Angelica would not treat Nell as a paid employee even though that was what she had been reduced to.

She washed and changed quickly into a plain, dark green gown, before seating herself at her dressing table. She reached for her brush, pulling it through her thick mass of curls. They had grown back quickly but then everything seemed to flourish here. She glanced up as a light knock fell upon the door. A plump, pretty maid came into the room.

"I do for you, Signora Marsdon?"

Nell smiled. Maria was another example of Angelica's kindness. Shocked that Nell had been travelling alone, she had employed the maid shortly after Nell's arrival and encouraged her to wait on her. Another luxury a mere companion should not enjoy. Maria was in her early twenties, amiable, and not above making herself understood.

"Thank you, Maria. In the simple style I showed you."

The maid took the brush from her, a knowing look in her eyes.

"No style can hide how beautiful is your hair."

"Even so," Nell murmured.

The maid shook her head but complied, pulling it severely back, plaiting and coiling it.

"Thank you," Nell said, reaching for the lace-embellished cap in front of her.

"What is this?" the maid said, frowning. "It is a… how do you say… un peccato?"

"A shame? A sin?"

Maria put her hands on her rounded hips. "Si, to wear it is both these things."

Nell rose to her feet and shrugged. "I am no longer a very young woman, Maria, and it is perfectly usual for a widow to wear such a cap in England."

"Bah! Me, I know why you wear this ugly thing. Signor Montovani, he looks. He will still look. You can hide your hair but not your face."

Nell frowned. "Your English is much improved, Maria, but you speak too freely."

A glimmer of mischief sparked in the maid's dark eyes. "But how else am I to learn?"

The tension left Nell and she laughed. "Very true."

"It is also true that the thing that is hidden becomes at once more… how you say… allettante?"

"Alluring," Nell said thoughtfully.

"Si. Take it off, I beg. Signor Montovani will offer you no insult in this house."

Nell removed the offending object. Maria was right. To suddenly change her habits might draw attention to herself rather than deflect it.

As she descended the stairs, she saw a fire had been lit at the far end of the long, low room that served both as entrance hall and dining room. A man of average height with curling golden-brown hair stood beside it, his arm resting on the mantle, his fingers tapping restlessly against the wood. Nell wondered what could have caused his impatience; it seemed at variance with the cheerful whistling she had heard not an hour since.

Not wishing for a tête-à-tête, she would have retreated and gone in search of Angelica if he had not just then glanced up. She thought the expression in his eyes rather calculating but conceded the dim light and her prejudice may have been responsible for this interpretation. He bowed and came to the foot of the stairs, holding out his hand.

"Signora Marsdon, you look delightful."

She laid her fingers lightly on his and he clasped them in a firm grip as he helped her down the remaining two steps. She felt a prickle of unease. There had been an odd emphasis in his tone when he had spoken her name.

"Thank you, Signor Montovani."

She attempted to gently withdraw her hand, but he raised it to his lips and dropped a kiss upon it. His blue eyes seemed to challenge her. She felt a pulse of anger as he again ignored her attempt to withdraw it.

"Sir, I neither need nor wish for such attentions. Indeed, it is most inappropriate for you to show your great-aunt's companion such observance."

He drew her hand through his arm and began to walk towards the fire. As Savio, Angelica's butler, just then came into the hall and began lighting candles, she was forced to submit. Angelica had asked her to try and like Bernardo, but he was making it very difficult. Her unease grew as he smiled down at her.

"I am merely showing you the respect you are due." He bent his head and murmured, "Lady Flint."

CHAPTER 3

I t might be expected that a marquess setting out on a European trip would preserve his dignity by providing himself with a large entourage to pander to his every whim. Lord Eagleton was not such a marquess. This did not cause his servants any noticeable dismay. His steward, who with Mr Winters, had long ensured that Alexander's interests would not suffer by his sporadic bursts of attention to his affairs, could not, of course, be spared from his duties. Nor could his secretary, a conscientious man quite used to dealing with various matters pertaining to the marquess, including his personal correspondence.

It was true that since the marquess's marriage, his duties had much diminished in that regard, something he was profoundly grateful for. Although his employer had always treated Mr Siddons well in his disinterested way, that gentleman had never approved of the string of lightskirts that had inevitably made increasingly avaricious demands on his employer's purse and time. Although he had never had the courage to voice his dissatisfaction in this regard, he believed it should never have been any part of his duties to purchase gifts for them, arrange assignations or inform them that their arrangement with his lordship was at an end.

Despite the callousness of this last duty, Mr Siddons could not deny that it had given him some satisfaction to perform it, nor could he deny that Lord Eagleton had always been generous when parting from his inamoratas. That the marquess had not yet resumed such undesirable habits offered his secretary small comfort; it could only be a matter of time. The absence of the marquess from England must, however, put off the renewal of these duties, and so he did everything in his power to expedite his departure.

Apart from his valet and his daughter's nurse, Alexander took only Timothy, a strapping footman from the household servants, who had the merits of being a favourite with Lady Francesca and an able bodyguard for her.

They travelled in the marquess's carriage and he in his curricle, both vehicles, his groom and coachman, making the channel crossing with him. This decision was a practical one. He doubted very much that he would be able to hire any vehicles as comfortable or well-maintained as his own, nor would he trust anyone who was not from his own stable to drive his daughter.

He set a hard pace and just over a week later, the party reached Cologne. His daughter had journeyed well but the same could not be said of her nurse. Despite the well-sprung carriage, eight days of being jolted over hard roads had taken their toll on Mrs Jane

Farley. She emerged from the carriage whey-faced and exhausted. Lundy, his valet, did not look much better.

Alexander frowned. "We will dine and then retire for the evening. Place Francesca's cot in my room tonight, Jane."

When she did not argue, he feared she might be ill and said as much.

"It's just a headache, my lord," she murmured faintly.

He frowned. "Why didn't you say something earlier?"

"It wasn't so bad then, and Timothy offered to amuse Lady Francesca. I thought it would go off. If I can just lie down, I'm sure it will."

But it did not go off, and Jane was unable to get up the following day. A doctor was sent for, and he reassured Alexander that it was nothing infectious, merely a migraine brought on by exhaustion. This relieved him greatly, for he had been watching his daughter closely for any signs of illness, barely letting her out of his sight.

He had found the experience quite taxing and felt a new appreciation for her nurse. How such a little person could consume quite so much of one's time was a revelation. He discovered that Francesca was not so easy to pacify during the day, and he looked up as his footman, no doubt alerted by her high-pitched cries, came into his private parlour, completely unaware of the look of unaccustomed helplessness in his eyes.

"I've tried everything, Timothy. She wants none of her toys and has been fed." He glanced down at the red-faced infant. "Do you think she is sickening for something, after all?"

"No," he said, the hint of a grin on his lips. "Give her to me, my lord. If she's been fed and changed, I expect she's tired, but sometimes the little mites need a bit of help to get to sleep in the day, especially if their routine has been upset."

Alexander handed her over and watched as his muscular servant began to rock her in his arms and softly sing a lullaby in a deep, pleasant voice. Francesca's wails faded away and she fell asleep. The marquess was surprised to discover a stab of jealousy shooting through him. He had come to think of the role as his own. He laughed softly at his foolishness. He had never given his heart to another, and yet this babe had crept into it and refused to be dislodged. When she fixed her peculiarly penetrating, trusting gaze on him, a fierce determination to be worthy of that trust and protect her gripped him. Perhaps it was because she was of his own flesh.

A soft, derisive laugh shook him. He had not had the same effect on his father. That gentleman had given the nursery a wide birth after the death of his wife and had steadily drunk himself to death over the following five years, leaving his son to the care of an uncle who had been both unwilling and incapable of executing the task thrust upon him with any degree of competence or goodwill. The only useful thing his father had done for him, was to ensure that he would be sent to Eton and Oxford, thus making Alexander aware that his upbringing was not typical and that his uncle was a cruel tyrant.

He looked at his sleeping daughter and a steely

determination took root. He would provide her with a mother, someone who was happy to accept a marriage of convenience and had a kind heart. She must also have enough strength of character to deal with a strong-willed child, for he was certain she would be that. As he had been. She would be tamed by love and reason, however, not by blunt force.

Mr Winters had been right when he said to know one is loved must change something. He and Lady Eagleton had had little in common and he would never have agreed to marry her if she had not been carrying his child, but for some inexplicable reason she had loved him, or at least the image of him she had created in her mind. Although he had not returned her feelings, he had found himself unwilling to fling them in her face by resuming his old way of life. He was honest enough to admit that he did not know how long his good intentions would have lasted, however.

"Lay her in the cot and stay with her, will you?"

"Of course, my lord."

Timothy laid her down and stood beside the cot, his hands behind his back, the gentle expression fading from his face as it took on its usual wooden look.

"For heaven's sake, sit down," Alexander whispered. "If you must take on the role of nursemaid, you may as well enjoy the privileges."

This time Timothy did not try to repress his grin.

Alexander went to his room to consult with his valet.

"I think we may need to reconsider our arrangements, Lundy," he said. "I do not wish Mrs Farley to suffer this malady again. Perhaps we should travel only a few hours a day once she recovers."

Although Lundy was used to the punishing pace his master insisted upon, he had no desire to immediately resume it. "Might I make a suggestion, my lord?"

"Please do."

"I went for a walk down to the river earlier and had a word with the boatmen there. We can take a boat along the river for a few days and meet the carriages at Mannheim. From there we can continue to Munich as per Mr Winters' suggested schedule. As the weather is holding fair, it should be a smooth ride and make a nice change. Apparently, the scenery is something to behold."

"Arrange it," Alexander said decisively. "We will set out in two days. The doctor assured me that Mrs Farley should be well again by then."

When Alexander had a goal in mind, he generally pursued it with ruthless efficiency. Once he had decided to visit his grandmother, the destination had taken priority over the journey. He had no wish to visit sights or linger in towns along the way. It might be expected then, that when the river journey took a week rather than a few days, he would become impatient and irritable.

His valet was both surprised and relieved when he did not. Lundy had not accounted for the number of times the boat would be forced to dock and be left waiting until customs officials deigned to check their papers. But although Alexander found this the least enjoyable aspect of the journey, his annoyance was ameliorated by the magnificent beauty that surrounded him.

As they had left Dover, he had stood on deck watching the white cliffs recede and wondered if he was running to his grandmother or away from England. He had decided it did not matter and had chosen not to examine his motives too closely. His spirits had perceptibly lightened, however, once the shores of his birth had disappeared from view.

Now, he felt curiously detached from himself and the urgency that had thus far driven him, dissipated. He was not romantic, the thought was laughable, but the alien landscape around him certainly was, and he found himself charmed by it. The wide river wound between steep hills dotted with picturesque towns, their craggy outcrops often topped with castles, and their slopes clothed in lush forests or vineyards. Through the early morning mists, thickly wooded islands would suddenly appear, turrets or church towers peeking above the foliage.

Unlike some of his more artistic compatriots, he had no desire to capture any of it in poetry or sketches, but rather lounged on deck, often with his daughter in the crook of his arm, simply absorbing it. He felt as if he had entered a hidden world where everything that had gone before or was yet to come was unimportant, where only that moment mattered. Although he and his small entourage were thrown into close proximity, an almost uncanny silence broken only by Lady Francesca's contented burbling fell between them for hours at a time, each of them seemingly as enchanted as he.

When they finally reached Mannheim, Alexander felt curiously reluctant to leave that world behind. When he again climbed into his curricle and took charge of the party, he felt something slip from him and struggled to identify what it was. Then it came to him. Peace. For the first time he could remember, he had felt at peace.

This brought the purpose of his journey back to the forefront of his mind. Would his visit bring his grandmother peace, or would it only trouble her further? Something close to a sneer touched his lips. If she knew how he had spent the majority of his adult life, she would no doubt disapprove of him as much as his uncle had. He could, of course, paint himself in a much more positive light but that would be a lie, and whatever else he had been, he had never been a liar.

With these thoughts, his restlessness returned in full, and he pressed on at his usual pace, reaching Munich in five days and Mittenwald three days later. Bad weather forced a two-day respite there at a posting house.

To make up for lost time, they left early on the third day. The rising sun illuminated limestone cliffs and snow-capped peaks in the distance set against a deep blue sky. As they climbed steadily over the next few days, he observed their summits bathed in sunshine, shrouded in mist or wreathed in storm-tossed clouds. These ancient giants looming over the earth were as indifferent to the vagaries of the weather or the cold rushes of water that bathed their sides, pooling now and then in deep lakes of icy blue, as they were to the forests of pine that marched up their flanks. He felt his insignificance and embraced it. He was but an ant crawling up their sides.

The rank that he had used to bolster his impor-tance and wield some small measure of power when at school and university, and later to keep a string of acquaintances and mistresses at his beck and call when he desired to be amused or distracted, meant nothing here. It had never meant anything but had been both a shield and a sword that kept the world at arm's length even as he had moved within it. It was true his estates had provided the means of survival for his tenants and servants, as the mountains allowed their gentler slopes to be cultivated, used as pasture, and suffered dwellings to be dotted amongst them, but he had been almost as distant and indifferent as them.

This reflective mood stayed with him as they made their descent and he saw the first hillside vineyards, the vines trained on long, low trellises. Maize, mulberries, quinces and nuts grew in profusion and the shrill sound of crickets crowded the air after sunset. He felt an unexpected thrill as the language gradually changed from German to predominately Italian, the musical cadence of the language calling to him.

As he made his way up a ridge, he observed fig trees growing beside the road and as he topped it, he glimpsed a profusion of olive trees. A long lake, hemmed in by soaring mountains stretched into the distance. It was a sublime view, but he did not linger. Dark clouds were rising behind their craggy peaks and a cold breeze whipped his unfashionably long hair against his cheeks. Below, lay the village of Torbole and he intended to reach it before the storm broke. Handing the reins to his groom, he reached under his seat, withdrew his greatcoat and donned it.

He did not quite make it, and he arrived at a waterside inn with rain dripping from the brim of his hat and his greatcoat saturated. The landlord looked surprised and then delighted as Alexander addressed him in his native tongue. He had learned Italian to spite his uncle, who had laid the blame for all his excesses on that part of his blood, conveniently forgetting that his father had been just as profligate. A small voice reminded him that it had also made him feel closer to his mother.

Alexander did not think it a good omen that he should be greeted on his arrival at Lake Garda by a storm. It passed quickly, however, and he made his way to the landing stage at the edge of the lake, watching the choppy waves crash over it. He had discovered that it was not possible to make the final part of his journey until the small hours when the wind would turn. His valet had already hired a boat and been assured that it would be safe by then.

He stood with his feet firmly planted, defying the strong wind that buffeted him, his mouth set in a grim line. It had better be; he would not attempt the boat trip unless the lake became much calmer. He may have courted danger many times during his lifetime, but his daughter would never be allowed to do so.

Now he was so close to his destination, he felt conflicted. Part of him longed to continue the journey, and part of him wished to linger. He did not know what he would find or even if his grandmother still lived. He had told Mr Winters only part of the truth. That he was going against both his father's and his uncle's wishes in coming here might afford him some petty satisfaction, but he had been forced to admit whilst amongst those lofty mountain peaks, that it was the desire to know more of his mother that had driven him.

His uncle had not hesitated when enraged, to lay her and his father's deaths at his door, and had claimed it was because the devil resided within him. In his darkest moments, he still believed it, but if his grandmother truly did not blame him for the loss of her daughter, then perhaps he might lay that ghost to rest once and for all.

A derisive smile curled his lips. He was still as selfish as he had ever been; he had not come all this way to give his grandmother peace but to find his own.

CHAPTER 4

Bernardo's smile grew as Nell's eyes widened. "You look surprised, Lady Flint."

"Do not call me that," she hissed.

"But it is your name, is it not?"

"Yes," she admitted, glancing uneasily at the butler, who was talking quietly to Luca, the footman. "I was asked my name when I was only half-conscious. I said Marsdon. It is my family name and I prefer to use it."

"I understand completely," he said, at last releasing her.

His softly spoken words did not reassure her. She sank into a chair and then wished she had not. He did not follow her example but stood looking down at her, a speculative look in his eyes.

"How did you find out?"

He glanced up. "Now is not the time, my great-aunt is about to join us."

She followed his gaze and saw Luca carrying her down the stairs.

"Smile," he said gently. "You must not distress my great-aunt. I shall be going out after dinner, but we shall talk again in the morning before breakfast, on the beach where we are unlikely to be heard."

He strode away, affectionate expressions of welcome on his lips as Angelica was set gently on her feet.

Nell's mind was in a whirl. When she had first discovered that Bernardo's estate was near Verona, she had felt some anxiety, but it had been allayed by his apparent acceptance of her. He had said that he was happy that Angelica had some company, that if he had known that she was quite alone, he would have gone against his father's wishes and visited her sooner. She had assumed that by reverting to her maiden name she had covered her tracks.

It had not been intentionally done but had happened as she said. She had not corrected the fault when she came to her senses because she had come to hate her husband's name, because it might lead her into explanations that were both painful and shaming, and because she had lost the means to complete her journey and needed employment.

Later, when she had come to love Angelica, she had felt a little guilty about her deception. Angelica had accepted her low spirits as natural in a widow, a status she had been forced to claim as her husband's ring had still been on her finger. To have revealed the truth had seemed increasingly impossible. It was not that she feared that Angelica would frown on her actions, although she knew society would, so much that she did not wish to add her own burdens to those Angelica already carried.

She was grateful that Bernardo was full of praise for the vineyard, his observations and questions to Angelica enabling Nell to get through dinner without the necessity of having to contribute much to the conversation. Indeed, she would have been quite incapable of doing so. Only the odd phrase floated into her consciousness. Bernardo's words were enthusiastic, his tone persuasive and Angelica's replies, patient and gentle.

"It is a very good harvest this year, but it seems that most of the village is engaged in gathering the grapes. I wonder if it is necessary to employ so many?"

"The villagers depend on the work, Bernardo."

"Signor Batiste seems to know his work well, but he is not getting any younger. Perhaps you should look for a younger man to oversee it."

"But with age comes experience."

"Indeed, but it is also easy to become set in one's ways. The orchard could certainly be made better use of. On the road from Verona to Venice I have seen vines strung between the trees and crops grown underneath. I have been considering trying it myself."

"Eduardo used to say that such methods ensured that the produce was of poor quality. One good crop is better than three poor ones."

Angelica seemed tired by the end of the meal of which both she and Nell had partaken only sparingly. She glanced at Nell.

"I think I will forgo tea this evening, my dear, and retire."

Nell was relieved. "As will I. My head aches a little."

This was true. She had been trying to understand if she stood in any danger from Bernardo discovering her identity. He had not threatened her and did not seem inclined to make his great-aunt aware of it, yet she felt uneasy. She was not sure why. What she had done might be thought reprehensible, but it was not a crime, or at least she did not think it was. Perhaps it was because she had stopped thinking of herself as Lady Flint months ago, and him calling her by that name had dredged up bad memories.

She had managed to block the worst of them at dinner, but her dreams were not so malleable, and they spared her nothing. Images of her brief, whirlwind courtship, her wedding day and the hope that had accompanied it flashed through her mind, followed by the crushing reality of what had followed. She again felt the relief she had known when her husband had left her behind at his country estate and gone to London to find, as he had callously informed her, women who knew how to please a man. His words had not hurt her as much as he intended; she already knew him to be a cruel, selfish monster and had been wrapped by then in a numb cocoon.

She again read the reply to the letter she had written her father, begging him to allow her to return to him, hardly able to believe that whilst he expressed his sadness that she was unhappy, he suggested the remedy was in her own hands and refused her sanctuary.

In the eyes of the law and God, you belong to your husband and must obey him. Nature, reason and scripture are as one on this. You were not forced into marriage and if you have now discovered that your husband is not entirely free of the infirmities of human nature, you must moderate your disappointment. Try to be a good, obedient wife and you will be rewarded on earth and in heaven.

She wept, wishing that her mother was still alive to advise her. She again felt the shock that her husband had already lost a large part of her dowry and they must journey abroad to avoid disgrace whilst the world still believed they were taking a delayed honeymoon. She relived the horrendous sea journey to Livorno on a merchant ship out of Bristol, the stint in Pisa, Florence and then Venice when she had been forced to attend various conversazione and assume a mantle of dignity she had not felt so that her husband might present a respectable appearance and gain access to those that might repair his fortune at the gaming table. She shivered in fear as, this plan having ultimately failed, they fled to Verona, and she faced the very real possibility that they might find themselves far from home without a feather to fly with.

These dreams came thick and fast, but the last one played slowly. She had been cooped up in her room for the two days they had been at the Due Torri, a smart hotel in Piazza Sant'Anastasia, quite unable to any longer maintain the pretence her husband demanded. Her nerves were stretched to breaking point and she felt quite ill. She had used this as an excuse to repulse the hand of friendship offered her by Lady Westcliffe, a fellow guest who had called upon her soon after their arrival. She had been kind and genuinely concerned.

"You do look pale and drawn, Lady Flint. Allow me to send for a doctor."

She had refused the offer, of course, and got rid of

her as soon as was possible. The urge to pour her troubles into friendly ears had been almost overwhelming, but that would have been a grave mistake. Her lord had thus far left her alone, saying that she did him no credit looking so haggard, but if she betrayed him, he would punish her.

Besides, it would have been a nonsensical thing to do. He had used their last letter of credit before they left Venice, and although she thought it highly unlikely he would be able to bring them about, there would be no chance of it if she advertised their circumstances.

Her thoughts and the four walls of her room seemed to close in on her, making her suddenly feel claustrophobic. She rose from her bed, donned a blue silk dressing gown, and slipped her feet into a pair of slippers. She needed a breath of air. She should get dressed, of course, but as her maid had baulked at the sea journey when she had seen the rough state of the sea, and Flint had said impatiently that the merchant vessel would not wait for Nell to persuade her, she had been left behind. Nell had had to make do with borrowing a maid at need from whatever establishment they had stayed in. Besides, it would take too long to ring for one to help her into a dress, and it was late. She would just stand in her doorway for a moment.

The rooms on her side of the hotel all opened onto a balcony that overlooked a central courtyard below, and seeing that all was dark and quiet, she was bold enough to step outside, closing her door gently behind her so that the faint light leaking from her room did not betray her presence. She laid her hands on the balustrade and closed her eyes, enjoying the cool, gentle breeze. She stiffened as an exasperated voice she knew all too well floated up from below.

"I would pay you if I could, but I can't. Give me a little more time; my luck must turn soon."

"Ah, but it is my experience that luck rarely favours those who need it. Besides, I must return to Venice the day after tomorrow. I left pressing business to track you down, Lord Flint."

Nell leant a little forward to catch the words. Unlike her husband's, they were softly uttered and yet held steel. The stranger's next utterance also held a threat.

"If you do not recompense me by then, you shall return with me and face the others you have fled."

Her husband's reply was laced with the bravado of one in his cups.

"I would not come. I am not such a fool."

"You are a fool and a coward," came the disgusted reply. "I will call again tomorrow evening. Do not disappoint me or I will arrange for your return to Venice, and I will not seek your permission. Good evening, Lord Flint."

Nell shrank back as the stranger strode away. In the dim light shed by the lanterns below, she saw that his stride was impeded by a heavy limp.

"Wait!"

The man paused and then slowly turned. Nell closed her lips against the gasp that threatened to burst from them. A flickering light threw his face into relief. One eye had a milky hue, and a puckered scar ran from above it down to one side of his thin-lipped mouth.

"Well?"

"When we last met you displayed some interest in my wife."

Nell's eyes widened. She was certain she had never met the stranger; she was hardly likely to forget such a face. It now held a keen interest. He retraced his steps.

"Of course. I never had the pleasure of being introduced to Lady Flint and have seen her only from afar, but she was much talked about by certain gentlemen of my acquaintance. How could it not be so? The paradox of a beauty with hair the colour of flame and yet so cold a demeanour could not fail to ignite a man's interest." He paused, and then added with taunting malice, "The image of that magnificent hair unbound, cascading over her pale skin must live in the dreams of all red-blooded males who know her."

Disgust twisted in Nell's stomach. Men were such base creatures and the honour and protection they pretended to offer nothing but a sham. Even so, her husband must surely act for her now. The stranger's scandalous speech touched his honour too. His response made her reel back against her door and slowly sink to the floor, her hands clasped to her mouth.

"You may experience that image for a price and for one night only. Tonight, if you wish it."

"That would be a poor bargain; the night already so far advanced. It must be tomorrow. You will bring her to my house on Via Pigna at six o'clock and then leave us."

"It will cost you considerably more than my debt."

"Name your price."

Not wishing to hear her worth as a harlot, Nell

twisted about and reached for her door handle. She crawled into her room and shut the door behind her, leaning back against it and, at last, allowed her sobs to escape.

How had it come to this? She had tried to keep her vows to her husband. She had been unable to love or honour him, but she had obeyed him. No longer. She would rather throw herself in the river than be any part of this plan.

Eventually, her sobs abated, and she slowly rose and went to her mirror, staring at her reflection as if seeking counsel. What was she to do? Her hazel eyes held no answer, only desperate, impotent anger. It was hopeless. She had only a few coins in her purse and no friends to aid her. The thought of throwing herself in the river might seem attractive but it would forever damn her in the eyes of God. It was enough that she must be damned in this life, she did not wish to be in the next.

Her eyes came to rest accusingly upon the long flowing locks she had once taken such pride in. With a shaking hand, she reached for her scissors, grasped a clump of hair and began to cut, fast silent tears pouring from her eyes. Her actions were at first controlled and measured but soon became frenzied.

When she had finished, she gave a slightly hysterical laugh. A chaotic cluster of unevenly cut curls that barely reached her chin made her look much younger than her three and twenty years. There was certainly nothing of the cool sophisticate about her. She froze as a soft knock fell upon her door. Had her lord come to gloat? Would he beat her for her rebellion? She neither knew nor cared.

Still, she felt tension grip her as the door slowly opened and her fingers tightened on the scissors still in her hand. It was not her husband, but a tall, elegant lady with black hair and grave, grey eyes. These rested for a moment on the long strands of hair that lay on the dressing table, Nell's lap, and the floor.

"I understand the impulse," she said softly, closing the door and coming forwards, "but it will not be enough to save you, I think."

Nell's mouth felt dry. "You heard?"

The woman nodded. "I could not sleep, and I stepped out for a breath of air." Her eyes dropped to Nell's hand, and she frowned. "Oh dear, you have cut yourself."

Nell glanced down and saw that it was true. Blood was dripping from the side of her hand.

Lady Westcliffe came slowly towards her, eased the scissors from Nell's fingers, and laid them down.

"Let me tend that for you. Do you have a handkerchief?"

Nell nodded and opened a drawer, sitting as if in a trance as Lady Westcliffe bound it up. When she had finished, Lady Westcliffe picked up the scissors.

"You still look very beautiful but let me tidy you up a little."

"I do not wish to be tidied up," Nell said on a sob.

"Do not despair," Lady Westcliffe said gently. "I will help you, but first I must make you look a little more respectable."

Nell looked at Lady Westcliffe in stunned disbelief. "You will help me?"

The woman smiled wryly. "I know our sex is not always kind to those more beautiful than they, but is it so hard to believe? I would be heartless indeed to abandon you in your current predicament." She set to work with the scissors. "You are unfortunate in your husband." The eyes that met Nell's in the mirror held a wealth of sympathetic understanding. "But you already know that. Has he done this before?"

Nell shook her head, dropping her eyes, hot colour rushing into her cheeks at the thought that Lady Westcliffe had contemplated the possibility.

Lady Westcliffe put the scissors down and laid her hands on Nell's shoulders. Nell raised her eyes and met a steady grey gaze.

"I would still have helped you. But I am glad for your sake that you have not been so violated. It makes it even more important that you escape before you are quite broken."

"How? I have no money."

"Do you have your passport?"

Nell nodded.

"Then you will do very well. Come, we must get you dressed and packed."

A bubble of hope began to burgeon in Nell's breast, and she allowed her would-be rescuer to help her out of her night things and into a dress. It suddenly burst as the reality of her situation hit her with the force of a physical blow.

"But I have nowhere to go."

Lady Westcliffe finished buttoning her dress and turned her around.

"When you reach England, go to Ashwick Hall."

She reached into the pocket of her cloak and withdrew a heavy purse and a card.

"The direction is on the card. I do not like you

travelling alone but that I can't remedy. You must travel by diligence wherever possible; the other passengers will offer you some protection. It will also be cheaper. If you are thrifty, you should make it to England. If you are given the opportunity to share a room with another female traveller, take it."

"Why?" Nell asked. "Why are you helping me?"

Lady Westcliffe suddenly embraced her. "Because I am very fortunate, Lady Flint. My husband rescued me from an impossible situation and understands my desire to help others less fortunate than myself. You will be safe at Ashwick and have time to heal and consider what you wish to do next."

Nell returned her embrace, hardly able to believe that for once, providence had shone its light upon her. "Thank you. That is exactly what I need."

She gasped as a foot sounded outside her door. Lady Westcliffe put a finger to her lips, and after a moment they heard the door opposite Nell's room close.

"Is that your husband's room?" she whispered.

Nell nodded.

"Then it must be his valet. I saw your husband leave the yard soon after the other man. It seems Lord Flint has gone out again. Is his valet sympathetic to your plight?"

Nell found her voice. "No. Renn is only loyal to Flint and will try and prevent me from leaving if he can. He despises me and doesn't try to hide the fact."

"Then we must hurry. My husband has gone to Venice to consult with the British Consul. Napoleon's escape is a worry, but he is not convinced that we must return yet to England. I received a note from him this afternoon, suggesting I join him there. We had already discussed the safest options open to us if we should decide to leave. It would be better to avoid France. We are very close to Lake Garda where you can take a boat to Torbole, and from there travel into Germany and Belgium before crossing to England. I have already called for my carriage." She put Nell from her. "Are you brave enough?"

The thought of travelling so far alone made Nell quake, but the alternative was even more unpalatable.

"Lady Westcliffe, I do not know how to thank you or if I will ever be able to repay you."

Her saviour was already packing dresses in a portmanteau. She glanced up.

"It will be payment enough if I find you safely ensconced at Ashwick Hall when I return."

"Is that your home? How will I explain my presence there?"

Lady Westcliffe extracted a second portmanteau from the wardrobe. "There is no time to explain, but you will find a welcome there I assure you, and you will be safe. I shall take you to Bardolino, and then go on to Venice. Unfortunately, there is only provision for one maid on my passport, but there is a large storage compartment beneath the seat of my carriage. It will be uncomfortable, but you need only hide in there when I must show my papers. That way there will be no record of your departure from Verona which will make it difficult for your husband to discover in which direction you went." She closed the portmanteau. "Now, my maid should have packed my things by now and I think we should go. I will take your bags, you put up the hood of your cloak and meet us in the square outside the hotel."

Nell awoke, the remnants of her dreams still clinging to her. Lady Westcliffe had bundled her into her carriage, and by the time they had reached Bardolino the sun had been rising, and she had made that fateful boat journey. The money Lady Westcliffe had so generously given Nell had been safely stowed in the pocket of her cloak. But when that garment had threatened to drag her down into the cold depths of the lake, she had been forced to discard it. The current had swept her towards the beach in front of Villa Montovani and the boat into Malcesine. The young boatman had been greatly relieved to discover that she had not drowned and had been able to at least restore her portmanteaux to her. The experience had frightened him, however, and along with his apologies, he had sent Nell an assurance that he would take up another profession.

Unwilling to slip back into slumber lest she relive the terror of being thrown into the icy water, Nell rose from her bed and donned her dressing gown. The storm had long since passed, and she stepped onto her balcony taking long, slow breaths.

It had been months since she had been troubled by nightmares and their re-emergence brought with them several questions. Where was her husband now? Had he looked for her? Had Lady Westcliffe returned to England? Would Nell still be welcome at Ashwick Hall when she eventually returned? And finally, would Bernardo's discovery of her identity force her to do so earlier than she had planned?

Angelica paid her a very generous wage, and she

now had the means to do so, but she did not wish to leave her. If the doctor was correct and she only had months to live, it would be a heartless thing to do. As her eyes turned northwards, she saw the faint light of a lantern. The night boat. Would it bring a letter for Angelica? She fervently hoped so.

Nell revised her opinion when the boat did not turn into the small port of Malcesine. A private traveller then on his way to Verona or Venice, who preferred the water route to the rough road through the mountains on the other side of the lake. Although the boat's sails were up, only the faintest breeze stirred the air and as the moon cast its silvery glow around the vessel, she was not surprised to see oars dipping into the water. The boatmen would earn their keep this night. A slight frown wrinkled her brow as instead of gliding past, the boat turned towards Villa Montovani's private quay. Perhaps the boatmen needed a rest.

A tall figure stepped ashore and began to walk towards the house. Had one of the boatmen decided to personally deliver Angelica's letter? It was impossible to keep anything a secret in such a small community as this, and as Angelica sent Luca into town every morning to see if a letter from her grandson had arrived, it was likely everyone knew of it. Besides, several of the servants lived in the town and little that occurred at the villa remained unknown. It was another reason she had not revealed her true story. She smiled. How kind of him.

CHAPTER 5

Alexander returned to the inn and went to his room to change for dinner. As he strode along the corridor, he heard footsteps behind him and turned swiftly. A comely chamber maid cannoned into him.

"I'm sorry," he said, grasping her shoulders and putting her at arm's length.

Her black eyes smiled saucily up at him. "There is no need to be sorry. I'm not. I came to see if there is *anything* you require, my lord."

Even if he had not spoken Italian, it would have been impossible to mistake her meaning. He sighed. He was used to such a reaction to his looks and his status; it had happened many times before, including on this trip, but he never succumbed to the lure of even the most attractive of inn servants. He was more fastidious. He preferred to know the history of his ladies and he had never been one to share their favours. He felt no contempt for the girl, however. She had an irrepressible air of mischief that suggested her unsubtle offer had been prompted by a desire to have fun with a handsome gentleman rather than out of desperation for money, although he was sure that must be a consideration. It was not his place to judge her, and he did not.

"You are most accommodating, but I have everything that I need."

"Very well." She pouted, turning away but cast him a look over her shoulder that held both regret and speculation. "If you change your mind, ask for Carlotta."

He tossed her a coin. "I will bear that in mind."

"Carlotta!"

The screech came from downstairs. She grinned, bobbed him a curtsy and hurried away.

He shook his head, a faint, ironic smile on his lips. He could not maintain his monkish existence indefinitely. He had been injured in a duel and had married shortly afterwards. It had taken him months to fully recover and by then his wife had been big with child and the doctor had assured him that intimate relations were extremely unwise. Would it have been so wrong to indulge in a little simple pleasure with a willing participant? The smile slid from his lips. Nothing was ever simple; there were always consequences.

He knocked on Mrs Farley's door, feeling a sudden need to see his daughter. She, at least, was a consequence he could not regret. Lady Francesca was seated on the nurse's lap but at sight of Alexander, held out her chubby arms and burbled something incomprehensible. He scooped her up, and she looked at him earnestly before continuing her babbling.

He raised an eyebrow. "You are not satisfied with your accommodation?"

Her forehead wrinkled and she burped.

He laughed. "I fear you may be right but console yourself with the knowledge that we will likely be gone in a few hours."

She smiled and grabbed one of his fingers, holding onto it tightly. He felt his heart squeeze in a most peculiar manner.

"Are you all right, my lord?"

He looked up in surprise. "Yes, of course, Jane. Why wouldn't I be?"

"I'm sure I couldn't say, but you looked as if you were in pain."

Alexander looked down at his daughter, a queer smile twisting his lips. "A touch of indigestion, Jane, that is all."

The nurse's lips twitched, and she murmured, "Before you have eaten, my lord?"

He returned the babe to her, ignoring the remark. "I suggest you try to get a little sleep once you have dined, Jane. You will get little enough this night."

As the boatman had predicted the water calmed, and a little after one in the morning, they set out across the lake. The mountains lurked tall and menacing in the shadows to either side of them, but a benevolent moon cast a silvery path that seemed to promise safe passage. A fair wind filled the sails, and they glided across the glassy surface, the silence only broken by the gentle hiss of water rushing past the bow.

An hour into the journey, the wind became fitful, and the sails began to flap. The boatmen reached for their oars, soon establishing a steady unhurried rhythm. The resemblance between them suggested they were father and son. Neither were large but they possessed a wiry strength equal to the task. The elder of the two sent Alexander several surreptitious glances that he neither acknowledged nor returned, his gaze fixed on lights flickering on high a little distance ahead.

"Is that our destination?" he said.

The boatman followed his pointing finger and laughed. "No. That is Scaligero Castle and its only occupants are a small company of Austrian soldiers who are repairing and strengthening it. Whether that is because they fear future invasions or wish to remind the people that they are subjects of the Austrian Emperor, I don't know."

"Do they need reminding?" Alexander asked dryly.

He shrugged. "Malcesine was part of the Venetian Republic for almost four hundred years, it is only during the last nineteen that France and Austria fought over Veneto like a dog with a bone. Life goes on much as it always has, however, and peace is better than war."

The boatman rested the oars on his legs for a moment and indicated a small light flickering beyond the town. "That is your destination, my lord."

Alexander nodded, although he could make out little in the darkness. Feeling the boatman's eyes still upon him, he glanced at him, raising one eyebrow.

"Is there something you wish to know?" he said softly, a hint of hauteur in the words.

The man shook his head. "I know all I need to. It's all there in your face. You are wondering how your grandmother will receive you." He laughed at Alexander's look of surprise. "There is only one person in these parts with your eyes, my lord." He nodded at a small oilskin bag at his feet. "It is well known that the old lady sends her servant into town every morning to see if there is a letter from her grandson, the marquess. That you've come in person will be a surprise, and I think her cup will be full." He chuckled as Lady Francesca let out a faint cry. "And when Signora Montovani realises she has a great-granddaughter, it will overflow. A child is always a blessing."

"You would think so," Alexander murmured.

The boatman once more pulled at his oars, and they soon neared the castle. Alexander could just make out a steeply sloping rocky incline on top of which grey walls soared skywards. It was an impressive edifice no doubt built in the days when warlords could both protect their citizens within its walls and repel the most determined of invaders from its ramparts. Now it was a symbol of their repression. It had had no power to protect the citizens it loomed over from the political decisions made when the spoils of war were divided amongst the victors of a battle fought miles away in another country, as after the victory at Waterloo, this region had been ceded to Austria at the Congress of Vienna.

And as he had had no power to fight the imposition of his uncle's rule over him and his home had become a prison. He could, of course, have adopted a more pragmatic stance and made his life easier by submitting to the tyranny instead of fighting it. Had his rebellion been worth it?

His gaze dropped to the dark, fathomless waters of the lake. There had always been a darkness inside him, a void. He had tried to fill it with many excesses but had only succeeded in deepening it. Although he had not allowed his uncle the satisfaction of dragging him into his mad world, he had done his best to forge his own path to destruction.

He found it both interesting and surprising that when the eternal abyss that must eventually swallow up every living being had opened its yawning jaws to him as a cold, steel blade had pierced his chest, he had discovered he had no desire to fall into it. It would have been the easiest of the options open to him, but he had chosen a woman who had schemed to entrap him and who carried his child over that tempting oblivion.

He had not been suddenly transformed, but he had decided that if he were to be given a second chance at life, he would try to do better. He had come to realise that Eliza had also been damaged by her upbringing and that although her actions had been dishonourable, she had acted out of a desire to be tied to a man she thought she loved. He, on the other hand, had taken what he wanted as a balm to his wounded pride when another lady who he had admired had rejected him. He had tried to right that wrong by marrying her, but his actions had still resulted in her death. Perhaps he was cursed.

Francesca's cries were growing louder, and he turned to Jane and reached for her. She snuggled against him and closed her eyes. He followed her example and drew a deep breath. If he was, he would find a way to break the curse. This small, helpless bundle in his arms was his path to redemption. He would protect her with every fibre of his being and ensure that she grew to adulthood happy and carefree, untouched by the cruelty he had endured.

He may not have been possessed by the devil, but that did not mean that he did not possess his own personal demon. It taunted him now. *How will you manage that when you are as twisted and stunted inside as the trees that grow on the moor?*

He growled low in his throat and quickly passed the child back to her nurse before his agitation could communicate itself to her.

I will find an innocent, kind-hearted woman untouched by misery who will be able to offer her the love she deserves.

She would bore you within a week.

His eyes snapped open, a flash of exasperation sparking through them. He saw they were passing a small harbour.

"Are you not forgetting your deliveries?" he snapped irritably.

The boatman chuckled. "Signora Montovani is well respected, and she has waited long enough for this family reunion. I will not delay the joy she will surely feel at your arrival."

Alexander's gaze moved beyond the town. The light the boatman had indicated earlier was brighter now, and he could just make out a lantern suspended from the corner of a building. As they drew closer, he saw the three-storey house was of moderate size and set close to the water. His eyes roamed over the building as they turned towards a small quay just beyond it, and he felt a prickle of unease at the base of his neck. Something moved in the shadows on one of the two balconies on the first floor. Someone was watching them.

"Wait here a moment," he said softly as they tied up to the quay. "I will see if we can gain entry without waking the entire household."

He stepped from the boat and strode towards the house, his eyes fixed on the dark figure, his unease growing with each step. His senses were on alert, his instincts telling him that danger awaited him. They had saved him on more than one occasion, and he had learned never to ignore them. He stopped at the corner of the house and tensed as the figure leant forwards. The lamp's flame flickered over tumbling, red gold curls surrounding a pale oval face. He could not see the colour of her eyes, but he felt a jolt of awareness as they connected with his own.

The figure paused as it neared the corner of the house, and Nell leant forward to call a quiet greeting. The words stuck in her throat as he glanced up at her, his features illuminated by the large lamp that hung a few feet above him. Nell's eyes widened and she suddenly found it difficult to draw breath. This stranger was most certainly not the boatman. His high cheekbones, straight nose and firm lips seemed sculpted by the hand of a master. She could not see the colour of his eyes, but she knew they would be green. She had seen those features before, captured in a portrait that hung in Angelica's sitting room. Set in a soft, smooth-skinned oval face they had been beguiling and breathtakingly beautiful, framed by a chiselled jaw and strong eyebrows they were striking, mesmerising, and devastatingly handsome.

Panic suddenly gripped her, and she stepped back into her room, closing the doors and drawing the curtains with unsteady hands. She had never thought the marquess would come in person, and she wished that he had not. The last thing she wanted was someone from her husband's world here.

Flint had not cancelled the papers when he returned to Town, and she had, at first, not been able to resist perusing them for news of him. She had soon learned not to. They had delighted in pointing out that although Lord F— had recently married, it seemed he found his wife wanting as he had not seen fit to introduce her into society and had already been seen in the company of a well-known opera dancer.

They had also mentioned a rather large loss he had suffered at the gaming table and speculated on the extent of her fortune, assuming it to be very large indeed as considering Lord F—'s well-known proclivities, a more unsuitable match for him than a vicar's daughter would have been difficult to imagine. They had assumed, quite correctly, that her portion came from her mother, whose identity they had yet to discover, and had pretended some sympathy for plain daughters who must bolster their husbands' coffers and then be left to languish in the country. It had occurred to her that there would be no point in publishing such stuff if there were not a large audience waiting to lap it up, and she had been thankful that she had at least been spared the humiliation of meeting that audience.

Whilst punishing herself in this way, she had also seen Lord Eagleton's name mentioned in connection to women and a large win he had had at Newmarket. Whilst it seemed the marquess was more fortunate than her husband, she assumed them to be of the same ilk. She would never have suggested Angelica send that letter if she had thought there was the slimmest chance he would visit her in person. No, she was not that selfish. She would, however, have left before his arrival if they had been given any warning of his coming.

The ringing of a bell in the distance sent her scurrying to her bed. Savio would do all that was required. She would put off meeting the marquess as long as was possible. He would not recognise her, of course, but she did not yet know if Bernardo would reveal her identity. She had toyed with the idea of stealing his thunder by revealing the truth to Angelica herself, but she could not do that now. Lord Eagleton would likely disapprove of his relative housing a woman who had condemned herself in the eyes of society. More importantly, he might betray her whereabouts to the world and then her husband might discover it. She huddled under her blankets and squeezed her eyes shut. Her hard-won peace was shattered, and she could see only one option open to her. She must leave.

The woman suddenly reared back and disappeared into the house, closing the doors to her chamber with a snap. Alexander stood looking up at the empty balcony for some moments, a small frown between his eyes. It seemed his instincts had played him false. What danger could a slender slip of a girl present to him or his daughter? His impression of her had been fleeting, but he felt sure she was beautiful. Who was she and why had she retreated so precipitately without speaking to him? He shook his head as if to clear it. No doubt she had gone to inform someone of his arrival.

He moved to the front door and waited. When no sound of hurrying footsteps came from within, he rang the bell. He would not have chosen to rouse his grandmother at such an hour, but it could not be helped. By the time he heard the bolts being drawn back, his luggage had been brought from the boat and his entourage had gathered around him.

"Savio is old," the boatman said, setting down the last trunk, "and his dignity would not allow him to come to the door before he dressed."

The door opened, revealing a grey-haired man, his lips pursed in annoyance.

"Savio," the boatman said cheerfully, "stop looking as if you have drunk sour milk. I have brought you precious gifts."

The man raised the candle he held in his hand and surveyed the marquess. Any doubts Alexander may have had about his resemblance to his family fled as he watched the butler's expression change.

"Mio Dio! You look just like your mother."

The boatman walked away chuckling.

Lady Francesca emitted a faint wail and the butler's eyes widened. "Come, bring the baby in, my lord. I will relight the fire whilst your rooms are prepared."

"Thank you," Alexander said, stepping across the threshold. "I would prefer my daughter and nurse be put in a chamber near my own. My valet and footman can help prepare the chambers if it will help."

"It will, my lord. Most of the servants reside in the town and will not be here for a few hours yet. Only myself, Signora Montovani's personal maid and one other stay here."

"It is a peculiar arrangement," Alexander murmured, following the butler to the far end of the room.

"It is not the English custom, I know, but most of them have families."

The embers of the fire were still glowing, and the man stooped towards a pile of logs stacked neatly to one side of the fireplace. Alexander did not miss the wince that crossed the old retainer's face.

"I will see to the fire, Savio. You may show my servants how they may help you."

He put the man gently out of the way and swiftly reached for two logs. He placed them on the embers, and they caught immediately.

"If you will take the child, my lord, I will also help make up the rooms," Mrs Farley said. "Timothy must carry up the luggage."

Alexander arranged his daughter in the crook of his arm and seated himself beside the fire. The baby opened her eyes and regarded the butler, who had leant down to observe her. He smiled gently and said in a voice suddenly thick with emotion, "Welcome, little one."

She wriggled and then let out an angry cry when she realised she could not release her arms. Alexander loosened the blanket that swaddled her.

"Do not be ungracious, my daughter."

The butler straightened, laughing softly. "Her grandmother also had a temper if she did not get her way."

A faint confused voice drifted down from the floor above. "Savio? Who is there? No doubt my mind is playing cruel tricks upon me, but I thought I heard a babe crying."

He turned and moved towards the stairs as quickly as his age would allow. "Do not try to come down, signora. You will fall."

"Leave it to me," Timothy said, mounting them swiftly.

Alexander stood, his stomach suddenly clenching. Mumbled voices could be heard above followed by the footman's firm tread as he descended. He emerged from the darkness, carrying a frail, white-haired lady. Timothy gently set her on her feet in front of the marquess. Her lightly bronzed, wrinkled skin was drawn tightly over high cheekbones, and her emerald eyes glowed from their sunken depths. They roved hungrily over his face before dropping to the baby.

She reached out an unsteady hand and he took it, but his usual address deserted him, and he could not force words past the lump forming in his throat. His grandmother did not seem to need them. Raw, powerful emotions simmered behind a veil of tears as her eyes rose again to meet his, and he discovered he could read every one of them. Sadness, regret, wonder and joy followed themselves swiftly until only one remained. Love. Pure, unconditional love. It communicated itself to him as clearly as that of his daughter, and he felt humbled before it. She offered it to him even though she thought he had ignored her existence, merely because he was of her blood.

Her fingers tightened on his. "You are the image of your mother. How proud she would be if she could see what a fine, handsome man you have grown into."

Her words broke the spell that bound him, and he grimaced. "I have done very little to make her proud, Grandmother."

She smiled gently. "That is not true. You have come, Alexander. That alone would make her proud. Now, help me to a chair and let me hold the child."

As the servants melted away, he did so. "Her name is Francesca."

Angelica stroked the tufts of black hair on the infant's head. "It is a beautiful name."

Francesca stared intently up at her great-grandmother, smiled and closed her eyes.

"She feels the bond," the old woman said, glancing up. "As do I, and as you do, I hope."

He could not deny it. He had felt a connection when he had read her letters, and the moment their eyes had met, it had deepened. He was not used to expressing his feelings, but he owed her something and so spoke the words in his mind.

"I felt it the moment I read your letters, Grandmother. They only came into my possession recently and I felt your pain. I am sorry for it… for everything that happened."

She observed him steadily for some moments and

then sighed. "My poor boy. I too feel your pain. Tell me all about it."

This was not what Alexander wanted or had intended. He did not wish to douse his grandmother's joy so soon, if at all.

"It is late. You must be tired."

She shook her head. "For the first time in a long time, I am not. There is another in the house who is dear to me and will not share her pain, and I do not press her because I do not have the right. You will tell me everything, Alexander, because you are my blood and I ask it of you. I have spent too many years wondering about your life, worrying about it. Now, I will know everything so that I may know how best to help you."

Mrs Farley returned for her charge, and Savio brought them each a blanket, wine and biscuits, allowing Alexander a few moments to gather his thoughts. It had been on the tip of his tongue to deny he wanted or needed her help, but he knew that was a lie. He would not reward her loving welcome with falsity or deny her right to know him.

They sat by the fire until the candles guttered in their sockets and the dawn sent fingers of light through the shutters. Once he started, he found he could not stop. As he stared into the fire, the dam he had built around his memories burst and they danced in the flames as he brought forth his history in an expressionless voice. He did not tell her quite every-thing, but his clenched fists and expression often revealed what his words did not. He, at last, came to an end, feeling drained and scoured. He looked up quickly, half expecting to see his grandmother had fallen asleep long ago.

She had not, but sat erect, her hands clasped on her lap and her expression distant and stony. His heart clenched and his stomach twisted. She despised him as much as he had feared she would. As much as he deserved.

"It is worse than I had imagined," she said, a thread of steel winding through her softly uttered words.

Alexander flinched.

"And if your uncle were not already dead, I would happily murder him. What was your father thinking?"

"He was not thinking," Alexander said, relief flooding through him as he realised her anger was not aimed at him. "He was too sunk in his despair and a bottle of brandy to consider anything, although my uncle was convinced he blamed me for my mother's death."

"That is nonsense," she said fiercely. "Do you blame Francesca for your wife's death?"

He thrust a hand through his hair, feeling suddenly unutterably weary. "Of course not, but then I was not madly in love with her."

Angelica sighed. "Alexander, you defied your uncle when he was alive, do not stop now that he is dead. You must purge yourself of his insidious poison. Your mother and wife died in or soon after childbirth; unfortunate events that were not in anyone's power to prevent. Your father drank himself to death in an orgy of self-pity rather than protect his child. That was his choice and his alone. You, on the other hand, have chosen to love and cherish

Francesca. You have wasted much of your life running from your responsibilities, but when it mattered you did not. You did the right thing, the honourable thing."

The shadow of a smile touched his lips. "It appears you are determined to champion me but to be fair, I was not given much choice. I believe I told you about the duel."

"That is a practice you will abstain from in future," Angelica said firmly, her eyes kindling.

He gave a soft laugh. "It is a pity you were not allowed to come to me, Grandmother. I believe I would have listened to you, perhaps even my father would have."

Angelica sighed. "It was my dearest wish, but it was not to be. I will have to be satisfied with you listening to me now."

"You are a fraud, Grandmother. You claimed in your letter to be old and tired, waiting only to hear from me before you embraced your last sleep."

A decided twinkle came into her eyes. "It was true enough, but your visit has achieved what none of the doctor's tonics could; it has revived me."

An indignant screech came from the staircase. "Signora! Are you mad? Have you been sitting here all night? You will kill yourself. I will have something to say to Savio for allowing this."

"Nonsense, Beatrice. I feel very much alive and had enjoyed several hours sleep before I was disturbed." She chuckled. "You are merely cross because you sleep so soundly you missed all the excitement."

The maid came out of the shadows, her dismayed

expression freezing on her face as she looked at Alexander. "Mio Dio!"

"Precisely," Angelica said, smiling. "It is I who have kept my grandson from his bed. We shall both now retire, however."

She rose to her feet as she spoke and accepted the arm Alexander offered her, patting it gently with her other hand. "You must sleep as long as you need."

CHAPTER 6

The rattle of china gently clinking penetrated Nell's consciousness and she opened bleary eyes. Maria was bent over a tray, her back to her.

"Maria," she murmured, "what time is it?"

"Almost eleven, signora."

Nell shot upright. "Why didn't you wake me?"

"You did not stir when I came in, and it seemed a shame to wake you when Signora Montovani is likely to sleep for some hours yet."

Nell threw back the bedcovers. "Is she ill?"

The maid turned, a cup of tea in her hand, and Nell saw that her dark eyes were sparkling with excitement.

"Beatrice seems to think she will be for she sat up all night." She passed Nell the cup, adding with a lift of her brows, "Talking to her grandson, the marquess."

Nell started and the cup tipped at a precarious angle. Maria swooped and took it from her before it slid off the saucer.

"It is a great surprise, no?"

"Yes," Nell whispered, as the vision of a man far more handsome than he had a right to be standing beneath her balcony swam into her mind.

"I have not seen him yet," Maria said, placing the cup on a nearby occasional table, "but Savio assures me he is the image of his mother. Me, I do not think Signora Montovani will be ill. I think she will be over-joyed! Is it not news of the most wonderful?"

"Is it not wonderful news?" Nell corrected absently.

It was, of course, from Angelica's perspective.

Maria opened a wardrobe and reached for a dress. "And he has brought his daughter. She is the sweetest bambina with eyes just like Signora Montovani's."

"A baby?" Nell repeated stupidly.

"Si, Lady Francesca. Her nursemaid, Signora Farley, told me that Lady Eagleton died soon after she was born. The marquess is unlucky, eh?"

Maria turned, holding up a blue muslin dress with gold trim. Nell nodded and went to the washstand, splashing her face to avoid answering. She felt confused. The man who had come all this way with his baby daughter to see his grandmother did not align with her image of a womanising gambler who indulged only his own selfish pleasures. Had he gambled away his fortune and hoped his grandmother could repair it or had marriage changed him? Had he loved his wife enough to change his ways? Was it her fault that her marriage had not prospered? Had she been lacking in some way?

"Signora? Perhaps it is you who are ill. You look very pale."

Nell realised she was standing there with water dripping off her chin and reached for the towel.

"I am perfectly well, Maria. I did not sleep well, that is all."

The maid nodded. "It is what I told Signor Montovani when he asked for you."

Nell suddenly remembered their assignation on the beach, and she felt dread lodge in the pit of her stomach.

"Quickly, Maria. Help me into my dress."

The maid tilted her head and regarded Nell in some surprise. "There is no hurry. He has gone to the vineyard but said he would be back around noon."

"Nevertheless," Nell said, "I must check that everything is going on just as it should."

The maid gave a knowing smile. "Did something happen last night that has made you change your mind about Signor Montovani?"

Nell pulled her nightgown over her head mumbling dryly through the cotton, "Not in the way you imagine."

The maid looked disappointed, but as she helped Nell into her gown, murmured into her ear, "Perhaps the marquess will be more to your taste. If he looks like his mother, he must be very beautiful."

"I think you mean handsome," Nell said, turning away. "And I have already told you that I cannot… will not marry again. You may leave me now, Maria."

The maid sighed, shook her head and walked to the door, pausing there a moment to look over her shoulder. "You must have either loved or hated Signor Marsdon very much."

Nell met her eyes in the mirror, unaware of the

shock and pain reflected in the glass. "Why do you say that?" she murmured.

"It is two sides of the same coin, no?" the maid said philosophically. "And for one so young and beautiful as you, signora, it is not natural for you to be alone unless you cannot bear to replace your husband with another. Only a great love or a great fear would make you so. Me, I have seen it. With my mother, it was a great love, but with my aunt, it was a great fear; her husband was a brute. They live together now and are happy enough." She gave a sad little smile. "And now you live with Signora Montovani and perhaps one day you will also be happy."

Nell sat staring at the closed door for some moments. She had thought herself in love with Flint, but it had been an illusion. She had not known him at all. Had she hated him? She had certainly felt fear, shame, contempt and disgust, but hate seemed too strong a word. Perhaps she was not capable of either emotion. She busied herself with the brush. It was better that way. If she had truly loved him, he would have destroyed her rather than merely causing her pain and humiliation.

She did not have time to style her hair and so simply gathered it in a clasp at the back of her neck. She felt the change in the house the moment she left her room. It hummed with anticipation. Maids huddled in corners, whispering and giggling, only returning to their polishing and sweeping when they saw Nell descending the stairs. There was a spring in Savio's step as he came into the hall to greet her and a smile on his lips.

"Is it not a wonderful day, Signora Marsdon? Have you heard the news?"

"Yes, to both questions," she said, feeling a little guilty that she had left the old retainer to organise everything. "I am sorry that I was not on hand to help you with the arrangements for the visitors, but perhaps there is something I can do for you now?"

"I have seen to everything," he said. "I have just sent Maria and Luca to fetch more provisions, and Lord Eagleton's servants did what was necessary when they arrived. There is nothing for you to do."

"Then I shall step out for a breath of air."

She walked across the short stretch of lawn in front of the house and down the steps onto the shingle beach. It was sunny but a chill wind blew, and she wrapped her arms about herself. She would miss this view, but she must leave, and it was nobody's fault but her own. She had been taught since a small child that lying was a sin, and she was now discovering that no matter the circumstances, it would come back to haunt you. She drew in a deep breath and her wild thoughts of the night before receded. It would be cowardly to leave under false pretences. Her reputation could hardly be compromised any more than it already was. She was sure that rumours of her flight must have reached England's shores, and she would lie no longer.

The crunch of gravel underfoot made her tense, but she pushed away the tendrils of fear that threatened to wind themselves about her heart, head, and tongue. When she had escaped her husband, she had promised herself that she would never again put herself in any man's power. If Bernardo thought he could blackmail her in some way, he would soon learn of his mistake. Raising her chin, she whirled about. Hazel eyes, blazing with defiance, met cool, assessing green ones.

She gasped and stumbled backwards, losing her balance as the pebbles shifted beneath her feet. One moment she was flailing her arms in a desperate attempt to avoid the ignominy of falling into the water in front of the marquess, and the next found herself hauled uncomfortably close to him. She froze, staring mutely up at him as he examined her face in a leisurely fashion. When he met her gaze, he frowned and released her.

"I did not mean to alarm you, Mrs Marsdon."

She took a hasty step backwards suddenly finding her tongue. "Then you should not sneak up on people, sir."

One dark eyebrow winged up. "It is not a habit of mine, I believe. And if I surprised you, I think it was because you were expecting someone else. As for saving you from a wetting in the lake, think nothing of it."

There was a drawl in his words that had not been there when he had first spoken, and she suddenly remembered the unwisdom of antagonising this man. Her limbs unbent enough for her to execute a slight curtsy.

"Forgive me, my lord. I am grateful you did not let me fall."

"Have we met before?" he said thoughtfully. "No, I do not think I would forget you. And yet you retreated in such haste last evening when I paused to speak to you that I wondered."

"I thought you were the boatman, and I was not dressed, sir."

A satirical smile touched his lips. "Ah, I see. You were not alarmed at the prospect of the boatman seeing you in a state of undress, but you were me. Do I deduce that although we have not met you know something of my reputation?"

"A very little," she acknowledged. "And only what I read in the papers."

"Have you been abroad long, Mrs Marsdon?"

"Since 1814."

"Ah, then you would not have seen the notice of my wedding or the lack of scandal thereafter. You have nothing to fear from me, I assure you. Even if I had not reformed my habits, I would offer no insult to anyone living in my grandmother's house."

That, at least, answered one of her questions. It seemed his wife had had the power to change his ways. What a pity he had lost her so soon.

"I am sorry that you lost your wife," she said.

"Thank you," he said. "And I that you lost your husband."

Her gaze dropped to the floor and colour flooded her cheeks. He sounded sincere and she could not accept his solicitude. She must end this charade.

"I did not lose him quite in the way you think," she murmured.

He bent towards her. "I think I must have misheard you. What did you say?"

"Excuse me, Lord Eagleton, Signora Marsdon, but Signora Montovani would like you both to join her for some light refreshments in her sitting room."

Nell glanced up in surprise. "She should be sleeping, Savio."

He chuckled. "You try telling her that. It was wonderful to hear her put Beatrice in her place when she suggested it. It was the Signora Montovani of old speaking."

Nell glanced at the house and saw Bernardo standing on the balcony of Angelica's sitting room, observing them.

"Well then, we must not keep her waiting."

She walked quickly towards the house, desirous of getting the forthcoming interview over as quickly as possible. She had no desire to upset Angelica, but at least she would have her family about her to support her. Unlike Nell. She would have no one to support her. No, that was not quite true. Lady Westcliffe had offered her a safe place to go until she could map out her future.

"Who was that on the balcony?"

The deep voice beside her made her jump. She had not expected the marquess to catch up with her. "He is Bernardo Montovani, your grandfather's great-nephew, so I suppose some sort of cousin to you. Like you, he has only recently made Angelica's acquaintance."

Surprise flashed in his eyes. "Why is that?"

"A family feud that started in your grandfather's time. When the glass business failed, Bernardo's grandfather was discovered to have been stealing from the company for some time. He denied it and claimed his brother was using him as a scapegoat. However it was, he made no attempt to mend the rift, nor did his son. Bernardo waited until his father died before he went against his wishes."

"My grandmother must have been delighted," he said in a colourless tone.

"She was pleased," Nell acknowledged, looking up at him. "But not as happy as your visit seems to have made her. What made you come after all this time?"

His eyes dropped to hers, their expression shuttered. "Are you always this inquisitive, Mrs Marsdon?"

He clearly thought her impertinent, and she supposed he was right to do so. It was not a companion's place to ask her employer's relative such a personal question. However, she was unlikely to remain a companion much longer and wished to know.

"No," she said coolly, stepping into the house, "but I am very fond of Angelica, and it is I who encouraged her to write to you again. I cannot help wondering why you came after all this time."

His jaws tightened. "Do you suspect me of ulterior motives, Mrs Marsdon?"

"Do you have any?" she countered.

A soft laugh shook him as they began to ascend the stairs. "Not in the way I think you mean. I have not gambled away my fortune—" He paused as she coloured. "Ah, I see that thought had crossed your mind. My motives are my own, ma'am, but as it seems I owe you something, I will satisfy your curiosity in some part. I did not come before because until very recently I believed both my grandparents to have died in a boating accident before my birth."

"Oh," she murmured, quite stunned.

"What a suspicious mind you have, ma'am. May I ask you how you came to be here?"

"I *was* in a boating accident and washed up on the beach. Your grandmother took me in."

They had reached the door to Angelica's sitting room when he said, "And did you have ulterior motives for remaining here?"

She felt his eyes burning into her but did not meet his gaze. "I stayed at first because I had to, and then because I wanted to."

She pushed open the door and Angelica greeted her with a radiant smile.

"Ah, you have already met my grandson, Nell."

She went to her, dropping a light kiss on her cheek. "It is wonderful to see you looking so well, Angelica."

She retreated as the marquess made his bow and was introduced to Bernardo, who professed himself delighted to meet his English cousin.

"Is it not strange that we should both meet our grandmother within a month of each other?"

"It is certainly curious," he replied civilly but without any noticeable warmth.

"It is as if fate has brought us together for a reason," Bernardo continued.

He was much younger than the marquess, somewhere in his mid-twenties Nell guessed, but his boyish enthusiasm seemed forced.

"Do you think so?" the marquess said softly. "I do not choose to put my trust in fate but prefer to shape my future and that of my daughter with my own hands."

Bernardo's smile did not quite reach his eyes. "I wish you luck with that, but it is my experience that what happens to us is not always in our hands. My family's silk business, for instance, was thriving before Napoleon's troops trampled the countryside and cut down many of our mulberry trees to use as firewood."

Nell had not heard of this before and was not surprised to hear bitterness lace his words.

"That was unfortunate," the marquess agreed, "but was the result of a power-hungry man, not fate."

"I thought you said your business was doing well," Angelica put in gently.

"It is once more thriving," Bernardo said, "but after many years of not doing so."

"Then your father did well," Angelica said, her eyes going to the portrait of her daughter. "Unfortunate things happen to us all, but we must rise above them."

Nell watched the marquess as he too looked at the portrait of his mother. For a moment his features seemed hewn from marble, but then she saw a muscle twitch in his jaw, and he walked slowly towards it. Angelica rose from her chair and went to stand beside him.

Nell felt like she was intruding on an intensely private moment and her eyes dropped to the carpet. She was not aware of Bernardo's approach until she saw his boots.

"You missed our rendezvous," he said quietly.

She did not meet his gaze. "I overslept."

"Are you really that unconcerned about my revealing your true circumstances?"

She sighed. "I doubt very much that you know them."

"I know a great deal that could harm you."

She glanced up angrily as his fingers encircled her wrist. "Let me go."

"Do not speak so loudly," he warned her. "You would not wish to upset my great-aunt."

"Neither would you, I hope," she said, glancing pointedly at her wrist.

He released her. "Of course not. You may ensure my silence by merely making yourself a little more amenable."

A look of revulsion crossed her face. "You disgust me, sir."

His face hardened. "You are a great fool, I think. I have only to drop a few words into certain ears and you will find yourself in a great deal of trouble."

"Drop away," she said through gritted teeth.

CHAPTER 7

A lexander's breath caught in his throat, and he felt gooseflesh rise on his skin as he stared at his mother's face. When he looked at his father's portrait, he saw a handsome stranger and felt nothing apart from a lingering resentment. This painting drew him slowly across the room as effectively as if his mother had called to him. She was so like him and yet so different. Her intelligent green eyes were the same shade as his, although the warmth, happiness and hint of mischief they held made them seem brighter. His, he knew, were often cold, assessing, and guarded.

She was not quite smiling, but her lips seemed to tilt naturally upwards as if she were perpetually on the verge of doing so. Her figure was slender and her posture confident and relaxed. Her skin had the soft sheen of youth and health.

"Her likeness was taken not long before she married your father."

Alexander glanced down at his grandmother. "Was she as happy as she appears?"

"Oh, yes. We used to call her our little beam of sunshine."

A half-smile touched Alexander's lips. "And yet Savio informed me that my mother had a temper."

Angelica laughed softly. "Perhaps, when she was very young. She liked to have her way, but she discovered quite early that charm was a more powerful tool than tantrums."

His gaze returned to the portrait. "Perhaps wisdom is passed down the female line," he murmured. "Francesca can already disarm me with a smile or glance. I hope she will hold herself with such confidence and exude a similar happiness when she is a young woman."

"You may need a little help with that," Angelica said gently.

"I know it."

A prickle at the back of his neck made him turn his head. Mrs Marsdon was as beautiful in her way as his mother had been, but she exuded wariness and a thinly veiled hostility. He frowned as he saw Bernardo Montovani take her wrist and bend his head to murmur something in her ear. She tensed, reared back and hissed something indistinguishable through her teeth. The same look of defiance she had worn when she had whirled around on the beach flashed in her eyes, and he knew it had been Bernardo she had been expecting. That she had not desired his company then or now was clear.

"Is something amiss, Mrs Marsdon?" he said, his cut-glass tones slicing through the tension that arced between the two of them.

"Bernardo?" Angelica said, a note of reproof in

her voice. "I hope you have not upset Nell in some way?"

He turned his hands palm up and shrugged. "I have merely been offering her a few words of advice."

"It appears she does not want them," Alexander said coolly.

Her defiance quickly faded, and Nell nibbled her bottom lip. She had the look of a hunted deer about to flee, and he would lay odds that whatever suggestion Bernardo had made had not been respectable. Her face was extremely expressive, and he watched in some fascination as a steely determination crept into her eyes. Her shoulders went back, her chin lifted, and she walked with graceful, measured steps across the room. Her eyes remained fixed on his grandmother and as she drew closer, he saw regret flicker through them.

"I am sorry, Angelica, but I have deceived you. I am not what… who I appear to be."

Alexander's gaze flicked to Bernardo, and he saw surprise, anger, and calculation swiftly chase themselves across his face. Had he tried to blackmail Mrs Marsdon by offering his silence over whatever revelation she was about to make for her favours? If so, it seemed she was about to sweep the rug from beneath his feet. He felt a flicker of admiration for the woman.

Angelica took both of Nell's hands and smiled. "Bless you, my child, you have not deceived me. I have always known that you were hiding some deep pain, and I hoped you would learn to trust me enough to confide in me. Would you like me to send the men away?"

"No," she said. "Bernardo has heard some part of

my story, I suspect, and Lord Eagleton is an interested party through his relationship to you. I would rather they heard the truth of the matter from my own lips."

"Go on," Angelica said softly.

Nell nodded and withdrew her hands, clasping them in a tight grip in front of her. "Although I was for many years Miss Marsdon, I have never been Mrs Marsdon. I was asked my name when I was ill, half-swooning and meant no deceit. By the time I regained my senses, it seemed too difficult to explain everything."

"That I can well believe," Bernardo said dryly.

Something tugged deep in the recesses of Alexander's mind, but the memory remained elusive. It was so long since he had taken any interest in worldly affairs.

Angelica frowned at her great-nephew before leading Nell to a sofa. "I thought it was strange you were travelling alone. Sit down, my dear, and tell us your story." She glanced again at Bernardo and then Alexander, a stern light in her eyes.

"I will brook no interruptions."

Bernardo leant against the wall and crossed his arms. Alexander nodded and sat in an armchair that gave him a clear view of Nell's face, or at least her profile, as she sat sideways, all her attention on Angelica as if hers was the only opinion that mattered to her. She began to play with her wedding band. Angelica's eyes dropped to it.

"Are you a widow, Nell?"

She shook her head. "No."

"Is that so——"

Angelica cut Bernardo short, her eyes never leaving Nell's. "No interruptions."

"But—"

Angelica sent her great-nephew a scathing glance. "Leave us or hold your peace. In my house, you will do as you are bid."

Alexander's lips twitched as Bernardo reddened. For all her kindness and apparent frailness, his grandmother had been and apparently still was a formidable woman. It appeared her companion had been put off her stride, however, and she seemed to shrink into herself.

"I… I don't know where to start," she faltered.

"At the beginning," Angelica gently encouraged. "I have seen the good, caring person you are, Nell, and I will not judge you whatever your story, but Bernardo and Alexander might need a little context to understand the predicament that led to your flight."

"You know that?" Nell said, pulling her hair over her shoulder as if it could shield her in some way.

The sunlight caught it turning it to flame and Alexander knew the urge to run his fingers through its silken length. Although he did not approve of his methods, he could not entirely blame Bernardo for his desire to know this woman better.

"Why else would you have been alone and unprotected? To attempt to travel to England in such a way was either an act of great foolhardiness or one borne of desperation, and I do not think you a fool, Nell."

A flush of colour infused her cheeks. "I have been a great fool, I believe, but I knew no better. I grew up in a quiet, rural parish. My father was the vicar, and he educated me after my mother died. The result was that apart from what our housekeeper taught me, I learned little that has proven of use to me. I certainly knew nothing of the ways of worldly men, and when one strayed into my orbit, I was naïve enough to believe that he was everything he appeared to be."

Alexander shifted in his chair and leant forward, his arms resting on his knees. He had a feeling this was going to be interesting.

Nell's voice broke a little. "My father was so proud on my wedding day. He had married above his station and always said that if one was patient, love would find you and overcome all hurdles. I believed him, for although my mother died when I was only twelve, I remember her as contented and happy. He never touched a penny of her fortune but insisted she used it for the fripperies he could ill afford to give her." She sighed and twisted a curl of hair around her finger. "There was little need of fripperies in the depths of Devon, however, and her fortune was settled upon me."

Alexander's gaze became intent. Devon? Had this beauty grown up in his own county and he had not known of it? His jaw tightened. It was just as well; he had never tried to seduce innocent ladies of quality, but he had to admit, she would have been a temptation.

"I never knew it," she continued. "How could I? We lived in a very simple style and were happy for it to be so."

"But did you never go into society?" Angelica asked.

Nell smiled wanly. "Thanks to Lady Larraby, I did. She was the wife of Sir James Larraby, the local squire, and a good friend of my mother's. It was very kind of her to concern herself with me, for she had six daughters to establish. However, when I turned seventeen, she insisted I be allowed to go to the local assemblies. She took me shopping, updated my wardrobe, and insisted I had dancing lessons with her daughters. It was all very pleasant, but by the time I was nineteen, I had lost the enthusiasm for such nonsense and was quite happy running my father's household and helping him with his parishioners."

Alexander's mobile eyebrow winged up. By God! Were there no red-blooded males in whatever part of Devon she hailed from? It seemed the same thought had crossed Angelica's mind.

"But, Nell, surely a stream of admirers paid you homage?"

"There were several, but my father did not encourage any of them." She smiled wryly. "Although they were respectable enough, and certainly not interested in my inheritance as no one apart from Sir James and Lady Larraby knew of it, they were not of the first stare."

"Ah," Angelica said gently, "I begin to understand. Your father wished for you just such a fairy tale as he had experienced. Your mother married beneath her status for love, and he wished for you to marry above yours for love."

Nell nodded, her eyes dropping as a flush of colour rushed into her cheeks. "I think you are right. He is distantly related to an earl, Lord Marsdon, and had once considered writing to him on my behalf in the hope he could find a female to sponsor my come out. But he decided against it."

Alexander's eyes closed on a sigh, and he felt pity snake through him as he finally captured the elusive memory he had been searching for a few moments ago. She had married Flint. He recalled that there had been a great deal of speculation about her. Lord Marsdon had been applied to but had said that if there was a connection, it was so remote he had no knowledge of it. When Flint had not brought his wife to Town, the general consensus had been that he was so badly dipped that he had married a woman too hideous for him to display. In the clubs, some had whispered that it was better if it was so, for then she might escape the attentions of one who was rumoured to have unusual tastes.

"My father always said that when the time was right, the correct suitor would appear. Lord Flint appeared to be him. He could not seem to keep away and was interested in everything about me, not just my looks but what I thought. He was gentle, kind, and never tried to steal a private moment with me or take liberties, although my father would sometimes leave us for a short while or allow him to take me for a walk or a drive. Then he stayed away for a few days, and when he did come, it was to take his leave."

He wooed you softly and then just when he was sure you were ready to fall into his palm, he raised the stakes, Alexander mused cynically.

"He seemed perturbed, unhappy, and when my father enquired if there was anything amiss, he admitted there was. He said it was a wrench to leave me, but he must. My father had been in hourly expectation of receiving an offer for my hand and asked him when we might expect to see him again." Nell gave a bitter laugh. "When I remember his performance, I feel positively nauseous. He said he felt like a cad for raising hopes in my breast that he could not fulfil. That if he were free to marry for love he would not hesitate to offer for me, but he was not. He explained that he had inherited debts, and although he was slowly bringing his estates back into order, it would be years before he could consider supporting a wife and family. He had told himself every day that he must not seek me out again, and yet whichever way he set out, he always found himself before the rectory gates."

Alexander was not surprised Nell felt sick; so did he. Machiavelli would have been proud of Flint's strategy.

"My father said he understood that Lord Flint had many responsibilities and he respected him for putting them ahead of his own desires. And then he looked at me, simply saying, *Well, Nell? If you could also marry for love, would you choose Lord Flint?*" She sighed, her fingers twining together. "You may guess my answer. It was then that my father revealed that I had twenty thousand pounds."

Alexander's jaw tightened. And you offered it to him on a plate, not realising that his debts would probably swallow half of it in an instant.

"He seemed shocked, and then a slow smile spread across his face. He said he felt as if he had stepped between the covers of a fairy tale, and that if I would trust him with my happiness, he would be

91

honoured." Her lips curled. "He fell upon his knees and took my hands, looking at me worshipfully. He said he could not in all good conscience touch a penny of my money but would be content with knowing that I would never go without the elegancies of life."

Alexander's lip curled. He parroted the vicar's stance. Masterful. Of course, Flint had known of her fortune all along. That sort of thing always got out, especially when the mother of six daughters held the secret.

"I would not hear of it. My father's circumstances were very different, and I did not wish my husband to be living under a mountain of debt. It would only have bred resentment and my father agreed with me."

Of course, he did, Alexander thought savagely. *He sounds as naïve and mawkish a man as ever I heard of.*

"As you may have already divined, our marriage was no fairy tale but rather a nightmare. My husband… I…" she paused, gulping, "we did not suit. I am convinced he somehow knew of my fortune from the start and that it is the only reason he married me, for soon afterwards he left me in the country whilst he went to London to squander it. When he returned some months later, we fled to the continent to escape his creditors."

Many men who would marry a woman as beautiful as her if she had not a penny, Alexander mused. *Flint was not one of them.*

"My husband continued to gamble in an effort to recoup his fortune. He did not succeed, could not succeed, for whenever he won, he would think his luck had turned and continue to gamble. The cycle repeated itself over and over again until he just kept losing, and when things became desperate, he… he…"

Alexander heard the catch in her voice, and glancing up, saw her head was bowed. He leant forwards to catch words uttered in barely more than a whisper.

"He offered me to a man in lieu of his debt and for some additional payment. I overheard the conversation and fled."

She had curled her hands so tightly in her lap that her knuckles were white as bone. Alexander knew a moment of searing anger. He recognised her shame, felt it, and empathised with it. His situation had been very different, but he knew well the feeling of being in someone's power, of having no one to turn to, and the shame that prevented you from seeking help. That she had had the bravery to escape rather than submit to the ultimate humiliation, despite the condemnation the world would surely heap upon her, deserved his respect.

"My poor child," Angelica said, covering her hands with her own. "You were very right to do so. Your husband is a monster."

"Was a monster," Bernardo said.

Nell's head snapped up and around. "What do you mean?"

"Lord Flint was found floating in the river Adige."

She stared at him for several moments in blank incomprehension.

"My husband is dead?"

"He is," Bernardo said. "When you proclaimed yourself a widow, you were speaking the truth." A smile curled his lips. "A coincidence, I am sure."

The gaze she turned on Alexander held amazement and a hint of hope. "Is it true? Am I free?"

He did not blame her for her lack of grief, he even admired her for not feigning an emotion she could hardly feel, but her candour surprised him, nonetheless. She seemed to realise it for she hurried into speech, colour flaming in her cheeks.

"I am sorry. That sounded callous, I know, and I never wished him or anyone dead, but neither will I pretend a fondness for him that I did not, could not feel. However, perhaps he was a friend of yours, in which case I apologise for my clumsiness."

"He was no friend of mine," Alexander said sharply, disgusted that she would think he might have been. She had some reason, he supposed. He had never tried to excuse or deny his past, but he found himself pointing out certain differences between himself and Flint. "I may never have been a pattern card of respectability, but I neither wasted my fortune nor continued in my previous lifestyle once I married."

"No... I see," she said a little uncertainly. "But is it true, Lord Eagleton?"

He took some small comfort in the fact that she seemed to trust his word above Bernardo's. "His death was reported in the newspapers. The article was brief, and as far as I can recall only mentioned that he had drowned and that his wife was missing."

Angelica looked at her great-nephew. "Bernardo? If you knew some part of this, why did you hide it from me?"

He straightened and shrugged. "I did not wish to upset you unnecessarily and I wished to discuss the matter with Lady Flint before I took any further steps. I made a few enquiries after my first visit. A lonely old woman is vulnerable, and I felt I must protect your interests."

"I hope you were discreet," Angelica said.

"Of course. I was away a great deal last year. My father wished to expand the business and I was given the task of finding new customers and so I had not heard of the scandal of the murdered baron."

"Murdered?" Nell whispered.

"Did you think he had thrown himself into the river when he discovered your absence?" Bernardo asked dryly.

"Perhaps… I don't know… I can't seem to think at all."

Nell's eyes were huge in her pale face, shock and bewilderment writ clear there.

"Be plain, man," Alexander snapped. "If you have something to say, say it."

Bernardo stiffened at this peremptory request, but after a moment continued. "His valet was greatly distressed when Lord Flint did not return to his hotel, and he set up a great hue and cry. His body was found two days later, and it was discovered that he had been stabbed before he was thrown into his watery grave. It seems there were several possible suspects as Lord Flint had some large debts outstanding, but they all had alibis." His eyes turned to Nell. "And then, of course, there was the conundrum of the missing wife. I was not sure, at first, that you and she were one and the same, but the timing of your arrival in Malcesine seemed something of a coincidence, and when I discovered certain other facts, I could not doubt it. I believe the mayor would be very interested in speaking with you. You are a loose end that he would very much like to tie up. It seems you managed to leave Verona without any record of it at any of the city gates."

CHAPTER 8

N ell felt sick. She rose to her feet, her legs feeling unsteady beneath her.

"I'm a suspect in my husband's death? That is ludicrous."

"Of course, it is," Angelica said. "And there is no need for you to return to Verona." She looked gravely at Bernardo. "You did not reveal that you knew Nell's whereabouts, I hope?"

"No. I was not sure what to do for the best."

Nell sent him a scathing look. What he should have said was that he was unsure how to turn the information to his best advantage. She would very much have liked to expose him for trying to blackmail her, but she would not go that far; it would only cause Angelica pain.

"You believed I was somehow involved, didn't you?"

He held up his hands. "I didn't know what to believe. I was hoping that you would enlighten me on several aspects of the case. You must admit that leaving the city without a trace seemed suspicious. Count Fringuello had been seen with your husband the night he disappeared and was the first to be questioned. He admitted that Lord Flint had offered you to him for a night. I do not know if it is the English custom, but it is not unheard of for Italian ladies to take a lover. It is highly unusual for their husbands to offer them to another man for payment, however. You had every reason to despise your husband, and if he came to you and goaded you with what he had done, it is entirely possible that you might have responded violently to such provocation. A crime of passion is understood if not condoned in our country."

"I am not a passionate woman, and I am never violent," Nell snapped.

Bernardo's eyes moved to her hair. "That is not the reputation of women who possess red hair. They are said to have a temper, and it appeared you had taken some pains to disguise your identity. You had cut your hair and left in a hurry. Long tresses of it were discovered in your room." He smiled. "When I discovered the colour of those tresses, I was almost certain that you and Lady Flint were one and the same."

"I was shocked and angry," Nell cried. "And I cut it off because I suddenly despised it and all the men who seemed to think it meant something that it did not."

"That is one explanation, certainly," Bernardo allowed.

His words offered Nell no comfort, for there was a speculative glint in his eyes.

"However," he continued, "spots of blood were

also found on the dressing table and carpet of your room."

Nell's heart began to thud in her ears. "I cut myself when I lopped off my hair."

"Bernardo!" Angelica said sharply. "You cannot believe that Nell murdered her husband. I know she is not capable of it."

Again, he held up his hands. "I am merely informing you what was discovered and why some people might think that it was so."

Anger began to fizz in Nell's veins. She felt sure he was enjoying her discomfort.

"How, pray tell, did I manage to carry him to the river and dispose of him?"

He shrugged. Nell was beginning to hate the gesture he used so frequently.

"A beautiful woman may drive a usually sane man to acts of madness."

"Bernardo!" Angelica protested.

"I am only repeating what I have heard said. I bear Lady Flint no ill will."

Nell did not believe him. He wished to punish her for spurning his advances.

"I must leave," she said, turning to Angelica. "As soon as is possible. It seems I have already been tried and convicted in some people's minds."

"Perhaps it would be better for you to go," Bernardo said. "You have cared for my great-aunt so well that I know you will not wish to cause her trouble and anxiety. You can write to her when you are safe."

"Where would you go?" Alexander said.

Nell was surprised at his question. "To England. Where else would I go?"

"You will also find things difficult for you there," he said bluntly. "There was a great deal of speculation about you before Flint's death, and it will only have increased afterwards. As Bernardo has pointed out, your disappearance looked suspicious, and as you are unknown to the *ton*, they have been free to speculate as wildly as they please."

"What are they saying?" she whispered, sinking back into her chair.

"I do not know. I do not read the scandal sheets, nor do I indulge in idle gossip." He sneered. "I have too often been the subject of it and in my experience, much of what is reported is false or grossly exaggerated. Besides, until I came here, I had not left Eagleton Priory for over a year, nor, apart from my man of business, have I been receiving visitors. I would be very surprised, however, if the whispers in certain quarters were not both salacious and malicious."

Nell sat as if turned to stone. She had had few options open to her before, but now it seemed as if she had none. She could hardly expect Lady Westcliffe to harbour a suspected murderer, neither could she bring such shame on her father. Was this her punishment for leaving her husband?

Angelica sent her grandson an anxious look.

"How did you discover so many details, cousin? Many of them were not reported in the English papers."

The marquess's words broke through Nell's despair, and although she did not look up, she listened intently.

"To give out too many details would have compromised the investigation. Apart from that, Verona has need of visitors; supporting a large garrison of Austrian soldiers is expensive and it would not have been in the town's interests to frighten away English visitors. Lord Flint's successor has been kept informed on every aspect of the case, however."

"You have still not explained how *you* are so well informed," Alexander reminded him.

"My father was a friend of the mayor," Bernardo said, a hint of self-satisfaction in his voice. "Signor Persico has many interests and invested in our business on the condition that he might experiment with more efficient ways of spinning silk and breeding silkworms. His input has been most beneficial. He recently invited me to dinner. Towards the end of the evening, with a little prompting, the full story came out. The mayor had recently received a letter from Lord Flint's successor, enquiring if there had been any developments in the case, particularly regarding Lady Flint's whereabouts, and so it was once again fresh in his mind."

Nell closed her eyes, willing the rapid beating of her heart to slow. She had never met her husband's younger brother. He was a soldier and had been abroad for years. There had been some fall-out between them, or at least that was what Flint had told her when she had asked him. Be that as it may, he must wish to bring his brother's murderer to justice. As he was so interested in her whereabouts it seemed that he too suspected her.

Her eyes sprang open as a gentle touch on the back of her hand made her start. Lord Eagleton squatted before her. His cool, clear gaze felt like an oasis of calm after a storm.

"What should I do?" she whispered.

"You must clear your name," he said calmly. "Even then, you may never be accepted into some circles merely because of your association with Flint. To waste one fortune is frowned upon, to waste two put him beyond redemption. However, you will garner some sympathy if it is proven that you had no hand in his death and were merely a victim of his machinations. He was not universally popular."

"Alexander is right," Angelica said. "You must not stand for this slander, Nell."

Nell glanced at her and was not surprised that she looked a little tired.

"I am sorry, Angelica. I never meant to spoil your happiness."

She smiled. "You could not do so. Being reunited with my family is a great joy and helping you will give me a purpose. I have been floating along in a malaise for too long, Nell, and I should never have given in to it. Everyone needs a purpose and people to care about. I will help you; we will all help you." Her gaze moved to her grandson. "You will help, won't you?"

He stood up. "I will do what I can to help Lady Flint—"

"Please," Nell said, a shiver running through her, "do not call me that."

"What then?" he asked. "Would you prefer I call you Mrs Marsdon?"

She shook her head. "Just call me Nell. As all the servants in this house are addressed by their first names, it will not appear overly strange."

Angelica's eyes flickered towards the door that led to her bedroom. "You are not a servant, Nell, and never have I treated you as one. It is true that the servants will think nothing of it, however." Her gaze moved on to her great-nephew. "And you, Bernardo? Will you help us?"

He came to her and took her hand, bowing over it. "I will do anything in my power to bring out the truth if it will make you happy."

"Good boy," she said. "Now, we will have some refreshments before we discuss what might be done. Ring the bell, Bernardo. Savio has been waiting for my signal."

Nell could not face any of the delicacies brought, but a cup of sweet tea did much to calm her nerves. Although her situation was worse than she had imagined, she was glad that she was no longer living a lie, and it was comforting that she had allies who believed her. She suppressed a grimace as Bernardo took a seat beside her; she was not convinced he was one of them.

"Allow me to apologise for any offence I may have caused you," he said softly. "I believe your mistrust of my sex may have led you to misconstrue my words."

She looked at him sceptically.

"Consider what I said for a moment. I only suggested that you be a little more amenable to me, nothing more."

"You also said that you knew a great deal that could harm me," Nell replied in a low voice.

"Yes, because it was true as you have discovered. That did not mean I would use it against you. I have explained that I wished to hear your side of the story before I decided what to do, but your reserve, your coldness, made that difficult. I only wished to suggest that you should unbend enough to trust me. If I expressed myself poorly, you must remember that English is not my native tongue."

Nell's brow wrinkled as she considered his words. Had her experiences made her automatically construe his words in the worst possible light? It was possible she supposed.

"If I was mistaken, I apologise," she said stiffly.

His relieved smile seemed genuine. "May we start again, Nell? I have promised to help bring the truth to light, after all. Apart from a desire for justice to be done, my great-aunt's goodwill is very important to me."

As he had always treated Angelica with respect and affection, she believed this last statement.

"Very well," she said, sighing. "I may have misconstrued your words, and I am grateful that you wished to discover my side of the story before revealing my whereabouts to the mayor."

Savio and Luca entered the room and took away the remnants of their luncheon. Alexander had been talking with his grandmother, but once they were alone again, he regarded Nell intently.

"Have you any witnesses who could support your story?"

"Yes," she said, hope burgeoning in her breast. "Lady Westcliffe. Do you know her?"

"I know of her," he said. "She is a philanthropist and has a property in Somerset that she uses to house orphans and others who are indigent."

Nell felt a spurt of surprise that he would know such a thing. "Is it perhaps called Ashwick Hall?"

"Yes, that's it. I am a little acquainted with Westcliffe. How do they come into this?"

"Lady Westcliffe also overheard the interaction between my husband and the count Bernardo mentioned."

"Count Fringuello," he put in helpfully.

"Yes, him," she said, her voice dripping with distaste. "I had just finished cutting my hair when Lady Westcliffe came to my room. She saw that I had injured my hand and bound it, tidied up my hair, and helped me escape. We were in a great hurry because although she had seen my husband leave the yard shortly after the count, we heard his valet go into his room, and it would not have been unusual for him to check on me. There was a storage compartment beneath the seat of her carriage, and I hid there whenever she was asked to show her papers. She took me to Bardolino before joining her husband in Venice."

"This is excellent," Angelica said. "You must write to her immediately, Nell, and ask her to send her account of what happened as evidence. We can take it to the mayor."

"You must certainly write to her," Alexander agreed. "However, I do not think you should wait for a reply to see the mayor. It will speak to your innocence that you went to him as soon as you heard he was looking for you."

"I agree," Bernardo said. "It will also put me in an awkward position if we wait so long. I can tell him that I was unsure of your identity until I spoke with you, but it will be more difficult to explain why I waited several weeks. As he has a stake in my business, I must be seen to be trustworthy."

Nell rose to her feet. "Very well. I shall go and

write to Lady Westcliffe immediately, and if I have to see the mayor, I would do it sooner than later."

"I suggest you allow me to warn him of your coming first," Bernardo said. "I expect your name will be noted at every entrance to the town, and you would not wish to be escorted to him by a custom's official or a soldier. I must return tonight and will arrange accommodation for you and send you word when all is ready."

"You may arrange accommodation for us all," Angelica said. "Nell will not face this meeting alone."

Nell was too relieved to object. The thought of having only Bernardo's support was unappealing.

Bernardo frowned. "Is that wise? I would, of course, be happy to accommodate you at my estate, but my mother is in mourning——"

"I quite understand," Angelica said. "We shall stay in Verona, but I would prefer to hire a house than use a hotel."

"At least allow the doctor to give you his blessing before you embark on a journey that may be injurious to your health," Bernardo said.

Angelica smiled. "Very well, if it will put your mind at ease."

"If you will excuse me, I will go and write that letter," Nell said.

Before she reached the door it opened, and a plain young woman came into the room carrying a baby.

"Is all well, Jane?" Alexander said quickly.

"Yes, my lord. I thought you and your grandmother might like to see Lady Francesca before I lay her down for her afternoon nap."

"Come in, Mrs Farley," Angelica said. "I would certainly like to see my great-granddaughter."

The nurse came further into the room, stooped, and laid the child face down on the carpet. "I had to shorten her dress for the occasion."

The infant pushed herself up on her arms, bent her legs a little beneath her, and began to shuffle backwards, burbling the whole time as if demanding all present observe her. When she reached her father, she walked her hands backwards and pushed herself onto her bottom. It seemed she had not quite mastered so advanced a manoeuvre, however, as she overbalanced. Reaching out a hand, she grabbed the silver tassel that hung from Alexander's glossy hessian boot. It came away in her hand, distracting her from the ignominy of her fall. She waved it in the air for a moment as if proud of herself before bringing it to her mouth.

"Well done, Francesca," Angelica said in doting accents.

Apparently undisturbed by this vandalism of his footwear, the marquess scooped her up, a soft laugh on his lips.

"So, you are on the move, Francesca, a feat worthy of an audience, I agree. However, whilst I have no wish to diminish your accomplishment, might I suggest it may be better if you move in a forward direction so that you may see where you are going?"

His words were delivered in clipped tones, but the gentle way he held her, the smile that still hovered about his lips, and the way his shoulders curved towards her revealed the tenderness beneath them.

"Bless you, sir," the nursemaid said. "She will soon enough."

Nell's eyes darted between them. She was surprised to hear amusement and something very like affection in the servant's voice. None of Flint's servants had ever spoken to him in such a way and they would have been quickly reprimanded for their presumption if they had done so. Lord Eagleton merely sent her a swift smile before returning his attention to his daughter. He removed the silver tassel from her hand. "Whilst I agree you deserve some reward for your endeavours, my lady, my valet will be most put out if I allow you to mangle this ornament."

Lady Francesca thrust out her bottom lip, clearly unimpressed with this reasoning. As her face creased, no doubt in preparation for a lusty wail of protest, Nell came forward, her arms outstretched.

"May I, my lord?"

"Alexander," he corrected. "We have cast aside such formalities, remember?"

Nell was a little startled. She had not expected him to reciprocate when she had asked him to use her name. She had never used her husband's given name; the expected permission had never come, and she had very soon lost any desire for it to do so.

"Here, take her," he said, passing the babe as a disgruntled cry issued from her lips. "Your timing is most propitious."

Nell settled the infant in her arms. "I agree, my dear," she said gently. "It seems most unjust that you must be deprived of your treasure, but gentlemen set such great store by their appearance that it was only to be expected. They become quite nonsensical over their wardrobe and there is no reasoning with them."

"Thank you," Alexander murmured dryly. "I am

sure my daughter will find your observations on my sex most enlightening."

It seemed he was correct, for even as Nell sent him an amused look, the cry died on the infant's lips, and her eyes opened wide as if Nell had just made a startling revelation. She reached out a hand, grabbing the long ribbon of hair that hung over Nell's shoulder, tugging at it and then gently stroking it. Nell's lips curled in a bittersweet smile as the pleasure of the interaction mingled with the sadness that she would likely never bear a child of her own.

"Do you perhaps have some experience with infants, Nell?" Alexander asked.

Her name sounded strangely intimate on the marquess's lips.

"Yes. I had many interactions with the children of my father's parishioners, but in addition to that, a poor little mite, who we named Joshua, was left on our doorstep. As it occurred at a time when influenza was running rife in the household, I was solely responsible for him for almost a month." She smiled wistfully. "And although I knew that I eventually must give him up, I found it surprisingly difficult to do so."

"I hope he went to a good home," said the nurse, a quiver in her voice.

Nell ran the back of her forefinger over Francesca's cheek. "Oh yes. I would not have been able to let him go if that had not been the case. There was a well-respected childless couple that lived in a nearby town who welcomed him with open arms."

Lady Francesca yawned as if this information could be of no interest to her.

"I apologise, my lady," Nell said. "It is so very

tedious to hear about people one has never met, isn't it?"

"Not in your case," Bernardo said, effectively banishing the mood of gentle raillery and bringing Nell to earth with a bump. "And it is quite ridiculous for you all to talk to the child as if she can understand you."

Francesca displayed her contempt for this remark with a burp.

"I quite agree, my child," Alexander drawled. "My cousin has execrable manners."

Bernardo laughed a little uncertainly and after a moment's awkward silence, bowed in the direction of the babe. "Forgive me, my lady, but if you had not woken me in the middle of the night, I might have more patience with all this nonsense."

Francesca blew a bubble.

"I wonder if you are right?" Alexander mused. "But whilst I agree that first impressions are impor-tant, it must be acknowledged that they can be misleading."

Nell could not help but wonder if his words were meant for Bernardo or her.

"I'll lay her down now," Mrs Farley said, coming to take her charge.

"I think I might follow her example and take a nap," Angelica said wearily.

"Yes, do that," Nell urged her. "And I must write that letter."

CHAPTER 9

As the ladies left the room, Alexander glanced at Bernardo. "Would you like to show me the vineyard?"

"Certainly. It will give us a chance to become better acquainted."

Bernardo had resumed his boyish tone, and his words were uttered with apparent delight. Alexander trusted it no more than Nell had.

"I will meet you downstairs in a few minutes," he said. "I must change my boots."

"What do you think of Montovani's man?" he asked Lundy a few moments later.

"He hasn't brought one, my lord," the valet said in an expressionless voice.

"Then he is either very self-sufficient or he doesn't trust his valet."

"I suppose that is possible," Lundy mused. "I have met a few in my profession who do not hesitate to share intimate details about their masters, especially after a drink or two."

His disparaging tone made clear his view on this subject.

Alexander sat down in a chair, thrust one leg out before him, and held up the tassel. "Before you get on your high ropes, it was none of my doing. Don't trouble yourself to reattach it but remove the other one. On reflection, I don't like them."

"Very well, my lord."

The valet donned a pair of white gloves and knelt down before him. "There are several other explanations for his valet's absence," he said glancing up. "He may have given him a holiday—"

"Is that a hint, Lundy?" Alexander said dryly.

"Certainly not, my lord," the valet said on a note of reproof. "The last time you granted me a holiday, you nearly got yourself killed!"

"Your concern is touching," he said softly. "And yet I cannot quite see the connection between those two events. Do you imagine that your presence would have made a difference? That you might have somehow stopped the duel?"

The valet eased his boot off. "Oh no, sir. There's never been anyone who has been able to stop you doing anything once your mind was set upon it. But perhaps my care in the aftermath might have expedited your recovery."

Alexander glanced down, a satirical smile on his lips. He had, in fact, received excellent care after the sobering event until he had been well enough to travel, but he allowed Lundy his delusion. He observed his valet's hair was thinning and flecked with grey, and there was a small bald patch on the top of his head. He wondered idly if he was responsible for it.

"Very true. What has made you stay so long with such a stubborn reprobate as I? It must be all of seventeen years since you entered my service."

"It is," the valet acknowledged, beginning to work on the other boot. "I'd not long been in my first position as valet to Mr Stevenage. You were celebrating your twenty-first birthday at The Pulteney, and he attempted to join your party. You took exception to his purple silk coat embroidered with gold thread." The valet glanced up, smiling wryly. "You were quite right. It was hideous, but I had not yet enough experience or courage to mention it."

"Ah, yes," Alexander said musingly. "I have a vague recollection of the popinjay. When I finally made my way up to bed, I met you on the landing, valise in hand, and with blood trickling down your face."

He smiled as if the memory was a fond one. Lundy picked up the hessians and went into a small dressing room, returning moments later with a pair of top boots.

"He'd thrown his shoe at you before dispensing with your services and the buckle had cut you just beneath the eye."

Lundy touched the faint scar that was testament to the encounter. "That's it, my lord. You said The Pulteney must be going downhill if it allowed brawling within its walls and asked me what I meant by it. When I explained what had happened you said I might as well make myself useful and help you undress."

A soft laugh shook Alexander. "Did I? My recollection is a little hazy. I was a callous youth, wasn't I?

In my defence, I believe I was a trifle bosky. You should have told me to go to the devil."

"That would have been a highly improvident thing for an aspiring valet to do, sir, and those aspirations had already been severely dented by being cast off without a reference."

"Oh, I doubt you would have found another position."

"That was my own despondent thought," Lundy admitted. "It is why I found the courage to offer you my services, my lord, fully expecting to have something else thrown at me. But you laughed, called me an impudent dog, and then said, 'Why not?', thus making amends for your hand in my dismissal, for it was your comments on my employer's coat that had led to it."

"I cannot claim such honourable motives," Alexander said dryly. "And if you had presented your case to me thus, I have no doubt I would have sent you on your way. That you didn't try to appeal to a better nature I did not possess stood you in good stead. I had already determined to surround myself with servants who would have reason to be loyal to me, however, and in that regard, you were a prime candidate."

Having helped the marquess into the top boots, Lundy stood and began to remove his glove, pulling gently at each fingertip in turn.

"I certainly had reason to be grateful to you." He removed the glove, laying it carefully down before starting on the second, his lips twitching. "Of course, gratitude fades over time. I have remained with you because you are a marquess, which circumstance is very good for my consequence."

"That's put me in my place," Alexander said, rising to his feet.

Lundy's eyes swept over his figure. "Of course, you also possess a fine set of shoulders and shapely calves, unlike Mr Stevenage, who required padding for the former and sawdust for the latter. These assets can also only reflect well on me, and if my suggestions that you allow me to add a little more colour and flair to your wardrobe have fallen on deaf ears, you have, at least, never hurled anything other than words at my head."

Alexander laughed. "I was right, you are an impudent dog!"

Lundy grinned. "Is there anything else I can do for you, sir?"

"As a matter of fact, there is. Find a way to attach those tassels to my daughter's cot. I wish her to be able to see them, perhaps even touch them, but not detach them."

"Very well, sir."

He found Bernardo pacing up and down in front of the house.

"I apologise for keeping you waiting, cousin."

"Think nothing of it," Bernardo said cheerfully.

They walked along a dirt track that led them behind the house and up a short but steep incline. After a few hundred yards they came to a crossroads, and Bernardo gestured towards the left.

"That way will take you into Malcesine. It is a fine old town, if a little rustic. The path ahead will lead you onto the lower slopes of Monte Baldo." He took the right fork. "The vineyard is this way."

Olive trees lined the path, their gnarled, knotted trunks twisted and scarred with age. Their branches seemed to shoot in all directions and were heavily laden with olives, some green, some reddish brown. They formed part of an ancient grove which lay to the left of the path. There appeared to be no uniformity to their planting, and the trees often leant at strange angles as if bending beneath the weight of their fruit. Among them, tussocks of scrubby grass sprouted between slabs of grey rock. In some respects, it reminded him of the wild stretch of moor near Eagleton Priory.

"Does the olive grove also belong to my grandmother?" Alexander asked.

"Yes. The olives will be picked at the end of October. As my great-aunt's closest living relative, I expect everything will one day be yours."

Alexander sent him a sideways glance. Had there been a hint of bitterness in his words? Bernardo's face held only a look of interested enquiry, however.

"I have no idea and had not given it any thought."

Bernardo laughed dryly. "Then perhaps you should. Lady Flint has become a favourite of your grandmother, and you would not wish her to cut you out."

"Angelica may do what she wishes with her property," Alexander said. "It can make no difference to me. I have more than enough for my needs."

"I admire your generosity of spirit, cousin," Bernardo said. "But would you really be happy for your grandfather's estate to pass out of the family? It is not the English way, I believe."

Alexander's lips twisted. "I never knew my grandfather and I have no very great opinion of family."

Bernardo laughed. "I shall try not to take your words personally."

"They were not meant to wound you, cousin. My opinion of you is not yet fully formed."

"But of your grandmother?"

A gentle smile touched Alexander's lips. "She and my daughter are the exceptions to the rule."

They had come to two large iron gates that were thrown open. A rough, stone wall stretched out on either side.

"We have arrived," Bernardo said. "You may not feel quite so disinterested after you have seen the vineyard."

It was vast, and unlike the olive grove, there was nothing haphazard about it. Long, leafy trellises stretched out into the distance in ordered rows. Many people hunched over them, picking the grapes, and young girls and boys hurried between them, heavily laden baskets in their hands. Several carts tethered to donkeys waited at the end of the rows to receive the bountiful harvest.

As Alexander took in the scene before him, Bernardo hurried forward to greet a man in a coarse shirt open at the neck. Sun, wind, and age had weathered his skin as they had the bark of the olive trees, but like them, he appeared sturdy and strong. His nut-brown eyes twinkled with humour, and his unhurried stride was confident. He shook hands with Bernardo, leaning forward a little to hear what he had to say. He nodded, his eyes turning towards Alexander, and executed an awkward bow.

"I am Signor Batiste. Lord Eagleton, you must forgive, my English is poor."

"My Venetian is worse," Alexander replied, resorting to the Italian tongue.

The man's face lit up. "We will do very well. It is a great pleasure to meet the grandson of Signora Montovani. Come, I will show you what happens here. No doubt you will have as many questions as Signor Montovani."

Alexander had drunk a lot of wine over the years, but he had never given much thought to its production. By the time it had been explained to him how the mild climate of Lake Garda was perfect for producing fine grapes, had been led amongst the vines and shown how they should be picked to avoid bruising them, and taken to the sheds where they were being pressed, he was far better informed.

He was surprised at the cheerful mien of the men, women, and children who chattered and laughed as they worked. When he mentioned this, Signor Batiste smiled.

"We are a small community, and harvest is an important time. Most of the workers have helped since they were children and know exactly what to do. It unites everyone in a common purpose, and when the work is done, there will be a big party with punch, food, and dancing. It is a time of joy and celebration for a job well done. I hope that you will come."

Alexander made a noncommittal reply, thanked Signor Batiste for his time, and he and Bernardo took their leave.

"Well, cousin?" Bernardo asked as they passed through the gates. "What do you think, now?"

"I found it all very interesting," Alexander said coolly.

"Bah! I find the English reserve that both you and Lady Flint possess very frustrating!" Bernardo complained, throwing up his hands.

Alexander glanced down at him, a satirical glint in his eye. "Yes, so I observed earlier. You should not have laid hands on her, you know. What was the advice you were attempting to give her?"

Bernardo shrugged. "Merely to be more amenable. It is very difficult to prise information from an icicle. I wished her to trust me enough to confide in me. She misunderstood me, and thought I was suggesting something entirely different."

"Indeed, she trusted you so little, she confided in us all. You must have expressed yourself very poorly," Alexander said dryly. "You relieve my mind, however. I must admit that the thought you might be suggesting something *entirely different* also crossed my mind. To dishonour a guest in my grandmother's house would not have been wise."

"I have already said it was not my intention, although what business it is of yours is unclear to me," Bernardo said resentfully.

"Then let me leave no room for misunderstanding. As you pointed out earlier; I am my grandmother's closest kin, therefore, I am in some way responsible for her. You will find me very interested in anything that concerns her happiness, including Lady Flint."

The words, though softly uttered, held a hint of menace. It seemed Bernardo recognised this for his eyes narrowed.

"I think I understand you."

"I somehow doubt it," Alexander murmured.

Bernardo offered him a brief bow. "It seems your

lack of sleep has made you unreasonable, cousin. I will leave you. I must go into Malcesine to arrange a boat for this evening, and I will also seek out the doctor and ask him to pay my great-aunt a visit."

Alexander watched him walk away, a frown between his eyes. He was not one to trust easily, and his instincts told him that in Bernardo's case, he had reason. He was volatile, his moods changing quickly, and although Alexander could understand that Nell's coldness might have irritated him, he did not believe Bernardo's explanation of his conversation with her. He was, however, beginning to doubt his initial inter-pretation of what he had observed.

He felt sure Bernardo would have used the infor-mation he possessed to try and persuade Nell to do something, but it seemed more likely now that he would have encouraged her to leave. He had agreed with her when she had suggested it, after all. His motive may have been to protect Angelica, but his reference to the inheritance made him doubt that. It occurred to Alexander, that before he had made an unexpected appearance, Bernardo might have hoped to inherit, in which case he had every reason to resent Alexander and by extension, his daughter. Was it his natural cynicism that made him think so? Perhaps, perhaps not. Either way, Bernardo would bear watching.

No one seemed to be about when he entered the house, and he decided to catch up on his sleep before dinner. He glanced into his daughter's room on the way, smiling as he saw the tassels suspended above her cot. Her arm reached up, her fingers just coming into contact with one, setting it swinging. Mrs Farley looked up from her sewing and smiled.

"It was an inspired notion, my lord, and has kept Francesca occupied for some time."

"I am glad for your sake, Jane," he said.

Lundy was not in evidence when he entered his room, but the gentle snoring that issued from behind his dressing room door betrayed his whereabouts. Unperturbed, Alexander removed his boots and went to his bed. A rosewood box sat upon his pillow. He removed it, rearranged the pillows, and climbed onto the bed, leaning back against them. He stroked the wood's satiny surface for a moment and then opened the lid. A pile of letters nestled within, and with a half-smile on his lips, he reached for the first one.

CHAPTER 10

It took Nell some time to pen her missive to Lady Westcliffe, and by the time she had explained all that had happened since she had bid her goodbye, she was exhausted. Her fatigue was mental rather than physical, but she lay down on her bed, telling herself that she would just close her eyes for a moment. She fell asleep almost immediately and awoke to Maria drawing the curtains on a darkening sky. She sat up, blinking in astonishment.

"Maria! What time is it?"

"Six and a half, signora."

"Half past six," Nell corrected.

"Si, that is what I said. Dinner will be served in half an hour." The maid turned and went quickly towards the wardrobe. "It was put back because the doctor has been with Signora Montovani and is amazed at the change in her. Did I not tell you it would be so?" She held up a white crape frock with a bodice of Pomona green, a dimple peeping in her cheek. "We must make sure you look your best. The marquess is very fine, no?"

"Not particularly," Nell said, determined to quell the maid's enthusiasm. "His clothes are certainly well cut but rather plain."

Maria laid the dress carefully over a chair, folded her arms, and raised her eyebrows. Nell read the amused challenge in them and suddenly laughed. "Very well, Maria, I will allow his appearance is impressive."

The maid came forward smiling. "His footman is also impressive and very handsome. With his blond hair and blue eyes, he looks like an angel. I spent some time with him today, and Timothy has manners of the most pleasing."

Nell felt her lips twitch. Maria's joie de vivre was infectious. She sobered as the thought that Flint had also been handsome and charming when she had first met him crossed her mind. She stood and turned so the maid could unbutton her dress.

"Be careful, Maria," she cautioned. "I would not like you to suffer a broken heart when the marquess's footman returns to England."

"It is very possible, signora, to flirt with a man without losing your heart. Me, I have had many flirts. It is an enjoyable game, nothing more."

Nell envied Maria's light-heartedness. Although it seemed a long time ago now, she had possessed it once. Most of the men she had met had been charming, and she knew some of them to be good men. She must remember that; it would be a mistake to colour all she met with the same brush.

The image of the marquess holding his daughter flashed into her mind. The scene had touched her. She had not forgotten that although he had apparently reformed his way of life after his marriage, he had been a womaniser and a gambler, but that he had not tried to charm her, was a point in his favour. Although he had offered her his help, he seemed cool, aloof even, and she was glad of it. She needed to trust someone, and she sensed that he would be a formidable ally or a dangerous enemy. For both her own and Angelica's sake, she must try to cultivate some sort of friendship with him.

Taking advantage of Nell's distraction, Maria set about arranging her hair in a way she had long wished to, piled high on top of her head, a few shorter strands clustered around her face, and a longer tress draped over one shoulder. It was not until she pushed a pearl comb into the front of the arrangement, her mouth curled in a satisfied smile, that Nell glanced up. Her lips parted on a gasp. She hardly recognised herself. She looked sophisticated, alluring, and in her opinion, altogether too conspicuous.

"Maria! I do not wish to draw so much attention to myself."

Maria clasped one of the few other items of jewellery that Nell still possessed – her mother's pearls – around her neck, a stubborn jut to her chin.

"There is no time to change anything. Besides, Signor Montovani has already dined and is sleeping as he will travel through the night, so you need not fear him looking."

"And the marquess?" Nell said, raising a delicately arched brow as she stood.

Maria retrieved the dress from the back of the

chair and eased it carefully over Nell's head and white satin slip.

"That one is different. He will notice everything but will not show it, I think."

Exasperation and amusement warred for supremacy in Nell's eyes. "Do not tell me you flirted with Lord Eagleton, Maria!"

The maid giggled. "I *tried* to flirt," she said. "It takes two, and the marquess pretended not to notice."

This outrageous admission drew a reluctant laugh from Nell. "You are incorrigible!"

"Me, I know this word," Maria said proudly. "We have one very like it."

"How do you know he only pretended not to notice?" Nell asked.

Maria waved a hand, adopting a nonchalant air. "I am very wise and just know these things."

As Nell continued holding her eyes with a steady gaze, she suddenly laughed and touched a finger to the corner of her mouth. "He twitched, just here, as if trying not to smile."

"Were you not afraid he might try to take advantage of you?" Nell asked in awed fascination.

"No," the maid said simply. "A man like him would not need to take his pleasure with a servant; he would have a mistress."

Nell felt a flush of colour warm her cheeks. "It is shocking to talk of such things."

"Why?" Maria asked, frowning a little. "It is life, and a man is a man, after all. If he does not have a wife, what else is he to do?"

"I had not thought of it quite like that before," Nell said faintly.

Maria clipped the matching pearl bracelet on Nell's wrist. "I did not mean to shock you. The women in the town often meet and talk openly about anything and everything when the men are not there. I grew up listening to them and although I did not understand everything, when I was old enough my mother or aunt explained things to me. So, you see, nothing can shock me."

Nell could not help but wonder if her mother would have talked openly to her had she lived. She had gone to the marriage bed knowing nothing but what she had gleaned from the animals in the fields about her home. She had somehow thought things would be different between a man and a woman, more tender and passionate, but she had been woefully mistaken. If she had known what to expect, perhaps she would not have found the experience so degrading and distasteful.

"Is it not the same with English women?" Maria asked curiously.

"Genteel women don't talk of intimate or scandalous things in front of unmarried ladies."

"No?" Maria said. "But with other married ladies?"

"I don't know," Nell admitted. "I never had any close female acquaintances after I married."

Maria looked at her in astonishment and sensing that she was about to question her further, Nell went to the door. "I must go down or I will be late."

As she went onto the landing, Angelica's maid came out of her room, wiping at her eyes with a handkerchief.

"Beatrice?" she said going quickly forward. "What is wrong?"

She raised her face from the lace confection, and Nell saw that she was smiling. Nell suspected that the lady's maid had always been jealous of her close relationship with Angelica, which explained why she had never tried to make herself comprehensible when Nell was present. It seemed that was a thing of the past for she spoke to Nell in English.

"I am so happy. This marquess, who is the image of my mistress's daughter, and of her when she was younger, has restored her health and her happiness. She is stronger than I have seen her in years. If you had not made her write to him again, this would not have happened. I am sorry that I have not always made you welcome."

Nell relaxed, returning her smile. "Think nothing of it, Beatrice. Signora Montovani's well-being is all that matters."

As if on cue, Angelica's deep, rich laugh issued from behind her sitting room door.

"I feared that I must be late for dinner, but I assume Lord Eagleton is with his grandmother?"

The maid nodded, wiping at her eyes again as they once more overflowed. "They have much to talk about. He has read all the letters that my mistress wrote to him when he was a child but did not send." She sniffed. "His family must have been very wicked to prevent him knowing his grandmother and to have forbidden her from visiting or writing to him. Signora Montovani is telling him stories of his mother."

"Then I will not interrupt them."

A delighted squeal came from behind an open

door a little farther along the corridor. "I shall pay my respects to Lady Francesca before I go downstairs."

Her eyes widened and a delighted laugh escaped her as she saw the silver tassels suspended over the cot swinging gently back and forth.

"As you see, ma'am, Lord Eagleton does not become nonsensical over his wardrobe," Mrs Farley said dryly.

"No, apparently not," Nell agreed, walking over to the cot. "You must forgive me, Lady Francesca, for maligning your papa."

The baby responded with a gurgle.

"He would do anything for her," Mrs Farley said.

Nell offered her hand to the child, and the baby clasped her finger. "I suspected as much. Have you been in Lord Eagleton's employ long?"

"No, but my grandmother was his nurse, as I am now Lady Francesca's."

"Oh? Did your grandmother grow old in his family's service?"

"She was let go when his lordship was still very young, but he found her later, and made sure that she was comfortable."

"I am pleased to hear it."

The nurse stood, leaned over the cot, and lifted the babe into her arms. Lady Francesca turned her head and nuzzled her nurse's dress, emitting a plaintive cry.

"She wants her feed," Mrs Farley said, a rather wistful smile on her lips. "It will be time to wean her soon."

Nell could sense the woman's sadness and thought she divined the reason for it. "You must miss your own child. Is your mother looking after your baby?"

The nurse sat down, undid a couple of buttons on her dress, and eased it down so that the babe had access to her breast. She stroked Francesca's head as she suckled.

"I was born out of wedlock and my grandma brought me up when my mother ran off with a gypsy. My husband and daughter were taken by a fever. Mary was but two months old. I miss them every day. If Lord Eagleton had not taken me in and given Francesca into my care, I think I would have gone mad."

Nell's heart ached with compassion for the woman. "I am sorry."

"It was God's will," the nurse said softly. "He tests us all, but we must trust in him and persevere."

Nell admired her faith. "You are wise. Good evening, Mrs Farley."

"Good evening, ma'am."

If Nell had needed another reason to trust Lord Eagleton, it seemed she had one. No one who took the time to search for his old nurse and ensured her future comfort and that of her family could be a selfish, heartless wretch. As she reached the top of the stairs, she heard the soft click of a door closing.

"Good evening, Nell."

There was nothing in the cool delivery of these words to alarm her, and yet gooseflesh rose on her arms. Telling herself it was because she had still not become accustomed to his use of her name, she turned towards him, a friendly smile on her lips.

"Lord—"

He cut her off merely by raising an eyebrow.

"Alexander," she amended.

"There, that wasn't so difficult, was it?" he said, coming forward and offering her his arm. "If it is any consolation, it is as strange for me to hear my name on your lips as it is for you to utter it. I came into my title at five years old and was referred to as Eagleton by my uncle and school friends and as my lord by the servants. My nurse, grandmother and now you, are the only people who have ever used my given name."

Nell laid her hand lightly on his sleeve, thinking how impersonal it seemed to always be addressed by your title. She knew that it was usual to address your husband or wife in a formal manner in public, but she had thought it would be different in private. Her parents had always used their given names, Elizabeth and Anthony, behind closed doors. Flint had usually addressed Nell as my lady, or if he was particularly annoyed simply as wife, but she thought that had been the exception rather than the rule. She removed her hand from the marquess's arm as they reached the bottom of the stairs and patted a stray hair into place.

"Do you like it?"

His cat-like eyes narrowed. "You look very fetching, as I am sure you are aware," he drawled. "If you have taken pains with your appearance to impress me, it was unnecessary. I have already said that I will help you and I needed no further encouragement. I rarely give my word, but when I do, I keep it."

Irritation and embarrassment brought a flush of colour to Nell's cheeks. "I was not referring to my appearance," she snapped. "I do not care a fig if you think I look fetching or not."

He looked at her intently for a moment, and then

his eyes lit with amusement and the corner of his mouth twitched, just as Maria had described.

"And now you are laughing at me."

She turned and walked quickly towards the fire at the end of the room. She should have insisted Maria restyle her hair. That he should think she would try to rouse his sympathy by using feminine wiles was insulting and ridiculous. It was true that she had decided it would be better to reach some sort of amity with him, but she had hoped that could be achieved through rational conversation. It seemed there was little chance of that now.

His measured tread sounded on the floorboards behind her.

"Forgive me, Nell. My wide knowledge of females may have led me into error."

She whirled about. "I can well believe it. I suppose you are used to them fainting at your feet or simpering and batting their eyelashes in an effort to engage you. I have not, nor will I ever, resort to such contemptible tactics."

"With your looks, I doubt that was or ever will be necessary."

Her eyes flashed with derision. "Do you not think it demeaning to be valued merely because you are rich, handsome, and titled?"

His lips twisted. "Not if it suits my purpose, and as my wealth, appearance, and title are all I have ever had to offer, it would have been unreasonable of me to grumble."

A long-repressed anger coursed through Nell's veins. "Money and beauty were not all I had to offer, but they were all my husband required."

They stood regarding each other for some moments, his eyes suddenly grave, hers simmering with angry tears. Finally, Alexander broke the silence.

"Flint always was a fool. My wife was very beautiful, Nell, and I did not love her, but I did try to get to know the woman beneath the veneer."

"And what did you find?" she whispered.

"That she had been brought up to value herself only for her beauty, that she was ill-educated, vain and shallow, but that in her own way, she loved me and wished to please me."

"And that made a difference?" Nell asked.

"Yes," Alexander confirmed. "That made a difference. Had she lived, I would have tried to close the gulf between us."

"For your daughter's sake?"

"For all our sakes."

Nell had not expected such frankness from either of them. She suddenly sank into a nearby chair, shocked at her behaviour.

"Forgive me. I am not usually such a termagant. I know that Bernardo said that red hair usually denotes a temper, but that is not… was not true for me. I don't recognise this version of myself."

"Do not apologise," he said softly. "You are changed, Nell. Hurt and pain will do that. I would rather you vented your spleen on me than turn your anger against yourself."

"Is that what you did?"

There was a long silence, broken only by the spitting of the fire.

"Yes," he finally said. "I suppose I did. I do not recommend it. Nothing that happened was your fault.

You will face these accusations and clear your name, Nell. You will go back to England with your head held high and forge a new life, a better life."

She almost believed him.

"When I asked you if you liked it, I was referring to you being addressed by your given name."

"It is strange," he said slowly. "I have been Eagleton for so long, that I do not yet know who Alexander Wraxall is."

"Are they so very different?"

He did not answer for a few moments, and his eyes took on a distant look.

"That remains to be seen. Let us hope so, but do not depend on it. A snake sheds one skin to make way for another but is still not to be trusted."

"You are honest, at least," Nell said.

"Yes," he said brusquely. "It may be my only virtue."

"Nonsense," Nell replied, rising to her feet as she heard Angelica's voice at the top of the stairs. "You also keep your word, remember?"

CHAPTER 11

Angelica refused to be carried downstairs but descended slowly with the aid of Luca on one side and Timothy on the other. Alexander was glad of the distraction. His conversation with Nell had taken far too intimate a turn.

Her unladylike show of anger had broken the accepted mores expected in polite society. It had also broken through his reserve. She had looked magnificent with her eyes blazing, her cheeks flushed, and her bosom heaving. When she had told him she didn't care a fig for what he thought of her appearance, he had believed her and felt both amusement and admiration. His amusement had swiftly died when she had mentioned her husband, and he had wished only to console, comfort, and advise her. This surprised and faintly alarmed him. He was unused to the role and thought himself singularly unfit for it.

It was not her delicate beauty that touched him, but the blend of vulnerability and strength she possessed. There had only been one other lady who had touched him so.

Miss Cressida Harrington had also not cared a fig what he thought of her and had possessed a similar frankness. He had been intrigued and had pursued her, at first, merely due to the novelty of having to exert himself to claim a lady's interest, and then because he had thought her affection might be worth winning. He had been set on having her for his wife. She had repulsed his advances, but her resistance had only made him more determined to have her. He had even been prepared to abduct her. Not to ravish her; he would not be that dishonourable, but so that he would have the time to charm her without the constant interruptions that always seemed to plague their meetings.

His arrogance, he reflected, had been astounding. She had divined his intentions and fled to Leighfield Park, the home of his old nemesis, Ormsley. He had followed her to a ball, still intent on changing her mind, but when he had seen Miss Harrington and Ormsley together, he had finally realised the futility of doing so.

He had not been desperately in love with her, had doubted himself capable of it, but had felt different in her company, no longer bone wearily bored or lonely. He had felt a degree of affection for her and had thought they might deal very well together. Until the moment he had seen Miss Harrington and Ormsley together, he had doubted romantic love existed, but he could not deny the evidence before his eyes and had finally accepted defeat.

His lips twisted in derision. Miss Harrington's love for the honourable, upstanding Ormsley had not prevented him challenging the man to a duel when the earl had knocked him down, and he had gone to that meeting with every intention of running him through. Miss Harrington's arrival on the scene had given him pause, however, and it was he who had been almost fatally wounded. As he had given his word that he would marry Ormsley's young stepmother, Lady Ormsley, if he should lose, his fate had been sealed, or so he had thought.

His eyes went to Nell, who was standing at the bottom of the stairs, offering his grandmother praise and encouragement for her efforts. He must guard against this odd desire to wipe the unhappiness from her face. She was not the woman for him, and he was certainly not the man for her. He suddenly wished they had not agreed to address each other by their given names. It made it harder to keep a barrier of formality between them, but maintain it they must, for both their sakes.

He walked towards the stairs as Angelica reached the bottom. Her breathing was rapid.

"Give a moment," she said breathlessly. "I am a little tired, but I shall be perfectly well in a moment."

"Whilst I am delighted you are feeling so much stronger," Alexander said, "perhaps you should not exert yourself so soon."

"Nonsense. It is only by exerting myself that I will grow stronger." She smiled at Nell. "I am delighted that you have done yourself justice for once, Nell. You look even lovelier than usual tonight." She glanced up at Alexander, a mischievous sparkle in her eyes. "Don't you think so?"

He hid a smile as Nell sent him a fierce look as if to remind him that it had not been for his benefit.

"As it is the first evening I have spent in Nell's company, I cannot say. I will allow, however, that she looks very becoming this evening."

"I was preoccupied, and Maria got a little carried away," she said sharply.

"You should allow her to get carried away more often," Angelica approved, releasing the footmen's arms. "I will do very well now. Give me my walking stick, Luca."

At Angelica's insistence, Alexander sat at the head of the table. Until the soup was removed, they talked of general matters and his impressions of the vineyard.

"It seems very well run, ma'am, and the atmosphere, though industrious, was a happy one. Signor Batiste was very knowledgeable, and I very ignorant." He smiled wryly. "He cannot have found me altogether contemptible, however, for he invited me to the harvest party."

"And did you agree to go?" Nell asked as Angelica nodded dismissal to the servants.

"I answered evasively," he admitted. "I did not know my grandmother's plans, after all."

Nell sent him a sceptical glance. She clearly thought him too high in the instep to consider attending such an event, that he was too arrogant and had too much pride. That there was an element of truth in these unspoken accusations only annoyed him further, which was nonsensical, for he should encourage her to believe the worst of him. Very well, he would play the arrogant marquess, and treat her impertinence with all the haughtiness it deserved. Whilst it was no bad thing that she emerged from Flint's hands wiser and stronger, she must understand her limits. It was not wise to cross swords with so expert a fencer. He raised his eyebrows.

"You doubt my motives, ma'am?"

Instead of looking abashed, her eyes flickered with amusement. "I doubt the Marquess of Eagleton would deign to dine with a group of rustics, what Alexander Wraxall would do remains to be seen."

Damnation! Why had he allowed her to be privy to some of his most private thoughts? She was already using them against him. Still, he had another card up his sleeve.

"Have you ever dined with rustics, Nell?" he drawled.

Still the flush of embarrassment did not come, but a bittersweet smile touched her lips. "When I was under my father's roof, I would sometimes share a meal with his parishioners, and I even cooked for them on occasion."

Of course, she had. For a moment he had forgotten her comparatively humble origins. It was hardly surprising. She looked as elegant and sophisticated as any lady of the *haut ton* tonight, yet the image she had conjured in his mind of her with an apron tied around her waist, her cheeks flushed with heat as she bent over a pot, was strangely alluring. He ruthlessly banished the vision. It was ridiculous to let her get under his skin in this way, and he had never considered such extreme domesticity necessary or desirable in a woman. He was about to utter something cutting to that effect, when Angelica spoke.

"Eduardo and I always used to attend together, and after he died, I went for many years on my own. Perhaps it is time to renew the tradition. If we are here, of course. They will not have finished picking the fruit for a week or two yet, and we may well be in Verona."

This reminder of her circumstances brought an anxious look to Nell's face, and although only moments before he had wished to lower her a peg or two, her anxiety afforded Alexander no satisfaction.

"You need not worry," he said curtly. "You will not be without protection. I shall be as top-lofty and arrogant as my rank allows, and if the mayor wishes to attract foreign visitors to his city, he will hardly wish to upset me."

"Or me," Angelica said. "I am not quite nobody, I hope."

"No, of course not," Nell said, straightening her shoulders. "And I thank you both for your support."

For the rest of the meal, she withdrew into herself, which circumstance also afforded Alexander little satisfaction. He could only conclude that he was far more contrary than he had hitherto imagined.

When the ladies retired not long after ten o'clock, having nothing better to do, he went to his room. Sleep eluded him, however, and he lit the candle by his bedside and again picked up the rosewood box. Angelica's letters had been full of little details about her life. One had been about the grape picking. He opened the lid and scattered the letters on the bedcover, rifling through them until he found the appropriate missive. He scanned the lines quickly until he came to the relevant paragraphs.

The grapes have ripened, and we have our best harvest yet. If your mother was still with us, she would have visited this year, and perhaps have brought you to us. I have no doubt you would have joined the other children who carry the grapes from the vine to the carts. You might think that beneath your dignity, but I assure you even I help pick them, as did your grandfather before he suffered his second stroke. You must not think him unhappy, although he is paralysed on one side. He sits and watches, and always has a smile and a kind word for everyone. He would have liked to see you running between the vines, shouting and laughing with the other children.

It is a time when old quarrels are forgotten, and the community comes together as one. When the last bunch has been picked and pressed, we have a splendid party outside under the sun, and later, the stars. I hope and pray that you will one day experience it, Alexander. I worry sometimes that you will inherit your father's pride. It is not enough merely to provide your people with employment, you must understand them, value and respect them. In return, you will receive much better service and loyalty.

He laid the letter down and leant back against his pillows. As Nell had done, and as he had eventually done when he had been able to employ his own personal servants. He had never, however, sat in any of his tenants' kitchens and discussed over a glass of ale their needs, or got his hands dirty by helping with the harvest. The thought had never occurred to him. The most he had ever done for his tenants was ensure he had a capable steward and offer them a nod and a brief greeting in passing.

He heard footsteps on the landing and as he had not heard Francesca crying, assumed it must be Bernardo leaving. His brows rose in surprise as a knock fell upon his door. He threw the covers back and donned his dressing gown before going to open it. Bernardo stood in the hall, a valise by his feet. He held out his hand.

"I just wanted to say goodbye, cousin. I did not wish to leave on bad terms. You must forgive me if I said or did anything that may have offended you earlier. I am sometimes quick to react to a perceived slight, even if none was intended."

"You did not offend me," Alexander said, shaking his hand.

Bernardo smiled wryly. "I am glad. Having put an end to one family feud, I would not like to start another. They are so stupid, don't you think?"

Not wishing his grandmother or daughter to be disturbed, Alexander agreed to this, wished his cousin a safe journey, and returned to the bed. He began collecting the scattered letters, folding them carefully and placing them in the box. He picked up the last one, laid it on the top of the pile and closed the lid. He frowned, and opened it again, glancing at the flowing script of the direction. His eyes had not played him false; the handwriting was different. Angelica had not written the letter.

He plucked it from the pile, laid down the box and sat on the edge of the bed. He was certain it had not been there before. He had carefully read each letter before he had visited Angelica. He opened it and picked up the candle to peruse its contents.

Eagleton Priory, January 15th, 1778

Dearest Mama,

I am quite out of charity with Eagleton. You would think he would be delighted by the prospect of a child and perhaps an heir, but he fumes and fusses by turns, saying that the child may go to the devil if only I come through the birth safely. It is most unnatural of him, is it not? I forgive him only because I know he cannot mean it and understand this little invisible being is as yet a stranger to him. It is not to me, however, but has so long been a part of myself that I love him or her prodigiously already and cannot wait to hold the babe in my arms. Judging by the way the darling miscreant wriggles, squirms, and kicks, it is a boy, (I shall refer to the child as he from now on, although I care not if is a girl), and he is as eager to make my acquaintance.

I declare Eagleton is jealous of the unborn child and perhaps he has reason. I talk to and of him incessantly, (in Italian when I am alone), and my husband feels sadly neglected. He must learn to share my attentions, however, for the child will be adored and loved as much as any child ever has been, but not suffocated.

My husband keeps me so close that I sometimes think I will run mad, but he has promised to take me to London in the spring so I will be patient. I know it is only because he loves me so much and is morbidly afraid that I will be taken from him.

I have been confined to my bed as I have become so huge that sleep, appetite, and strength have quite deserted me, and both my back and head ache. The accoucheur Eagleton has installed at the priory assures him that it is quite normal at so advanced a stage of pregnancy, but he will not be reassured. He frets and vexes me with his constant hovering. I can bear anything, however, if only my child be born healthy.

I comfort myself with the reflection that when his fears are proven groundless, my lord will be so relieved that he will become more reasonable about you and Papa coming to us. How I wish you were with me now, Mama, to advise me and give me courage. If anything should happen to me, (you see how Eagleton's fears begin to infect me), I would ask that you make sure my darling child is made aware of how very much I loved and longed for him.

My best love to you and Papa,
Your loving daughter,
Livia

Alexander's hand was not quite steady as he folded the letter. He did not return it to the box but slipped it under his pillow, shed his dressing gown, and slipped into bed. He closed his eyes and let out a long, low sigh, feeling his long-held resentment towards his father slip out on the exhalation.

His mother had been loved, perhaps to the point of madness. Alexander might not have experienced that strength of feeling towards his wife, but he loved his daughter, and if anything happened to her, he too might run mad. He quite understood his father being more concerned for his mother than for him; until Francesca had been born, she had been a stranger to him, it was not until he had held her that he had felt something inside him shift.

Had his father ever held him? Alexander suspected it would have made no difference. His resemblance to his mother could have offered his father no comfort but must have been a painful reminder of all he had lost, like scouring an open wound with a wire brush. He had tried to cauterise it with brandy, that too,

Alexander understood; had he not done it himself many times over?

He thought it likely that his father had blamed himself as much as Alexander for Livia's death, as he had felt guilty when Eliza had died. He may have shown little or no interest in his son, but from all Alexander had discovered that was hardly unusual; many gentlemen had little interest in the infantry. He had provided him with a nurse who had been kind to him, however, and he could not have known how cruel his brother would become.

When he finally slipped into a deep sleep, Alexander's dreams were all of his mother stroking her swollen stomach and talking to him in Italian. The sound of Lundy moving quietly about in his dressing room eventually woke him. Fingers of light seeped between the cracks in the blinds. He sat up with a start, threw the covers back, and made haste to the door.

"Jane?" he called urgently, stepping across the hallway and thrusting open the door to the room she shared with his daughter.

"Yes, my lord?" she said, hoisting Francesca onto her shoulder as she stood and offered him a curtsy.

"Thank God!" he murmured, taking three quick strides and plucking the child from her grasp. "When I realised she had not been with me last night…" He broke off, unwilling to utter aloud the fear that had gripped him. It was ridiculous to think anything might have happened. He was as overanxious a parent as his father had been a husband. "I slept unusually deeply last night and did not hear her cries. You should have brought her to me."

Mrs Farley smiled. "She didn't wake, either. You stayed up the whole night when we arrived, and I let her cry herself to sleep. It seems to have done the trick and broken her of the habit."

Alexander was not at all sure he wished her to be cured of the habit. He had needed her as much as she had needed him. But he too had slept soundly and without nightmares. Perhaps they were both cured.

CHAPTER 12

N ell was seated before her dressing table pulling a brush through her hair when she heard Alexander's anguished cry. Had something happened to Francesca? The thought worried her, and she dropped the brush and raced from the room. She found the marquess clasping his daughter, her cries muffled as her head was pressed so tightly against his shoulder.

"Be careful," she said quickly, "you do not wish to suffocate her."

He glanced at her, a stunned expression on his face, and then handed the infant back to her nurse.

"No, I must not do that."

Nell's eyes widened and her cheeks coloured, her own state of undress forgotten as she registered his. She, at least, wore a dressing gown that covered her from neck to toe; his nightshirt came only to midthigh, revealing muscled legs. It was open at the neck, the strong column of his throat exposed. His tousled hair and sleepy eyes made him seem strangely vulnerable.

Her heart started to thump, and she took an involuntary step backwards.

"I shall leave you. When I heard you cry out, I thought Lady Francesca might be ill. I came to see if there is anything I could do to help."

A dull flush darkened the high line of his cheekbones. "That was kind of you," he said, his voice rough. "I apologise for disturbing you. I think I must still have been half dreaming. Stay if you wish. I must dress."

He strode from the room on the words. Nell sent the nurse an enquiring glance.

Mrs Farley chuckled as she laid the baby in the cot. "It was only because she slept through the night, ma'am. She only has to squeak, and he comes and takes her to his bed."

Nell's brow wrinkled in thought. "He is a doting father, no doubt, but that seems a little excessive, and why would he think her silence meant something had happened to her?"

The nurse sighed. "He has lost so many of his family…"

"As have you," Nell said gently.

"Yes," Mrs Farley agreed, "but I never blamed myself for their deaths."

"He blames himself?" Nell said, shocked.

The nurse nodded. "His wife died giving birth to his child, his mother giving birth to him, and his father drank himself to death from grief."

"But he could not help any of that," Nell said.

The nurse's brow darkened. "No, but I've heard him cry out things in his sleep that make me suspicion someone made him think he was in some way responsible for his parents' deaths, at least. And I'm sure I know who. My grandma says as how his uncle, who became his guardian, was a cold, cruel man, and he sent her away when she tried to stop him whipping his lordship when he was no more than seven years old for nothing more than a boyish prank."

Nell's appalled expression seemed to give the woman pause.

"I've said too much," she said. "His lordship is a very private man, and he wouldn't thank me for blabbing about him."

"No, of course not," Nell said.

As she made her way back along the landing, she saw Beatrice outside Angelica's door, balancing a tray holding her mistress's chocolate in one hand, her other on the door handle.

"Let me take it in," she said. "There is something I wish to discuss with Signora Montovani."

"Very well, ma'am," the maid said, pushing open the door. "Just send word when she wishes to get up."

"You may be sure I will."

Angelica sat very straight in her bed, her eyes fixed on the door.

"Nell? Did I hear Alexander cry out?"

She smiled, coming forward and laying down the tray. "Yes, but only because his daughter slept the night through. He is an anxious parent."

She passed the cup to Angelica and pulled a chair to the side of the bed. The old lady sighed and laid back against her pillows.

"You wish to know why?"

"Mrs Farley explained it a little." She frowned. "I do not mean to pry, but I have already been quick to anger twice in your grandson's presence. Perhaps if I understood him better, I might be able to temper my reactions." She gave a rather bemused laugh. "He told me that he had been a marquess since he was five and did not yet know who Alexander Wraxall was, which I quite understood. I am in a similar situation. Much of who Ellen Marsdon was is gone, and I am not at all sure I much like what is left. I never used to be so combative, so easily roused to anger."

"Circumstances change us all, Nell, but they rarely change the essence of who we are." She regarded Nell intently. "How did my grandson respond to this anger?"

"He said he would rather I took it out on him than on myself. He tried to comfort me, and in the next breath warned me not to trust him." Her brow wrinkled in thought. "When I realised he had come in person, I was glad for you but afraid for myself. I thought him to be like Flint, knew that he had had mistresses and gambled—"

"I believe neither habit is uncommon, Nell," Angelica said softly.

"No," Nell said. "And I had judged him before I had met him. Now I don't know what to think, and yet I feel as if I can trust him."

"Of course, you can," Angelica said. "It is himself he does not yet trust." She sipped her chocolate thoughtfully. "As he has all of your story, I think it only fair that you know some part of his. Be careful how you use that knowledge, Nell. Alexander does not wish for sympathy or pity. If he is to discover who Alexander Wraxall is, he will need to be challenged and tested." She smiled and added, "As will you, I suspect."

When Nell left Angelica's room a little over an hour later, she had much food for thought. When she entered her own, she saw that Maria had made her bed but was no longer in evidence. She went to her wardrobe and absently picked out a white, muslin dress, her mind mulling over what she had discovered.

Although she felt an aching compassion for the boy who had undoubtedly suffered much cruelty, she felt conflicted about the man he had subsequently become. She had been wrong to judge him so hastily, but there were similarities between him and Flint. They had both wasted their lives indulging in selfish pleasures rather than using their position in society to do some good. That went against everything she had been brought up to believe in, and it faintly appalled her. She was the last woman on earth to admire a rake, even a reformed one.

She was fair enough to recognise the differences between her husband and Alexander, particularly regarding their motivations. Mrs Pinkerton, the house-keeper at Flint Hall, had felt some sympathy for Nell and had shaken her head over Flint's treatment of her and the way the estate had been run down over the years. Her words echoed in Nell's mind.

His parents would be heartbroken. Master Rupert was the apple of their eye and spoilt and indulged from the moment he was born. And look what has come of it.

Flint's behaviour had been driven by his belief that the satisfaction of his desires was all that was impor-tant, Alexander's by the need to distance himself from his past or perhaps punish himself for it. It had taken him almost being killed to try and reform his way of life, and whilst Nell did believe in such transformative moments, she could not help but wonder if they were permanent.

As she discarded her dressing gown, she recalled a man in her village who had been addicted to strong drink. Mr Withers had let his family half starve in order to pay for his habit, but when he had become dangerously ill from it and then recovered, he had said that God had forgiven him his sins and from that day forth he would never touch a drop of liquor again. He had kept his word for over a year, but when one of his children had died from a putrid fever, he had taken to it again and had drunk himself to death. As Alexander's father had. Was such unsteadiness hereditary? Would his good intentions be overthrown at the first sign of adversity? She hoped not. His depth of feeling for his daughter was palpable, and if, God forbid, anything happened to that child, she dreaded to think how he might react.

Frowning, Nell donned her dress and sat down to gather her hair into a simple knot. She was in no doubt that Alexander had offered to help and support her to please his grandmother, but it had been good of him, nonetheless. She wished to help him in turn, but how?

The sound of laughter outside distracted her from her thoughts, and she rose and went onto the balcony. Timothy and Maria were too close to the house for her to have a clear view of them, but their voices carried clearly to her.

"Leave me be," Maria said, laughing. "I am trying to… how you say… shine the door knocker."

"I think you mean polish," came the footman's amused voice. "And you've missed a bit."

"Where?"

"Here, look."

There were a few moments of silence and then the maid squealed.

"It is you who need polish!" she said, in mock outrage. "And I will give it to you!"

"No! You must not dirty my uniform!"

"You should have thought of that before!"

Laughing, Timothy ran around the corner of the house, Maria chasing him waving her duster. Smiling at their antics, Nell glanced over the lake towards Limone. The sun glimmered on terraces of tall, white pillars amongst which the lemon trees grew. The pillars supported wooden planks in winter to protect the trees.

Her smile faded and her eyes grew distant as she tried to grasp the threads of thought forming in her mind. They were all products of the circumstances in which they grew, she supposed. Alexander had grown up without warmth and protection, she with perhaps too much, and when she had been transferred to a very different situation, she had not known how to adapt and had withered. Here, where the climate was mild, the scenery beautiful, and the people kind, she had begun to recover, and now she was beginning to put out new shoots; they might need training, but they were new shoots, nonetheless.

A smile flickered over her lips as the kernel of an idea began to take root. In her mind, Alexander Wraxall was the man who adored his child, searched for his nurse, and spoke gently to his grandmother, and on occasion to her. The Marquess of Eagleton was the man with the flying eyebrow, narrowed eyes, and purring drawl. The two were entwined, but as an uneven shrub could be reshaped by the weak side being pruned hard back and the stronger side only lightly, perhaps his less desirable traits could be too if she put her new prickly shoots to good use.

The sound of the door closing firmly below her made her start. Maria had no doubt returned to finish polishing the door knocker. She wondered if Timothy had escaped her retribution. She doubted he would mind either way. It was not Maria, however.

A firm tread sounded on the hard-baked track that separated the house from the sliver of garden and Alexander came into view. He did not glance up but strode purposefully away from the house. Even garbed in an olive-green coat cut more for comfort than style, fawn pantaloons, a pair of serviceable top boots, and a shallow crowned hat, he was an impressive figure, but Nell gave him credit for not trying to cut a dash. In such a backwater as this, he would only have made himself look ridiculous. If his destination was the town, he would still garner a great deal of attention, however. She wondered if he would deign to notice. She would discover soon enough; Maria was a fount of knowledge.

The thought seemed to conjure the irrepressible maid, for as Nell stepped through the balcony doors, Maria came into the room, a breakfast tray in her hands.

"Excuse me, ma'am."

"Well done," Nell said. "I see Timothy has at least helped you with your English."

"Si, Signora," she said, unabashed. "I would have brought you your breakfast sooner, but I had not realised you were no longer with Signora Montovani."

Nell offered her an understanding smile. "Of course, you didn't. You have been too busy trying to polish Timothy."

The maid grinned. "That one needs to be put in his place. He runs too fast."

"Oh?" Nell said, purposely misunderstanding her. "Did you not catch him then?"

Maria laughed. "It does not do to rush these things. The anticipation of a kiss is usually more exciting than the thing itself."

"Is it?" Nell murmured, frowning. In truth, she had no idea. Flint had never kissed her on the mouth.

If she did not catch her words, Maria caught her expression. "You disapprove of my flirting? I assure you it does not interfere with my work."

If Maria had been a servant at Flint Hall or her father's rectory, she would have disapproved and taken her to task, but things were different here and Maria was not her servant but Angelica's. Neither did she wish to dampen the girl's spirits.

"Just be careful, Maria. I would not like you to be taken advantage of."

The maid laughed. "I will not be. It is nothing more than a pleasant game and if you fear for my virtue, you need not. Me, I am a good girl."

"I never doubted it," Nell said, becoming very interested in the contents of her breakfast tray. "But gentlemen sometimes take what they want without regard to a female's wishes."

Maria nodded wisely. "It is true, but Timothy is not such a one."

Nell tended to agree with her. Despite his powerful build, there was something gentle about the footman. She chose a small pastry from the tray and nibbled it, although her appetite had quite deserted her. As the maid left the room, she laid it down and sighed. It had been Flint's right and she was fortunate that he had exercised it so rarely.

She drank a cup of tea and then went to Angelica's room. The old lady had cast aside her habitual blacks and wore a lavender gown, a purple pelisse, and a straw hat.

"You look wonderful," Nell said.

Angelica smiled. "It was time for a change. I am fortunate that Beatrice has kept my long-neglected wardrobe in good order. Go and put on your hat, Nell. We are going to the vineyard. I have already sent Luca to bring around the cart."

By the time she had donned a russet pelisse and a broad-brimmed hat of the same colour, Angelica was already halfway down the stairs on Timothy's arm. He lifted her into the cart and bowed as she thanked him, before turning to offer Nell his hand, his countenance wooden.

"Thank you," she murmured, laying her hand in his. She looked into his guileless blue eyes and added softly, "You have been trained well; your performance is so very... polished."

She bit back a smile as he coloured. It would do him no harm to know that she was alive to his antics.

The cart was drawn by a recalcitrant donkey, who

stopped every few yards to chew on the scrubby grass that grew by the edge of the road.

"She is old," Angelica said, unperturbed. "And like me has grown lazy." She smiled as they passed the olive grove and pointed at an ancient specimen with a huge girth. "Eduardo and I used to sit under that tree in the evening with a glass of wine and discuss our day."

Nell touched her hand. "You have many fond memories to look back on."

"For many years that is all that has sustained me," Angelica said, "but now, I shall enjoy making new ones." She turned her hand to clasp Nell's. "As you should."

CHAPTER 13

Alexander walked quickly, eager to put some distance between himself and the house. He felt Nell's eyes following him but did not acknowledge her presence. She had made him feel foolish, a sensation he did not enjoy. Was she laughing at him? A low growl escaped him. She would not laugh if she knew the jolt of desire that had shot through him at sight of her in that elegant dressing gown, her little pink toes peeping beneath its hem and her unbound hair streaming about her shoulders. She would feel as contemptuous of him as of all the other gentlemen who had admired it. Her words echoed in his mind. *I cut it off because I suddenly despised it and all the men who seemed to think it meant something that it did not.*

She had meant, of course, that she was not a passionate woman; she had stated as much. A grim smile curved his lips. It had not appeared that way to him when she had raged at him the evening before. He recognised the spark between them if she did not. That was not his arrogance speaking but his experience. He had noticed the way she jumped when he touched her hand, the flush that had crept into her cheeks when she had observed him that morning, and the delighted glint in her eye when she had sparred with him at dinner.

It would not do. He must keep her at arm's length. In her own way, Nell was as wounded as he. It was why he had warned her not to trust him. He would help her for his grandmother's sake, but he could not and would not be responsible for her happiness. Her trust must be reserved for someone who was everything Flint had not been: honourable, kind, and gentle. He paused at the crossroads, and after a moment's indecision, strode towards the vineyard. As before, Signor Batiste came out to greet him.

"Good morning, my lord. I expect you want to see the books. You'll find everything in order, I assure you." He smiled ruefully. "Whatever Signor Montovani has told you."

Alexander regarded him in blank astonishment. "My cousin looked over your accounts?"

A look of uncertainty crossed the man's face. "You had not then arrived, my lord, and I thought it only natural that Signor Montovani wished to interest himself in his great-aunt's affairs. He had much to say about how many people we employed and the wages we pay them. I thought perhaps he had mentioned it to you."

"We discussed nothing of that nature," Alexander said. "And it would be a great impertinence for me to interfere in something I know so little of. I expect my grandmother knows what you're about."

Signor Batiste looked relieved. "Yes, my lord. I

consult with her regularly, and it is she who has the final say on everything. If the grapes are not picked before they grow too ripe, they do not make good wine, which is why so many come to gather them. But it is only for a few weeks a year, you understand, that we employ so many."

Alexander nodded and began removing his coat. "Then there is no more to be said. I find myself in need of activity and have come to offer my services as a grape picker."

The old gentleman's face creased as he laughed. "It is fitting. Your grandfather would have approved. He was a fine gentleman, but he was not above getting his hands dirty, nor was your grandmother before she grew too frail." He took Alexander's coat. "I will take this into the office."

He returned a few moments later, carrying two baskets. "I will work with you until you feel confident to continue by yourself. Come."

Alexander translated this to mean; I will work with you until I am persuaded you will not make a botch of it. Signor Batiste led him among the vines, uttering words of praise and encouragement to anyone they passed. Alexander smiled and nodded as their eyes turned enquiringly upon him.

"I think I will take you a little apart," Signor Batiste said. "You are causing something of a distraction."

"I apologise," Alexander said. "I came to help not hinder."

"They will get used to you soon enough." He reached out a hand and grasped the shoulder of a boy who was hurrying past. "Giuseppe, you will collect our baskets."

The boy grinned. "Si, Signor Batiste."

He ran off calling to his friends that he was to work with the marchese.

"News travel fast," Alexander murmured.

Signor Batiste smiled. "It is a small community, and Giuseppe is Luca's son."

"My grandmother's footman?"

"Yes. Giuseppe is already an admirer of yours. As you have brought your own footman to help with the work, his father is able to return home earlier each evening. His wife is expecting another child, and he does not like her to tire herself. Now, let me show you."

Alexander watched as Signor Batiste took a narrow-handled knife with a sickle-shaped blade from his basket.

"Hold the bunch gently in your palm, cut here, and place the grapes in the basket."

Alexander copied him, feeling a little self-conscious.

Signor Batiste smiled. "Very good. Now, you continue on this side of the vine, and I will work on the other."

Alexander soon lost himself in the work, finding a simple pleasure in the repetitive activity. When Giuseppe arrived with fresh baskets, his was only half full, however. He straightened, rubbed his neck and smiled ruefully.

"It is good for first time," the boy said slowly.

Alexander's eyebrow flew up. "You speak English."

The boy grinned, his teeth white against his sun-bronzed skin. "My papa teaches me. I also speak a little German."

"You are destined to be a great man, I think," Alexander said gravely.

"Si, like you."

Alexander's lips twisted. "Much greater than I, I hope."

The boy laughed, picking up his basket. "I can never be a marchese."

He watched the boy scamper away. "Is there a school in the town?"

"No," Signor Batiste said. "Although Don Carlo holds classes after church on Sunday. The children learn what they need from their parents."

"I see," he said absently, rolling up his sleeves. "Well, if I am not to disappoint Giuseppe, I had better get busy."

"I will leave you," Signor Batiste said. "Most of the pickers have been here since first light and there will be a break in about half an hour when lemonade and cakes will be served. I will see you then."

Alexander went back to work, and when Giuseppe returned for the next basket, it was two-thirds full, and on the third occasion full. His back was aching, however, and he was pleased when he saw a trail of people making their way towards a long table that had been set up outside the pressing barns. A group of them had stopped to huddle around a cart, and although he was several hundred yards away, their excited chatter carried on the clear air.

"It is my father," Giuseppe said, abandoning his basket and running off.

Alexander felt dread settle in the pit of his stomach. Why would Luca come to the vineyard? Had something happened to his grandmother? He instinctively wished to run after the boy, but unwilling to embarrass himself twice in one day, he allowed reason to prevail. Someone would have come directly to him if there was anything amiss rather than standing around chattering.

As he neared the cart the crowd parted to reveal Angelica, smiling and laughing as comments flew at her from all directions. As there was no step, Luca was waiting to lift her down, but he was impeded somewhat by the press of people wishing to greet her and Giuseppe who had thrown his arms about his waist.

Luca spoke sharply to his son, but Alexander strolled forward, saying, "Giuseppe is a credit to you, Luca."

The footman bowed. "Thank you, my lord. He is a good boy, but I am working."

"Very true," Angelica said. "And I insist you go with Giuseppe to find some chairs for me and my companion. My grandson will take very good care of us." She smiled approvingly at Alexander. "I see you have been busy."

He smiled wryly. "I have merely been continuing the family tradition."

Angelica stood and Alexander put his arm about her waist and lifted her down.

"Thank you for all your kind words and your hard work," she said to the crowd. "But I insist you take your rest now."

As Angelica's well-wishers departed, Signor Batiste hurried up to her. "Signora, how happy I am to see you here." He offered her his arm. "May I?"

As they moved off together, Alexander turned to help Nell down from the cart.

"Thank you," she said primly as he stretched up to grasp her waist, "but I will do very well with just a hand."

"As you wish," he murmured.

Before he could take her hand, however, the donkey, who had stood passively thus far, decided to follow the crowd toward the refreshments. As the cart lurched into motion, Nell fell forward. As she had her skirts gathered in one hand, she would have landed face down in the dirt if Alexander had not taken the only option open to him. Grabbing her outstretched hand, he pulled her to him and wrapped his other arm around her. She was not heavy, but her momentum as she landed against him made him stagger backwards a step or two. His hold tightened as her forehead crashed into his nose.

She went rigid in his arms, hissing, "Put me down. I am not one of your fancy pieces."

"No," he agreed, his eyes closing on a wince as he unceremoniously released her. "I daresay any number of them may have wished to give me a bloody nose, but none of them ever succeeded."

"Oh," she exclaimed as she landed heavily on the hard-baked earth.

He opened his watering eyes and then closed them again as she landed on his foot.

"If I am ever in danger of succumbing to a chivalrous impulse again, Nell," he murmured, "I shall be sure not to yield to it."

"Oh!"

He ventured to open his eyes again. "Is it the

concussion you have given me, or has your vocabulary become woefully inadequate?"

"You *are* hurt," she said, ignoring this sally. "And as I do not have my reticule with me, I have no hand-kerchief."

"Really, Nell," he drawled. "You give your sex a bad name."

"Don't talk to me in that detestable way," she said, bristling. "The blood is dripping all over your neckcloth."

With deft fingers, he untied the knot and dabbed at his nose with one end of his ruined cravat. "I wonder which of your complaints is the greater crime?" he mused.

"There can be no doubt it is the former," Nell said, a spark in her eye. "You cannot help bleeding, but you can help how you speak!"

"Is it I who am at fault or is it that you lack humour?" he countered.

Nell's eyes narrowed. "It is not what you said, but how you said it. You only use that drawling purr when you wish to appear superior or put someone in their place."

"If I had wished to put you in your place, Nell," he said softly, "I would have let you fall."

This reminder of the service he had done her had its effect. After a few moments stilted silence she said, "I'm sorry."

He regarded her with cynical amusement. "For snapping my nose off, making that appendage bleed, or assuming I was trying to ravish you in front of half the town?"

She nibbled on her bottom lip, eyeing him resentfully. "The last two."

Alexander's gaze strayed towards his fellow grape pickers, and he discovered that dozens of dark eyes were turned on him and Nell, their owners' tongues unnaturally quiet.

"Wonderful," he muttered. "They will think, quite rightly, that we have been arguing, and I will, no doubt, be the villain of the piece."

If her apology had been rather half-hearted, Nell at least had the grace to look a little shamefaced.

"Do not concern yourself," he said bitterly. "I am used to it, although I had hoped to escape my reputation here, if not for my sake for my grandmother's."

Nell suddenly stepped towards him, took his arm and smiled radiantly up at him. If she had punched him in the stomach, she could not have robbed him of breath more effectively.

"What are you doing?" he said through gritted teeth.

"I am showing everyone that we have not fallen out," she said in reasonable accents. "And I will explain precisely how your nose came to be injured." A glimmer of wry amusement flashed in her eyes. "I really would be doing myself and my sex a disservice if I allowed everyone to think I had purposefully injured you, although how they think I might have done so, is beyond me. Even if I wanted to hit you, I doubt very much I could reach. Now, come along, you must sit down until the bleeding stops."

He blinked, allowing himself to be led towards his grandmother. He was not sure if his head was spinning from his injury or the rapidly changing faces of the woman beside him. She insisted he took the chair meant for herself, before smiling ruefully at Angelica and animadverting on the unpredictability of donkeys, her own clumsiness, and praising Alexander for his gentlemanly instincts and his stoic acceptance of his injury.

He closed his eyes and uttered a faint groan, undermining her last assertion somewhat. God save him from well-meaning females. Signor Batiste was doing his best to translate what she was saying to the interested onlookers and judging by their knowing smiles, Nell had only succeeded in planting a different species of speculation in their minds. He was transformed from villain to hero and Nell into his damsel in distress. He suspected his grandmother had wisdom enough to see through her rather animated performance, but the onlookers clearly suspected a romance.

Nell was aware that her performance was a trifle exaggerated, but in truth, she was a little ashamed of herself and wished to make amends. When she had found herself clasped in Alexander's arms, she had experienced a peculiar blend of panic, exhilaration, and anger. How she had had the audacity to throw his mistresses in his face she did not know.

She should have apologised, at once, of course; what she had said was shocking. He had not been shocked, however, and his mocking amusement had only inflamed her further. She could tell herself that taking him to task for that horrid drawl was fair enough, that it was all part of her plan, but the truth was she had enjoyed brangling with him. It was not until he had reminded her that he had saved her from falling that she had remembered the fact.

Her lack of moderation and her willingness to argue in a public place was both surprising and concerning to her. She could have achieved the opposite of what she desired. She wanted Alexander to see the best of himself reflected in people's eyes, not the worst. He had made a very good start by working alongside these people, and she could have ruined it all.

She appeared to have recovered the situation, however. She saw the admiring glances that the women, in particular, were sending Alexander's way. She must modify her plan. This did not mean a full retreat, but she would learn to be more subtle. There must be some middle ground between polite submissiveness and outright war.

CHAPTER 14

It was not until the following evening that Nell learned of the speculation already running rife in Malcesine. Maria tripped into the room, two thin strips of green ribbon in her hand.

"Signora Montovani gave me these to wind through your hair."

"That was kind of her. It will match my green silk perfectly."

The maid went to the wardrobe and retrieved the gown. "Si, that is what she said."

It was not until she was dressed, and Maria plaiting her hair, weaving a strip of ribbon between the strands, that she noticed the air of repressed excitement hovering about the maid.

"Maria? Is there something you wish to tell me?"

The maid shook her head. "This is intricate work, signora, and I cannot concentrate if I talk."

Nell regarded her suspiciously; in her experience, the maid never did anything without talking. She waited until she had circled her head with the delicate braid, however, before trying again.

"That is lovely, Maria, thank you." She stood, smiling at the girl. "Now, what is it that has stilled that unruly tongue of yours?"

"It is only gossip, signora." The maid clasped a hand to her mouth in dismay.

"Come," Nell said, half amused, half exasperated. "Tell me, or I will begin to think this gossip is about me."

The girl's eyes widened, confirming her words. Nell felt a nervous flutter in her stomach.

Maria ran to the door. "I am sorry, my lady, but Signora Montovani told me to say nothing."

The maid whisked herself out of the room before she could be questioned further. Frowning, Nell slowly followed her. She went to Angelica's room. Beatrice admitted her, offering her a curtsy before leaving. The lady's maid had never shown her such observance before.

"Angelica?" she said, crossing the room.

The old lady sighed, clipped an amber drop to her earlobe and stood, turning to greet Nell with a wry smile.

"I thought Maria's silence might be too much to ask for."

"She has told me only that there is a rumour. And that only because I pressed her. She fled before I could discover what it was, however." She frowned. "It is not Beatrice's habit to curtsy to me. Angelica, has Bernardo betrayed my secret?"

"No, child, it was not he. I am afraid that when you begged Alexander not to call you Lady Flint or

Mrs Marsdon but Nell, one of the maids overheard you. Pia did not eavesdrop on purpose. She was cleaning my room and noticing that the door to my sitting room was ajar, closed it. I observed her do it and later sent for her. Her English is still rudimentary, but she understood what she had heard. There was no point in denying it, but I asked her not to repeat it."

"But she could not resist sharing such a titbit," Nell said dryly.

"To be just to the girl, she did resist it. It was not until another rumour began to circulate that the temptation to reveal your identity overcame her."

"I cannot imagine what it would be," Nell said bemused.

Humour sparked in Angelica's eyes. "Where there is a beautiful woman and an attractive man in close proximity, rumours will always abound. The smile you offered Alexander at the vineyard was witnessed by many, and then you extolled his praises so warmly that it is only natural that some would speculate as to the nature of the relationship between you."

Nell stared at her. "There is no relationship between us."

"Yes, well, Pia's mother asked her about the two of you. She suggested that although you are beautiful, a marquess would look higher than a companion for a wife, and Pia could not resist informing her that you were a lady."

"This is ridiculous!" Nell declared. "I only behaved as I did because we had been arguing and he suggested that everyone would assume he was the villain of the piece."

Angelica's lips twitched. "Do I take it he was not?"

"No," Nell admitted colouring. "At least not completely. I did not react quite as I should when I found myself caught by him, and then he spoke to me in a way I found unacceptable…"

"I see," Angelica said, interested. "Did you tell him so?"

"Yes. I had already decided to take him to task for his less desirable traits, but I should not have done so in public…" Her cheeks grew warmer. "This is preposterous. Outrageous! How can I behave in a natural manner with the servants watching our every interaction?"

Alexander paused outside his grandmother's door when he heard voices. *I had already decided to take him to task for his less desirable traits, but I should not have done so in public…*

So, the vicar's daughter intended to offer him correction, did she? His mouth set in a grim line. What right did she have to question his behaviour? If she had not been under his grandmother's roof, he would have been tempted to teach her a salutary lesson. He grimaced. He could offer her no cruelty. He was sure Flint had offered her lessons enough.

This is preposterous. Outrageous! How can I behave in a natural manner with the servants watching our every interaction?

She should have thought of that before praising him to the skies. He wanted neither her praise nor her censure.

"I suggest you ignore the speculation," he said, walking into the room.

"Eavesdropping is a bad habit," she said, flushing.

He regarded her coolly. "If you would prefer not to be overheard, I recommend you learn to shut the door. And if you would prefer not to give rise to further speculation, I encourage you to follow my advice."

Her eyes flashed. "In your *vast* experience, does ignoring rumours make them go away?"

"Not necessarily," he acknowledged, "but neither does denying them. People generally believe what they want to believe. It is unlikely you'll be given the opportunity to confirm or deny our romance." His lips twisted. "However preposterous, because no one will ask you directly. It would be an impertinence."

"You clearly don't know my maid very well," Nell said dryly.

Alexander raised an eyebrow, "No, how should I?"

They glanced at Angelica as she chuckled, as if surprised by her presence.

She gave Nell an understanding smile. "However annoying this situation may be for you, Nell, I would remind you that it is not of Alexander's making. No one here knows anything about your husband, but they do know you a little and will assume you had very good reason to keep your identity secret." She smiled ruefully. "It is true the mystery will only add to the romance, but you need not bear the scrutiny for long."

Nell paled. "You have heard from Bernardo?"

"Yes, I received a letter this afternoon. The house he has hired will be available next week. As his mother has gone to visit her sister, he has offered us two maids from his household and hired a cook. I suggest we go the day after the harvest celebration."

"Yes, of course," she said, anxiety clouding her eyes. "But one form of scrutiny will only be replaced by another far worse."

Alexander's expression softened. "That scrutiny will clear your name, however, and that knowledge must bolster your courage. Now," he said offering each lady an arm, "shall we go down to dinner?"

His grandmother accepted his escort, but Nell pretended not to notice and left the room.

Angelica patted her grandson's arm. "You are doing Nell a great deal of good."

He glanced down at her, a satirical gleam in his eyes. "By inspiring her with a zealous desire to rid me of my bad habits?"

"So, you heard that, did you?"

"Clearly, and she is doomed to disappointment if she thinks there is the remotest chance of her doing so."

Angelica laughed. "I am sure you are right and that you think her impertinent for even thinking of attempting it, but I assure you that it is not impertinence that prompts her but a genuine desire to help you find your better self."

"I wish you would not encourage her in such a foolish endeavour."

"I have not done so," Angelica said, unperturbed by this accusation.

"Perhaps not," Alexander said, "but neither did you discourage her."

"No," Angelica agreed, unrepentant. "As I said, you have done Nell a great deal of good. Before you arrived, she was pleasant, kind, and attentive, but also subdued, as if her spirit had been extinguished.

However misguided she might be in her handling of you, Alexander, I cannot but rejoice in the revival of it. I see it as a sign that she is finally recovering from the shock of her marriage to Flint."

He eyed her a little resentfully. "Do you expect me to tolerate her criticisms?"

"Not at all. I expect you to continue to duel with her, but when you do cross swords, make sure your tongue parries rather than cuts."

He laughed dryly. "It is a very skilled fencer who can avoid inflicting injury whilst receiving none."

"It will certainly require some restraint," Angelica agreed, "but as you have never yet slain your opponent, I must assume you have experience enough."

His eyes narrowed. "My opponents are generally of the male variety, and if you expect me to remain within the bounds of what is recognised as gentlemanly behaviour, I will be at a severe disadvantage."

A glimmer of mischief sparked in Angelica's eyes. "I am not so unreasonable as to expect *that*."

A lopsided grin twisted his mouth. "A home thrust!"

Alexander had very little opportunity to spar with Nell over the next week, however. He spent his days at the vineyard and only saw her at dinner, at which time she treated him with polite reserve. He discovered this annoyed him as much as it had Bernardo, and he frequently felt the urge to pierce it, but he made no attempt to do so. It was one thing to react to provocation, but quite another to instigate an argument out of nothing. Besides, he liked his sparring partners to be up to his weight, and Nell was looking decidedly peaky.

Although Alexander could not know it, Nell was also finding their encounters frustrating. From the start their exchanges had been characterised by a frankness that was unusual, faintly alarming, and, she had to admit, rather exciting. The polite indifference she was determined to maintain in order to defuse the rumours of a romantic attachment between her and the marquess was imposing some strain on her nerves.

When Alexander answered Angelica's questions about his day, Nell found herself surreptitiously watching the expressions flit across his face and had to bite her tongue to prevent herself asking a dozen others. When he carved a slice of chicken for her and placed it on her plate, she had to curb the desire to smile as she thanked him lest it be misconstrued by a hovering servant, and when she went early to bed, she found herself longing to be downstairs again.

The trip to Verona was looming ever closer, and she would have liked to discuss with him what might happen there. She was not looking forward to revisiting the place where she had been so humiliated or having to relive it through her interview with the mayor. She knew Alexander could allay her fears if he chose to, and if only she did not allow him to provoke her newly discovered temper, there was no reason why he shouldn't. But the house was not large, and it was impossible to have private speech with him without adding fuel to the fire of speculation that was already blazing quite happily on its own. Maria might not have openly questioned her yet – Nell was certain she had Angelica to thank for that – but she had several times sent her speculative glances.

Comforting herself with the knowledge that she was no longer friendless, she tried to put her worries from her mind, but by the afternoon of the harvest party, she felt exhausted and little inclined to join in the festivities. She was still Angelica's companion, however, and could not allow her to go unattended. That lady continued to grow stronger every day, but she had not yet been tried by such a strenuous event, and so, when she discovered Maria laying out a dark green sleeveless dress, its skirt embroidered with white flowers, and a round-necked chemisette, she pasted a smile on her face.

"What is this?" she said, stroking the skirt's soft folds.

"Everyone is of equal importance at the party," the maid explained. "And so you must dress as the other ladies. This is traditional dress for the harvest celebration."

Whilst Nell could appreciate the sentiment, she was not at all sure the garments would fit or suit her. The waist of the dress was much lower than she was used to and its flounced hem very wide.

"It belongs to Signora Montovani but is too small in the middle now. It will be perfect for you, Lady… signora."

Nell ignored the slip, saying breezily, "Let us see, shall we?"

Maria turned the full-length mirror in the corner of the room and did the same with the smaller one on the dressing table.

"You must not look until your toilette is complete."

The bodice of the dress was cut low and without the chemisette would have been quite scandalous. Green ribbon crisscrossed it at the front so it could be tightened to fit the wearer.

A small smile of approval touched the corners of Maria's mouth as she stood back to look Nell over. "It will do very well. Please sit so I may arrange your hair."

Maria wove some strands from the side and top of Nell's head into a plait which she knotted, leaving a riot of curls hanging over her shoulders and down her back. She finished with a wreath of leaves and small white flowers.

"Now," she said, going to the mirror, "you may see."

Nell blinked at her image. The chemisette was like no other she had worn and had not provided her with the coverage she had hoped for. It clung to the top of her arms rather than covering her shoulders, and the bodice of the dress pushed up her breasts so that more of her décolletage was showing than she would have liked.

"Maria," she said uncertainly, "are you sure this is what the other ladies will be wearing?"

"Certamente, si."

"Oh, you look wonderful," Angelica said coming into the room. "I knew it would suit you. I am so glad I did not throw it away." She smiled a little mistily. "It is many years since I have worn that costume, but it brings back fond memories."

Angelica was wearing a more conservative version of the dress and a long-sleeved chemisette that rose to her throat.

"I think I would be more comfortable wearing something with a higher neckline myself."

"Nonsense," Angelica said, dismissing her complaint. "You must rejoice in your youth and be grateful that you don't have to hide a myriad of defects, my dear."

Beatrice came into the room and draped a cloak about her mistress's shoulders.

"Thank you," Angelica said. "The harvest feast always begins at four and so we must be on our way. Alexander will meet us there; everyone brings some food to the celebration, and he has taken our contribution. Luca is waiting outside with the cart and Timothy is waiting to help me downstairs."

Maria picked up a fine woollen green cloak she had draped over a chair. "Take this," she said, "you will need it later."

"I need it now," Nell said, donning it and fastening the gold clasp at its neck. She at once felt more comfortable.

CHAPTER 15

When they arrived at the vineyard, Nell spotted Alexander immediately. He stood head and shoulders above everyone else and was moving easily amongst the crowd, shaking hands and smiling, his teeth flashing white against his lightly tanned skin. He looked more relaxed than she had ever seen him. Like all the other gentlemen present he wore buff-coloured breeches tied just below the knee with a green ribbon, white stockings and black shoes with golden buckles. A wide band of green silk was wrapped around his trim waist, and above it, he wore a white shirt with billowing sleeves. It was open at the neck, the space filled with a green-knotted silk handkerchief. Over the shirt he wore a tan waistcoat intricately embroidered with tiny vine leaves. He should have looked ridiculous, but he did not; he looked earthy, masculine, and devastatingly attractive.

It very soon became clear that she was not the only female present to think so, for as they approached the long trestle tables laden with food and big earthenware jugs, two giggling young women each plucked a bunch of grapes from the table and held them up. The people around them began a slow, steady clap their faces wreathed in smiles. Alexander laughed and bent down, offering his cheek first to one and then the other so that they might kiss it.

"He is in his element, I see," Nell murmured dryly.

"It is a tradition," Angelica explained. "Only women may initiate the ritual, although I must admit they don't usually start doing so until the wine punch served with the meal loosens their inhibitions."

"How very unusual," Nell said, a sharp edge to her voice, "does it not incite jealousy?"

Angelica sent her a sideways glance. "Occasionally; if a girl kisses the same man twice, it is an indication that she is interested in a romantic relationship, and that can sometimes cause a disagreement with a rival for his or her affections."

"Then this might prove to be an enlivening evening," Nell muttered.

Signor Batiste came up to them. "We are honoured that you have joined the celebration this year, Signora Montovani." He smiled at Nell. "And you too, of course, signora."

He led them to the first trestle table, their progress hindered by the greetings offered by all they passed. The sun blazed above them, and Nell was uncomfortably hot by the time they reached the chair set at the head of the table for Angelica. As she took her seat, Alexander came to his grandmother, lifting her hand to his lips.

Signor Batiste turned to Nell. "Let me take your

cloak, signora. You will not feel its warmth later if you keep it on."

Nell would have liked to keep it close, but as it appeared she would have to sit on one of the long benches set on either side of the tables, there was nothing convenient for her to drape it over. Besides, Maria had spoken the truth; many of the young women present were dressed as she. Reluctantly, she undid the clasp and allowed him to take it. "Thank you."

Alexander lightly kissed Angelica's hand, murmuring, "Your timing is excellent, grandmother."

Angelica chuckled. "Do not tell me you object to pretty, young ladies kissing you for I will not believe you."

He grinned. "Perhaps not, but I will admit I prefer to be the hunter rather than the hunted, and how am I to remember who has kissed me before? If I allow it to occur a second time, I could find myself in hot water."

"That is true," Angelica said, "Nell has already foreseen that possibility."

His eyebrow flew up and his smile turned wry. "I expect you mean she saw that probability."

He straightened, glancing across at her as she turned her head to thank Signor Batiste who was removing her cloak. He stilled, his eyes skimming over the riot of curls that tumbled over her pale, finely boned shoulders. He felt his mouth go dry as they lingered for an instant on the soft swelling of skin and the hint of a shadow at the neckline of her chemisette before travelling on to the impossibly small span of her waist. His hands curled into fists, and he closed his eyes as he felt the blood coursing through his veins and his heart begin to race.

Good God! He was no stripling to be overwhelmed by a beautiful woman. He had known dozens of them, intimately. None of them or the other young ladies present had provoked such a reaction in him, although their charms were more blatantly on display.

He turned as he felt a tap on his arm and accepted the earthenware goblet of wine punch offered him. He quickly tossed it off and began to choke as the spicy liquid burned his throat.

The boy holding the tray laughed along with several other people in the near vicinity.

"You must drink it very slowly, or you will become very silly," the boy said.

"I can well believe it," he gasped. "What is in it?"

"Apart from wine, I don't know. It is a secret known only to Signora Fratelli who makes it. Would you like another glass?"

"Not just at the moment, thank you."

He would need to keep his wits about him if he was not to betray himself. Nell would not welcome or appreciate his admiration, he felt sure. At least the drink seemed to have restored his wits.

He turned back to the table and met Nell's suspicious gaze. Had she seen his swift scrutiny? He did not think so and made sure his eyes rested only on her face. It was no hardship, after all. If he only regarded her from the neck up, her delicate features, flowing locks and flower wreath made her resemble a fairy princess or a wood nymph.

He bowed, and not daring to comment on her appearance, searched for something mundane to say. "Good afternoon, Nell. I would recommend you drink only lemonade. The punch has quite a bite."

"As you drank it as a man dying of thirst, I am not surprised," she said tartly, accepting a goblet from the boy who now hovered behind her. She took a cautious sip, regarding him defiantly over the rim of her glass. He repressed a smile as she grimaced.

"It is an acquired taste," Angelica said. "But it grows on you. I would recommend, however, that you also partake of the lemonade; the punch is rather potent." She smiled as Signor Batiste, having disposed of Nell's cloak, reappeared. "Sit next to me, Georgio, we can reminisce about the old days."

Alexander breathed a sigh of relief and moved farther down the table. The thought of having to sit opposite Nell through the meal was untenable. However honourable his intentions, he found her beguiling, and he doubted he could have prevented his gaze from straying where it should not go. He found a spot between Signora Fratelli, a fat, jolly matron and her lean, weathered husband.

They greeted him affably and with no ceremony and after a few moments he turned to the matron and saw she was regarding him with a humorous twinkle in her eyes.

He grinned. "I am happy to have provided you with some amusement, Signora Fratelli. I have drunk a variety of punches, made a fair few too, but I must admit, I have never tasted such an interesting concoction as you have brewed. Might I know the ingredients?"

Something between a laugh and a cackle escaped her. "You may not. The secret has been passed from mother to daughter in my family for generations." She leant towards him and spoke in hushed tones. "My great-grandmother was a wise woman, and she created the recipe when she was asked for a love potion."

The cynical thought that the love did not generally outlast the headache induced by such potent concoctions crossed Alexander's mind, but he curbed his tongue. The effort proved to be unnecessary as the stout dame beside him read his thoughts.

"You do not believe, but you will see," she said, her eyes straying in Nell's direction.

Alexander could not resist glancing down the table and frowned as he saw Nell take another sip of the punch. She rarely finished the glass of wine served with her dinner, and if she was not careful would find herself quite cast away. Signora Fratelli misinterpreted his expression.

She laid a plump hand on his arm and gave it a slight squeeze. "Do not worry. Whatever has caused this coolness between you will be a thing of the past by the end of the evening. Many love matches have been made on this night, even where there was no attachment before."

Alexander knew it would be futile to point out that there was no question of a love match between him and Nell and so merely smiled faintly and surveyed the platters of foods before him. It was a simple meal consisting of a variety of meats, raised pies, cheeses, fruit, vegetables and vast quantities of freshly baked bread. The air soon sang with lively conversation and laughter, which grew louder as the meal progressed, no doubt thanks to the diligent refilling of glasses by a handful of volunteers under Luca's supervision. Perhaps he should have allowed Timothy to come; he could have kept an eye on Nell, but even in this quiet backwater, Alexander would not leave his daughter unprotected.

He did not hear Nell's voice in the hubbub, and he felt a twinge of guilt as he glanced again down the table. Angelica was deep in conversation with Signor Batiste, and he suddenly remembered that Nell's Italian was rudimentary, making it difficult for her to follow the fast-flowing conversations going on around her. She did not look unhappy, however, and although she was not contributing much to the conversations, she was nodding and smiling at her neighbour, a swarthy young man, who in Alexander's opinion, was leaning a little too close to her.

Her eyes suddenly met his, and he silently cursed as he saw they were bright and sparkling. No wonder the young man was taking such pains to make her understand him. The moment the violins struck up, Alexander rose to his feet and stepped back over the bench. Exercise was just what Nell needed; it would clear her head. Before he reached her, however, her unknown would-be swain was leading her into one of several circles that were forming. Alexander put his hands on his hips and watched her progress with narrowed eyes.

He glanced down as a hand slipped through his arm. One of the girls who had kissed him earlier was smiling up at him. He had not meant to offer her any further encouragement but found himself saying, "Would you like to dance, Mariela?"

She laughed and pulled him towards the circle. The dance was simple and its steps easy to master. They moved a few steps to the right, partners then linked hands and turned, before returning to their original positions. A couple then entered the circle, and whilst the onlookers clapped, the man knelt and offered his hand to his lady, who ignored him, raised her hands above her head and pirouetted around him, her twirls growing ever faster as the music picked up pace, the wide skirt of her dress swelling and rising a few inches with each turn.

"It represents a lover's quarrel," Mariela said, sending him a speculative glance. "The rise and fall of the skirt suggests the woman's flight."

It did not appear she was destined to escape, however, for after her fourth circle of her partner, he suddenly stood and stamped his foot. She turned away, her arms outstretched and her body swaying as if she were dizzy, which she most likely was. Her lover reached for her hand, she turned, and they walked in a circle around each other, their hands joined above their heads, their eyes locked in a battle of wills. The woman's right hand then fell to his neck, and she gathered her skirts in the other. His left hand moved to her hip, he wrapped his right arm about her waist and lifted her from her feet, turning slowly before setting her down again. She lowered her head and sank into a curtsy, the man bowed, and they returned to the circle. This was the cue for the couples to face each other before weaving in and out of the other dancers, but at, it seemed to Alexander, the random clapping of a hand, the circle stopped, and the sequence was repeated with a new partner.

On the sixth repetition, Alexander found himself next to Nell.

"Are you enjoying yourself?" he said as they moved to their right.

"Very much," she said coolly.

When they joined hands and turned, she did not meet his gaze. The clapping began and looking up he saw all eyes were upon them. Apparently, it was their turn to enter the circle, although how this was decided was a mystery to him. He heard Nell gasp.

"I can't do it," she said, finally looking up at him.

He took her hand. "It is certainly not as restrained as our country dances," he murmured, a spark of humour in his eyes as he imagined what the society matrons of the *ton* would think of it. "Perhaps next time you will curb your eagerness and look before you leap. I expect the punch affected your judgement, but it is too late to draw back now."

Her eyes flashed. "I have had only one cup."

"I suggest you don't have another." He suddenly grinned as those hazel orbs positively smouldered. "You are playing the part to admiration already. The dance represents a lover's quarrel."

"I had worked that much out for myself," she hissed through her teeth as he led her into the centre of the circle. "But the woman concedes to the man in the end, and I doubt very much I can carry that off."

He knelt before her and held out his hand. "I see it more as a mutual concession myself. You should try it some time."

She whirled away from him, her arms rising gracefully. From his lowered position he saw her neat steps and enjoyed a view of her slender ankles as her pirouettes grew ever faster and her skirts billowed. He timed his moment to stand to perfection and stamped his foot with conviction. He had a fleeting glimpse of flushed cheeks and heaving bosom before Nell turned away, stretching out her arms and swaying gracefully. He reached for her hand, and she turned promptly as if glad of the support. Their eyes locked as he pulled her to him so forcefully that Nell's body pressed against his. They stood thus for a moment before he raised their linked hands.

He had thought himself master of the situation, that his earlier reaction to Nell had prepared him for anything to come, but as they slowly circled, he found himself drowning. Her eyes seemed to glow bronze, green flecks dancing in their depths. The battle he fought was with himself not her, and he was losing.

As her hand moved to his neck, her fingers seemed to trail fire. Clenching his jaw, he wrapped his arm about her tiny waist and lifted her against his side. Heat coursed through his veins, and turning his head, his gaze dropped to her parted lips. They were inches from his and it took every ounce of control he possessed to keep from kissing them.

The sweet torture seemed to last for minutes rather than seconds, but at last, he set her gently on her feet. She swayed for a moment as if unsteady, her eyes huge in the narrow oval of her face, then she lowered them and sank into a deep curtsy, finally releasing him from her spell. As he bowed before her and helped her to her feet, he realised the clapping had stopped, but as they walked back to the circle, wild applause broke out.

Nell clung to Alexander's arm as he led her out of the circle and back to the table. Her breathing was rapid and her heart pounding in her chest. The drama and intensity of the dance had left her light-headed and shaken. Her legs trembled beneath her, and her wits were scattered; even so, she knew the moment he left her side.

"Drink some lemonade, Nell," Angelica said. "You have overexerted yourself, although your performance seems to have excited much admiration."

She smiled tremulously and picked up the goblet of lemonade she had requested moments before she had been asked to dance. She put it to her lips and took several gulps, needing something to calm the tumult inside her. The liquid burned her throat and set her coughing until her eyes watered.

"Are you all right, Nell?"

Angelica's voice seemed to come from far away.

"Yes," she spluttered. "I drank too fast, that is all."

Her head began to spin unpleasantly. She must have drunk from the wrong goblet. She reached for another and cautiously sipped it, breathing a sigh of relief when the cool, refreshing drink proved to be lemonade. She drank it in a more moderate manner, feeling her head begin to clear.

She did not understand what had just happened, had no words to describe the sensations that had over-powered her during the dance, but she was honest enough to admit it had been no mere performance. The tension between her and Alexander had been very real from the start. She tried to pinpoint the moment it had changed from anger to something entirely different.

When she had been twirling about him, a heady exhilaration had come over her. The self-consciousness she thought she would feel with dozens of eyes watching her had not manifested itself. She had only been aware of Alexander's eyes following her movements and the knowledge had brought with it a frisson of excitement. The moment her eyes had locked with his excitement had turned to something else. To look away and break the connection had been as impossible and undesirable as to stop breathing. When he had spanned her waist with his arm and lifted her from her feet, holding her close against his side, there had been nowhere else she wanted to be, and when his eyes had dropped to her lips, hers had dropped to his, her pulse fluttering wildly.

"Would you like to dance, signora?"

She glanced up and saw two lines were forming but shook her head at the young man who was regarding her with hopeful eyes.

"Thank you, but I am a little tired."

His disappointment was clear, but he bowed and moved off. Nell shivered; the heat that had warmed her from the inside only moments before dispelled. The sun had dipped behind the mountains and the sky had darkened to the deep blue of twilight. Angelica had already donned her cloak, and she decided to follow her example. Rising, she smiled at Signor Batiste and asked him where he had put it.

"I will get it for you immediately, signora."

"Please, do not get up," she said, smiling. A walk was just what she needed.

He gestured towards a door at the end of a large barn. "It is in the office."

"Thank you."

Enveloped in the soft wool of the garment, she wandered towards the vines where Alexander had toiled for the best part of a week. It had done him a great deal of good, allowing his Italian side to emerge from behind his reserve. It was she who had maintained it, and she now admitted to herself that it was not just because she wished to dispel the rumours surrounding them. A soft laugh escaped her. That was now a pointless endeavour; no one who had seen them dance would believe there was nothing between them.

The vine rippled as she absently tore a leaf from it, and an overripe bunch of grapes fell to the ground. She had promised herself there would be no more lies, but she had been deceiving herself. There had always been something between them she realised as she bent to pick up the fruit. She overbalanced and fell to her knees. As the vines seemed to be swaying in the most peculiar manner, she decided to stay in that position. She picked one of the grapes and popped it into her mouth. The truth was Alexander Wraxhall touched something in her she had not known existed. A word or look could inflame her temper as effectively as a spark to dry tinder, and she no longer thought it had anything to do with his or her past.

She had admired Flint when she had first known him; he had appeared to feel just as he ought on a number of topics and had been at ease with her father.

She had respected his restraint when he had never offered her more than a chaste kiss on the cheek even after they had become betrothed. She sighed. What a foolish girl she had been. It had not been restraint; it had been disinterest.

She had told Alexander that she did not wish to be admired for her beauty, and yet when he had been more interested in the punch than her, and then had seated himself some distance down the table, she had felt an unreasoning resentment. She popped another grape into her mouth and chewed reflectively. How contrary she was.

A bemused smile touched her lips. Alexander was not disinterested like Flint. The attraction she had hitherto denied was mutual. She had felt the hairs rise on the back of his neck when she touched it, had seen the desire in his eyes. It had been far more potent than the punch. She suddenly hiccupped and giggled. At least before she had partaken of her second cup.

She looked down in surprise as she felt something cool running down her fingers. The mangled skin of a grape was squashed between them. She dropped it, retrieved a handkerchief from the pocket of her cloak and wiped them. Whatever insults Flint had thrown at her, the fault had not been all hers. She was not cold and incapable of passion, she had just been with the wrong man.

"Nell?"

She pulled her hood over her hair and waited for him to leave. Desire did not equal love, and frankly, it was an inconvenience. The Marquess of Eagleton would not wish to marry someone whose reputation was damaged beyond repair, and he was a rake. She never again wanted to be in the position of wondering where her husband was or what he was doing.

"Lord Eagleton!"

Alexander's groan was audible. "Mariela. What are you doing here?"

Nell peaked over the top of the vine. It was the girl who had kissed him earlier, and they were standing only a few feet from her.

"Did you not want me to follow?"

She took a step closer and raised her face to his, closing her eyes.

Nell held her breath, waiting to see what he would do. She smiled as he took a step backwards, a frown furrowing his brow, and began a conversation with herself.

You must be fair to him, Nell, he is a reformed rake.

Yes, but he still has women following him about.

He was looking for you.

This internal dialogue came to a halt as Mariela's eyes popped open, a ludicrously disappointed expression on her face. Nell closed her lips on a giggle. There was something irresistibly funny about a rake, however reformed, being chased against his will.

A deep, rough voice came out of the gloom. "Mariela!"

The girl jumped and whirled around as the young man who Nell had refused to dance with hove into view. Pushing the girl to one side he fired words at Alexander. Nell picked out three; *la mia donna.* Mariela, suddenly finding her voice, vociferously objected to his claim that she was his woman, as well as to several other things judging by the length of her speech.

When she finally paused to draw breath, he answered her complaints just as comprehensively.

When the opportunity came, Alexander spoke, his tone confident and earnest. It did not have the desired effect for the man had worked himself up to such a degree he put up his fists. Mariela shrieked, her cry coinciding with the last notes of the violins. The dance was over, and Nell decided it was time to put an end to this scene before they attracted attention. If Alexander was going to keep his reputation intact, he really must be a little more careful; she would not always be on hand to rescue him. She emerged from her hiding place, waving her arm in an Italianate manner, and saying in the voice she had used with naughty children in her father's parish, "Basta!"

CHAPTER 16

Alexander quite agreed. He had had enough of this contretemps. It was not of his making, not that he expected Nell to believe it. She pushed her hood back as she came up to them, the motion knocking her flower wreath a little askew.

"What are they arguing about?" she asked peremptorily.

"Can't you guess?" he drawled. If she was going to believe the worst, he might as well add fuel to the fire. It was not irritation at the tone she so hated that flitted across her face, however, but a look that was almost affectionate. Her lips tilted and her eyes softened.

"There is no reason to be so defensive. You really are very silly to have put yourself in this position, but I saw what happened and have indeed guessed some part of the problem. The girl threw herself at you and the young man is jealous." She held up a hand, as the thwarted lover began to talk. "Un momento per favore."

Her voice whilst calm was firm, and he subsided,

confusion wrinkling his brow. Alexander laughed softly, a glimmer of admiration sparking in his eyes.

"He was angry with Mariela for kissing me earlier and so did not ask her to dance. To teach him a lesson, she asked me. He thought he would repay her in kind by asking you for the next dance."

"I see," Nell said, smiling wryly. "It is a blow to my vanity, of course, but I think I will recover from the disappointment."

His lips twisted. "Content yourself with the knowledge that there were a host of others waiting for their chance. Something you would have discovered if you had not so unwisely wandered off."

She raised her chin a little. "Unwisely?"

His jaw tightened. "Someone might have followed you."

"Someone did," she answered a little tartly. "You. I only wished for a few moments alone to recover my equ... equ..." For some strange reason, she found herself unable to form the word and it suddenly occurred to her that it might not be wise to. She amended her sentence. "To recover my breath."

Alexander had suspected she had been as shaken as he by what had passed between them but hearing her almost admit it sent a surge of exhilaration through his veins.

"But we stray from the point," Nell said. "I assume Mariela followed you to inflame..." she gestured towards the young man, "him further?"

"She has denied it. She has also claimed she wanted a few moments alone, but it is the logical conclusion." He smiled. "I am sure my pride will also recover."

Without warning, Nell unleashed her wide smile upon him, and stepping closer, reached up a hand to cup his cheek. He sucked in a deep breath. She brought her other hand from behind her back and held up a bunch of grapes.

"What…"

Her hand moved and she laid a finger briefly against his lips. They tingled. Good God! Did she have any idea of what she was doing to him?

"Play the game," she murmured. "I don't believe that young man was in our set and so he will not have seen us dance. He must believe you when you explain that it was me you came to meet and that I hid when I heard footsteps, which is why Mariela accidentally stumbled upon you alone."

He could not argue with her logic and obediently bent to receive her kiss. As her cool lips brushed softly against his cheek, an irresistible impulse overwhelmed him. As she began to withdraw, he turned his head and pressed a swift kiss on her mouth, feeling an almost savage satisfaction when he saw her eyes flare with surprise, their pupils growing so huge that only a sliver of colour surrounded them. He half expected she would slap him, but she merely sighed.

"Trust you to break the rules," she said softly.

"A minor transgression," he murmured. "And quite involuntary."

It transpired that there was no need for him to explain anything. As he straightened, the young man turned to Mariela and pulled her into his arms. She squeaked a protest, but the moment his lips touched hers, she threw an arm about his neck and surrendered. Alexander felt a pang of envy.

"Let's leave them to it," he said brusquely. "It is time we took my grandmother home."

"Yes, of course," Nell agreed.

They had not gone many paces when she stopped and turned to him. She nibbled her bottom lip. He had noticed she often did that when she was worried or uncertain.

"What is it, Nell?" he said gently.

The moon was just bright enough to show the pink that crept over her cheeks. "About you breaking the rules…"

He frowned, suddenly feeling like a cad. "Do not let it trouble you. I meant you no insult, Nell. Put it down to the punch, the moonlight… whatever you will. I apologise unreservedly…"

"Don't," she said. "Don't apologise. You said it was involuntary, after all, and…" Her eyes dropped as if she felt suddenly shy. "And perhaps I was a little to blame."

A queer smile touched his lips. "My compliments, Nell. You are the most surprising woman I have ever met; I never know what you will do or say next."

"I am afraid that you are a little to blame for that," she said. "I react to you in ways that surprise me."

Good Lord! What would she say next? Deciding it would be safer to focus on the less desirable ways in which she responded to him, he said, "Well, don't let that trouble you either. I believe I told you I would rather you took your anger out on me than yourself."

She drew in a deep breath and raised her eyes to his. "Let there be honesty between us, Alexander. I have done with lies. You know it is not just anger that you provoke in me. As neither of us wishes to marry the other, this attraction between us is both inconvenient and inappropriate, but it is there, nonetheless. I expect you are used to being attracted to people and know how to deal with it, but I do not. Perhaps you can help me with that. Ignoring you does not appear to have helped."

"It rarely does," he said dryly. "It only makes the feeling more intense when you again come into that person's presence."

She looked at him for a moment and then nodded. "Yes, of course. That is what happened tonight. The best solution would be for us to part company, but that will not be possible for some weeks."

The ludicrousness of the situation did not escape him. She was asking a former rake how to deal with her attraction to him. He ran his hand through his hair as a myriad of emotions swept through him. Whilst he admired and respected her honesty, it also exasperated and tormented him. It was one thing to expect him to restrain his impulses, but quite another to ask him to take responsibility for hers. She should have used that waspish tongue of hers to good effect for stealing that kiss, let him know in no uncertain terms that she had neither wanted nor enjoyed it. It did not matter if it was true or not; it was the way the game was played.

"If it is honesty you want, you shall have it. You are a fool to ask my advice on this matter or to trust me."

There was that gentle look in her eyes again. Was she not listening?

"Perhaps, but you assured me at our first meeting that I had nothing to fear from you and that you would offer no insult to anyone living in your grand-mother's house."

"We are to leave my grandmother's house tomorrow night," he said harshly,

Nell sighed. "That is mere pedantry, but perhaps it will help. I will have more important matters to consider, after all."

Why did that sting? "Very true. It might also help if you would refrain from throwing yourself at me on the merest provocation."

The gentle look was vanquished, and a flash of anger took its place. "I did not throw myself at you…"

"Now who is the pedant?" he drawled.

Her eyes narrowed. "You know very well what I was trying to do."

This was much better. An irate Nell he could deal with. "I neither want nor need your protection."

Her hands curled into fists. "I wish I had let that man hit you. It is no more than you deserve."

A cynical smile curved his lips. "At last, we are singing from the same page. But the only person I deserved hitting me was you, Nell." He bent down and offered her his cheek for the second time that evening, his eyes challenging her. "If you don't want to be taken advantage of it is a habit you really ought to cultivate."

She gasped, opened her mouth, shut it again, and stalked off.

"You might want to straighten your wreath," he called after her. "Or people might wonder why you are so disarranged."

Nell came to an abrupt halt, staggering a little to one side as she did so, straightened the accessory, and then carried on her way. He laughed softly as he realised she really had had a little too much punch. That explained everything. Words much better left unspoken often escaped under the influence of strong drink.

I expect you are used to being attracted to people and know how to deal with it, but I do not. Perhaps you can help me with that.

There were only two ways he knew how to help her with it; the first was to take the attraction to its natural conclusion which was not an option, and the second was to give her a disgust for him, something he felt sure was well within his power but would make things rather awkward.

Nell awoke with a thumping headache and only a vague recollection of the evening before. This made her feel uneasy.

"Maria," she murmured as the maid opened her curtains. "Close them again. I feel a little sick and my head hurts."

The maid did as she was bid and came to the bed.

"It is the punch," she said. "Some years it is stronger than others. This year it was very strong. Signora Garibaldi, our neighbour, would not let her husband into the house because he was so drunk, and he had to sleep in the square. I nearly tripped over him when I came to work this morning."

"Oh," Nell said, her heart sinking. "Did you put me to bed, Maria?"

"Yes, of course. You were not very late."

Nell's sense of unease grew. "Did I say anything that seemed strange to you?"

"No. You were very sleepy." She chuckled. "Perhaps that is why you slid off the bed when I was trying to remove your shoes."

"Oh dear," Nell said. "I apologise."

"It was nothing."

It alarmed Nell that she had no recollection of this mortifying event. What else might she have done? It was cowardly of her, but she did not know if she wished to find out. "Would you mind informing Angelica that I have a headache and will stay in bed this morning?"

Angelica was most understanding and sent her a posset which relieved the worst of her symptoms and she fell back into a fitful sleep. When Maria roused her again, it was early afternoon. Although the pain in her temples had subsided, she still felt sluggish.

"I have prepared a bath for you, signora. It will make you feel much better."

"Thank you," Nell murmured. "It is just what is required."

Maria reached down and plucked something from her hair. When Nell saw the small, white flower dangling from her fingers she frowned, trying to catch an elusive memory. It was too much effort and she let it go.

She shed her nightgown and climbed into the tin tub, easing herself back. After a moment, she raised her knees and slipped under the water, feeling her hair fan out about her. She closed her eyes and Alexander's face, inches from her own as he held her against him and slowly turned around flashed into her mind. She sat up hurriedly sending waves of water over the side of the bathtub.

"Signora?" Maria said, rushing over to her. "Is something wrong?"

"No," she gasped, blood pounding in her ears. "I think I must have stayed under the water for too long."

Maria dropped the towel she was holding over a puddle of water and retrieved another. "You are not yourself, signora. Let me wash your hair for you."

The gentle rhythm of the maid's fingers massaging her scalp calmed Nell, but the feeling that she had somehow embarrassed herself last evening refused to leave her. If anyone would know, Maria would.

"I did not see you at the harvest party, Maria," she said. "I am sure you would have enjoyed it."

Maria began to scoop water from the bath and rinse Nell's hair. "I kept Timothy company," she said nonchalantly. "Lord Eagleton insisted he stay to protect Lady Francesca." She sighed longingly. "It is a shame because I would very much have liked to have seen you dance with the marchese. They say it was a performance most believable."

"Who says?" Nell said, opening her eyes and then closing them again as soapy suds stung them. She held out her hand. "The towel, please, Maria."

"But I have not finished."

"Never mind." She stood, wiped her eyes, and wrapped the towel around herself. "Who says it was a remarkable performance?"

The maid's eyes widened at her defensive tone. "My friends, Julia Bianchi and Lara Rizzo. It was a compliment, signora. It is not easy to play the part of enemies to lovers, but they said you and Lord Eagleton did it perfectly, especially the second part."

Nell stepped from the bath. "We are not and have never been lovers, Maria, and you may tell your friends that."

"I cannot tell them anything, signora, because I am to come with you to Verona tonight and be a proper lady's maid. Besides, they would not believe me."

Nell drew in a deep breath. She was determined that Maria, at least, would believe her. If she was to accompany them, she had better tell her the truth; Maria would find out soon enough. "The first rule about being a proper lady's maid, Maria, is that you must keep all your mistress's secrets."

Maria's eyes sparkled. "Si, certamente. What secrets?"

"As you are to be with me in Verona you may as well know that the rumour that I am Lady Flint is true."

Maria nodded eagerly. "Si."

"My husband was not kind to me, and I left him."

"I knew it!" the maid said as if this snippet of information pleased her greatly. "Did I not say that only a great love or a great fear would make you wish to not be married again?"

Nell was beginning to shiver. "You did. Bring me my shift, if you please."

"Of course."

As the maid was lacing up her stays, Nell said. "My husband died soon after I left Verona."

The maid gasped. "How?"

Nell winced as the maid pulled the laces too tight. "I cannot breathe, Maria."

"Sorry, sorry."

"He was stabbed and thrown in the river."

"Mio Dio! It is very terrible but if he scared you, it is good that you were made a widow," the bloodthirsty maid said.

To her surprise, Nell felt a smile touch her lips. The maid's ridiculously simplistic interpretation of the situation made it seem less terrible somehow.

The smile faded as Maria threw Nell's petticoat over her head. "I never wished for his death. The mayor wishes to talk to me because my leaving looked suspicious."

Maria yanked the petticoat down with some force. "Bah! It is what you said last night."

Nell's brow wrinkled. "I thought you said I didn't say anything last night?"

"I said that you did not say anything strange," Maria said. "It is true that men are sometimes stupid creatures."

"Did I say that?" Nell said.

"Si, but you did not say why. I expect you and Lord Eagleton argued and are enemies again."

"We are not enemies," Nell protested.

"Good," the maid said emphatically. "Because if he cares for you, he will help you. He has tied his daughter in a shawl to his front like a peasant woman and taken her for a walk. He is not one who is afraid of what people might think."

"He will support me because he is fond of his grandmother," Nell corrected her. "It is Lady Westcliffe who will aid me the most. She helped me escape and will write to confirm my story."

"This is very good," Maria said. "But until her letter arrives, it is the marchese who will protect you, no?"

"Probably," Nell said reluctantly. "Along with his grandmother."

Maria waved this addition away. "Here in Malcesine, Signora Montovani is honoured and respected, but in Verona, she will just be an old woman who is not even Italian."

"Neither is Lord Eagleton," Nell pointed out.

"He has Italian blood in his veins," Maria said, going to the wardrobe and taking one of the few dresses that had not been packed. "And even if he had not, he has… something."

Nell lifted her eyebrows. "Arrogance?"

Maria nodded. "If you will, but it is more than that. He is not a man to be crossed. He is… how you say… a force. Like the wind that governs our lake, he may blow one way or another, but you take no notice at your danger."

"At your peril," Nell muttered.

"Si, that is what I said. You be nice to him, Lady…"

Nell sighed. "Just call me signora."

Maria laid a hand on her arm. "I understand. I am your friend and I want only what is best for you. Whatever is between you and Lord Eagleton, you should make him your friend also."

Nell knew Maria was right. She did not know what Alexander could do to help her through the coming ordeal, but she felt certain that he would. His mere presence would bolster her confidence, and, as she must eventually return to England, it would be unwise to alienate him. Yes, she would certainly need powerful friends, and if he added his voice to that of Lady Westcliffe, some of the malicious gossip that surrounded her might be dispelled.

CHAPTER 17

I t had been decided that they would dine early at four, so they might get some sleep before the journey. Alexander's walk around the ancient, cobbled streets and squares of Malcesine had taken longer than he had expected. He had not taken into account the interest Lady Francesca would arouse. Acquaintances and strangers alike had not hesitated to approach him and coo over the infant. By the time he had washed and changed, the footmen had already escorted his grandmother downstairs.

He had not seen Nell that day although his mind had drifted to her several times. Her illness that morning had been unfortunate but predictable. He could not help but wonder what her thoughts had been when she had awoken that day. Had she regretted her frank words? Would she pretend nothing untoward had happened, or would she still be angry?

He was fully prepared to do battle with her; had even decided it would be for the best. Angelica had given him permission, after all. He had not come to this decision for Nell's sake alone. He wished to be free of this attraction as much as she did. He may have decided that he must marry again for Francesca's sake, but it would be a marriage of convenience, and to be leg-shackled to Nell would not be convenient at all. There would be nothing lukewarm about any union between them. It would be passionate, unpredictable, and ultimately doomed to failure.

When Nell had said she had so much more to give than her wealth and beauty, she had meant her love, of course. What she had not said but had been implicit in her words was that she had hoped for love in return. That was something he could not give her. He had meant it when he had said that his wealth, appearance, and title were all he had to offer. He might, unlike his parent, possess the instinctive love a father felt for his child, but he suspected that if he ever allowed himself to love a woman, he would be only too like his sire; selfish, possessive, and jealous. That was not the type of love Nell needed; it could hurt her as much as Flint's neglect.

His lips curled cynically. There was no question of love on either side. His attraction to Nell was heightened because he should not, could not, act upon it, and none knew better than he how quickly desire could fade once sated. Faults easily overlooked whilst in its thrall, became magnified when it died. He had faults enough and a history that was bound to breed mistrust in a woman already slighted at the hands of a rake. Something it seemed she was well aware of. *As neither of us wishes to marry the other, this attraction between us is both inconvenient and inappropriate, but it is there, nonetheless.*

To make her dislike him must be an object with him then. She need only give him an opening and he would be completely insufferable.

As he stepped onto the landing, so did she. She saw him immediately, hesitated for a moment, and then began to walk towards him. He met her halfway at the head of the stairs, his face a mask of aloofness. He was about to greet her coolly, but she spoke first, her voice hesitant but warm.

"Alexander, I am so pleased to have a moment alone with you."

His eyebrow winged up.

"Oh dear. How awkward this is."

"Is it?" he said unhelpfully.

Pink infused her cheeks. "Yes, for I can see by your expression that I am in disgrace."

Her eyes seemed to plead with him for forgiveness. When he said nothing, she began to nibble at her bottom lip.

"I see you are not going to make this easy for me."

His lips twisted derisively. "It might help, ma'am, if you were a little more precise about what *this* refers to."

It was not the act of a gentleman to make her repeat the shocking things she had said, and he hoped that would infuriate her.

An uncertain smile waivered on her lips. "The thing is, I cannot perfectly remember."

That gave him an unfair advantage, and he was surprised to discover he could not bring himself to take it. "Then how do you know you are in disgrace?"

She sighed. "I don't know. It is just a feeling. That dreadful punch must have affected me more than I realised. I have never woken up feeling so ill nor have I ever suffered such a memory lapse. It is most disconcerting."

Not as disconcerting as asking me to help you overcome your attraction to me. "I believe I advised you to stick to the lemonade," he said sternly.

"Did you?" She looked rueful. "I am very sorry I did not listen to you." She stepped a little closer and laid a hand on his arm, her eyes again pleading with him. "Please, put me out of my misery. I know that we danced…" She gulped. "And I remember a very little of it, but nothing afterwards."

A crooked smile touched his mouth. "There is nothing to remember that need concern you. You went for a walk, and I came to recover you as my grandmother wished to return home. I did not think you would wish to keep her waiting."

"Oh," she gasped, her shoulders sagging in relief. "I am so glad. I expect you…" She closed her lips and shook her head. "Never mind."

"Your restraint is admirable, Nell," he said wryly. "You are right, however. I have many times woken up with a thumping head and an imperfect memory, but not, I might add, for quite some time."

Colour pulsed again in her cheeks. "I am sorry… my wretched tongue. I was brought up to speak my mind, and it was not until I married Flint that I… that I…"

"Learned to curb it," he finished for her, his stomach clenching at the thought that she had been too afraid to voice her thoughts to him.

"Yes," she said. "And if I do sometimes say things I should not to you, it is in part a reaction to that. I never wish to be subjected to such tyranny again. Can you understand?"

He could, all too well. In truth, he felt a little honoured that she did not fear to speak her mind to him, however exasperating he found it.

He looked at her quizzically. "I think so. But do not think I am giving you carte blanche to take me to task every time I say or do something you do not like. There are reasons why I too dislike being chastised."

Her sympathetic smile suggested that his grand-mother had told her some part of his story. He did not know how he felt about that. He certainly did not want her sympathy. He had never wanted or sought compassion, quite the opposite; he had gone out of his way to ensure no one ever suspected there was any reason he deserved it.

"I will *try* not to, but you, in turn, must try not to give me cause. If I do say something you do not like, you must take no more notice than you would if a close friend of yours did so."

His eyes turned cynical. "I have no close friends, and none of my acquaintances would dare take me to task. They would have too much to lose."

Nell's brow furrowed as she considered this. "I expect you mean they hang on your sleeve, that your consequence adds to theirs."

"Something like that," he agreed.

"Perhaps, then, you should make some new friends when you return to England."

"Perhaps I should," he murmured. "Do you have many close friends, Nell?"

She shook her head. "No. It is one of the many reasons I am grateful to Angelica. I was very lonely before I came here." She took a breath, looking very much like a penitent child. "And I am very grateful also that you are to stand my friend when we go to Verona."

A gleam of amusement sparked in his eyes, and he laughed softly. "It is you who now wish to hang upon my sleeve and trade upon my consequence, which is, of course, why you are suddenly so amenable."

She laughed a little guiltily and took the arm he offered. "Very true. What other reason could there be?"

Shortly before midnight, two boats collected the travellers from the quay outside Villa Montovani. As well as Maria, Beatrice and Savio accompanied Angelica and Nell, but unwilling to wrest her footman from his family, Luca was given a holiday. The majority of the baggage had been sent to Torbole the previous day, and Alexander's curricle, coach and another hired vehicle had taken a route through the mountains and would meet them at Bardolino in the morning.

A good, steady wind favoured them, and Nell, who had not managed to sleep after her protracted stay in bed that morning, dozed off. She awoke to find her head on Maria's shoulder and the maid's arm about her waist. The dramatic mountains that hugged the northern end of the lake were here replaced by rolling hills, and the pink-golden light of sunrise warmed the villas that lined the shore of Bardolino.

The carriages waited for them on the shore, and

Nell, not waiting for assistance, stepped from the boat, feeling disorientated for a moment as the ground seemed to sway beneath her feet. Alexander helped Angelica alight, and Nell was pleased to see she seemed to have taken no ill from the journey.

"You look fresher than I feel," she said, stretching her aching neck.

"It has been too long since I made the journey," Angelica said, smiling. "Is not the lake magical at night? It is so peaceful, and the stars shine so brightly."

"I am afraid I slept for most of the journey," she said.

"It is probably for the best. I feared you might be anxious after your last boat trip on the lake."

Nell was surprised to realise she hadn't been. Her eyes strayed to Alexander who was now holding Lady Francesca as Timothy helped Mrs Farley to alight. It was because of him, she realised. She had an unreasoning belief that she would always be safe when he was near. It did not matter that she had no basis for her faith in him, it was enough that it gave her the courage she needed to face the coming weeks.

As it was so early, they decided to press on and breakfast once they reached Verona. Alexander had taken charge of their papers and led the way in his curricle. The view of increasingly fertile plains and lilac-smudged mountains in the distance was pleasant and it was not until they swept up to the city gates shortly before ten o'clock, that Nell's fortitude began to waiver. She clasped her hands in her lap and drew in a startled gasp as a soldier appeared at the window of the carriage.

"Do not worry, Nell," Angelica said. "The mayor is expecting us, after all."

The man glanced down at the papers in his hand, sent Nell a curious look and disappeared again from view. Nell released the breath she had been holding.

Angelica patted her hand. "There, what did I tell you?"

Despite this reassurance, as they passed beneath the city walls, she felt as if she were entering a prison from which she might never escape. On her first visit to Verona, she had arrived and left in darkness and spent the interim in her room. She turned her head, her eyes staring so blindly out of the window that she only gained a vague impression of streets, busy squares, and noble public edifices. Too many questions were circling her head for her to concentrate on her surroundings. Would the mayor believe her story? Had Lady Westcliffe received her letter? Would hers exonerate Nell? Had she been a fool to come?

When they drew up outside a terrace of four elegantly proportioned mansions, she took a deep breath and silenced the panicked voice in her mind. As she stepped down from the carriage, she saw the street was only just wide enough for the carriage, and mossy grass grew between the cobbles. The dwellings were all marked by faded grandeur. Paint peeled from doors whose brass knockers were dull from lack of polishing, and some of the closed shutters were cracked or hanging from their hinges.

Alexander jumped down from the curricle and strode to join her and Angelica. He frowned. "Is this the best Bernardo could do?"

"Remember he had very short notice," Angelica said gently. "And at least it is quiet."

A dark blue door opened, and her great-nephew appeared. He ran lightly down the steps a smile of welcome on his face.

"The wind must have been kind. You are a little earlier than I expected."

Alexander looked at him sceptically. "Do I take it that if we had been an hour or two later the door would have been painted and the knocker gleaming?"

He laughed ruefully. "You are disappointed, but you should not judge before you have seen all. I have arranged for stabling at the Due Torri, but as it is not far distant, that should not cause you any great inconvenience."

Nell's stomach clenched at mention of the hotel, but she did not think Bernardo guilty of meaning to discompose her. He seemed unaware of his tactlessness and gestured towards the house.

"It belongs to a cousin of my mother who fell out of favour when the city was under French rule. Many fled at that time, and not all have yet returned." He shrugged. "It remains to be seen if the Austrians will be any better than the French but at least they have allowed Italians to have some say in the governance of the city." He pointed to the last of the four buildings. "That is the only other occupied at the moment."

Nell was surprised to hear the house was occupied for it had the shabbiest frontage of them all.

"It belongs to Signor Conti. He is old and will not trouble you. Now, let me show you around whilst cook prepares breakfast."

They filed into a dark, marble-floored entrance

hall with three doors leading off it. Apart from a large round table set in the middle and a few chairs ranged around the walls it was empty.

"This level and the one beneath houses the kitchen, laundry and servants' quarters," Bernardo said, leading the way up the stairs.

He threw open a door to his left and gestured for them to enter, following them in and going to open the long shutters at the end of the large, gloomy room. There were two sets, each of them concealing double doors that led onto a balcony.

Light flooded in revealing walls covered in faded frescoes of mythological scenes. Decorative stucco mouldings covered the ceiling, framing paintings with a religious theme. Elegant sofas, chairs, and gilt-legged tables, all in surprisingly good condition, were scattered about the room, a group clustered together around a large fireplace with fluted marble pillars and mantel.

"My mother has kept the interior in good condition. She sometimes stays here if she wishes to visit her friends or go to the play." He opened the doors onto the balcony, sending Alexander a sideways glance. "What you could not guess from the front of the house, but will not find contemptible, I think, is the view."

Even before she stepped out, Nell heard the hiss and spit of water. Her eyes remained fixed on the long view of houses and crooked streets, cypress trees, the ramparts of a castle, and gently rolling hills beyond. Eventually they fell to the winding green ribbon of the river, at first focusing on the bridges that spanned it, and the water wheels that floated on rafts upon it. At last, placing her hands on the stone balcony, she leant a little forward, her eyes dropping to the white foaming waves that whirled and danced around hidden rocks directly below. A strange buzzing in her ears muted their roar as she imagined Flint being tossed and turned in the rapids.

"Nell?"

She was dimly aware of the voice but could not tear her eyes from the river. Imagination seemed to become reality, and she saw him floating just beneath the surface, his eyes closed and his face pale. Pity and horror warred for supremacy in her breast, but then his eyes snapped open, their stare accusatory and bitter, and there was only horror followed by darkness.

CHAPTER 18

"Is it not a magnificent prospect?" Bernardo said.

His cousin's eager expression reminded Alexander of a puppy seeking approval. "I will allow it to be impressive."

"I thought you would be pleased."

"It is not I who you need please," Alexander said dryly.

Bernardo turned his head to regard Angelica. His satisfied smile faded as he saw her thoughtful look.

"Great-Aunt? Do you not like what you see?"

Her gaze was fixed on the river. "It is a wonderful vista," she said, "and such a surprise. However, considering Lord Flint's unpleasant demise, it might have been kinder to Nell if the river was not a part of it."

Alexander glanced at Nell. Her eyes were wide and her skin preternaturally pale.

"Nell?" he said.

Her mouth suddenly opened on a scream cut short as her eyes rolled up in her head. Pushing Bernardo roughly out of the way, he took one large stride and caught her as she fell backwards. Lifting her, he stepped back into the drawing room and went swiftly to a sofa, laying her gently down.

"Bring me a cushion, Bernardo," he said curtly.

"Yes, of course," he said, thrusting one into Alexander's hand. "I would not have this happen for the world... I did not think—"

"Perhaps you should have," Alexander snapped, his tone harsh but his movements gentle as he slipped his arm under Nell's shoulders and raised her enough to place the cushion beneath her head.

Bernardo began to justify himself. "How could I have known? It is not as if she ever saw Flint in the river—"

Alexander turned on him. "If you have not yet discovered that imagining an event can be far worse than the reality, you are fortunate indeed."

Something in his expression made Bernardo take a step backwards. He put up his hands in a conciliatory gesture, his expression grave. "I do know it, and I apologise. I will try and find another house immediately, and if I cannot you must come and stay at my estate. Now my mother has gone to visit her sister..." He broke off, colouring, his eyes going to Angelica.

A sad little smile tilted her lips. "Do not worry, Bernardo. I had already guessed that she did not wish to see me."

"There is no need for you to find another house," Nell murmured, her eyes fluttering open. "It was not your fault, Bernardo. Even I could not have guessed that I would react in such a foolish way."

He bowed. "You are very kind."

She sat up and swung her feet to the ground. "I am better now."

"Even so, you will not try to stand just yet," Alexander said sternly, dropping a hand on her shoulder.

Nell wriggled out of his grasp but remained seated.

Scurrying footsteps sounded in the hall.

"It sounds as if your things are being taken to your chambers," Bernardo said. "If Nell would like to lie down, I will alert her maid." He smiled apologetically at her. "You will be glad to know that I did not give you a room facing the river."

"Thank you," Nell said. "But I do not need to lie down."

"Where have you put Mrs Farley and my daughter?" Alexander asked.

"In the room opposite yours, of course. I knew that is it what you would want." He sent Nell a sympathetic glance. "I am afraid it is only separated from yours by a dressing room and so you will most likely be disturbed."

"It is not at all likely," Alexander said. "Lady Francesca no longer wakes at night."

Bernardo laughed. "If I had been aware of that fact, I might have been tempted to stay here myself."

"You are very welcome to," Angelica assured him.

He shook his head. "It is not wise for both my mother and me to be away from home. Besides, it is only half an hour's ride and I enjoy the exercise. If Nell is feeling strong enough now, I will show you all to your rooms so that you may freshen up before breakfast."

Nell rose to her feet. "I am perfectly recovered."

She swayed slightly and Alexander scooped her into his arms. "More bottom than sense," he muttered.

"I do not believe I have ever heard that term," she said, a little stiffly. "But it does not sound at all complimentary."

Her irritation reassured him as her words had not. "Bernardo, make sure my grandmother is safely escorted to her room, will you? I will find my own way."

"But of course," he said. "I have given my great-aunt the bedchamber on this floor. It used to be a parlour, but my mother's cousin is very fat and could not manage two flights of stairs for fear he would expire from the effort."

"Let us hope that that fate does not await you," Nell murmured.

Alexander strolled from the room, pleased at so rapid a recovery of her spirit. "I am many things, but fat is not one of them."

"And I do not have a large…" A tinge of pink relieved her pallor as she halted mid-sentence.

He laughed. "I was not referring to a part of your anatomy, I assure you. It means to have more courage than sense and is often used in male circles when someone attempts something beyond their capability."

"You should not use cant in the presence of a lady," she said, her protest lacking force and her eyelids drooping over her eyes. "And I am perfectly capable of walking."

"Already correcting me, Nell?" he said softly. "And without the least provocation."

She nibbled her lip. He did not blame her; he would have liked to nibble it himself. He squashed the thought. Perhaps it would be better if he allowed her to nag him; it would be a constant reminder of what an interfering, impertinent chit she was.

"I see it is too much to expect you not to criticise me at all, and so I will allow you one free hit per day. As you have suffered a shock, I will not even count this one." They had reached the top of the stairs and he set her on her feet. "Is that not gentlemanly of me?"

She smiled wanly. "Yes, and thank you for your help. I will do very well now."

Francesca's gurgling guided them to their rooms. Nell's door was open and Maria already busily emptying her portmanteaux.

"Take care of your mistress," he said. "She has suffered a shock."

Maria took one look at Nell, dropped the gown she was holding, curtsied and came hurrying forward. "You may leave everything to me, my lord."

He nodded and moved on to Francesca's room. Timothy was just placing her cot next to a large bed tented with yellow silk.

"Have you everything you need, Jane?" he said.

Mrs Farley smiled at him, jiggling the baby on her lap. "Yes, my lord. More than enough. When you do banish us to the nursery, I won't know how to go on without such luxury."

"You will be delighted, and you know it." His eyes fell to his daughter. "Perhaps when we return home, I will allow it."

"I think that would be best, sir," the nurse said. "Whilst Lady Francesca is still too young to notice."

His smile twisted. It was one thing to know he should do it, and quite another to give his consent to the separation. He was determined not to suffocate Francesca and infect her with his fears that she might be taken from him, to put a healthy distance between them, but it was easier said than done. The remoteness of his home and his many conversations with his grandmother might have put his past in perspective, rid him of any lingering guilt even, but the fact remained that those he was closely connected to tended to die.

He turned and left the room, a grim laugh escaping him as the thought he should probably forewarn his future bride of that circumstance crossed his mind.

Nell was more shaken than she liked to admit. She allowed Maria to strip her to her shift and tuck her up in bed, docilely drinking the cup of coffee laced with brandy that she brought her, although she did not touch the bread and butter on her tray. The maid eventually gave up coaxing her to eat and removed it.

"Try to get some sleep," she said. "It is being tired that made you see things that weren't there."

Nell agreed but did not close her eyes as the maid left the darkened room. She did not dare. This was the city where she might well have been raped and where her husband had suffered a violent death, and she had been foolish not to consider the effect returning to it might have on her. Alexander might be able to protect her from physical harm, but he could not protect her mind from its worst imaginings.

He would understand that. How he had borne living in a house where he had suffered cruelty and neglect, where so many of his family had died in unfortunate circumstances, she did not know. She supposed he had no choice; a marquess could not rid himself of his family seat, after all.

She sighed. He had been kinder to her than she deserved. As he had been standing by the sofa when she had regained consciousness, she assumed he had caught her when she had fainted and carried her there, as he had carried her up the stairs. She should have been grateful, not waspish. Her embarrassment at misunderstanding his slang was not solely responsible for her reaction. She had liked being so close to him, had been aware of an urge to snuggle into his shoulder and wrap both arms about his neck. Sparring with him had seemed the safer option, however half-hearted the attempt.

Despite her misgivings, she did fall asleep and suffered no nightmares. When Maria woke her and offered her another tray, she discovered her appetite had returned. She ate two pastries, dressed, and went to find Angelica. Whether she liked it or not, she was in Verona and she could not spend her time cowering in her room.

As she reached the foot of the stairs, she heard Angelica's rich chuckle issue from a room on her left. She opened the door and stepped into a library. A fire had been lit and Angelica sat beside it on a sofa, but it was not Alexander or Bernardo who had caused her mirth. A stranger was sitting opposite her, his greying dark hair just visible above the back of the wingback chair.

She was about to back quietly out of the room when Angelica glanced up.

"I am sorry," Nell said, "I did not realise you had a visitor. I will leave you."

"No, don't go," she said. "I want you to meet our visitor. His father was a friend of Eduardo's, and I knew Signor Persico when he was a little boy in Venice. It is a fairly common name and so it was a delightful surprise to discover that he and the Podestà of Verona were one and the same."

As the man rose to his feet and turned towards her, Nell took half a step back, suddenly nervous. He was tall, his face long and serious, but as he rose from his bow, she saw that his eyes were kind.

"Lady Flint, it is a pleasure to make your acquaintance, at last."

She smiled uncertainly. "I wish I could say the same."

"Nell!" Angelica protested.

"I'm sorry," Nell said, clasping her hands tightly before her.

"No, it is all right," Signor Persico said. "The circumstances are difficult and if it was not a polite response, at least it was an honest one."

"I meant no disrespect," Nell said. "I am a little nervous."

"You need not be," he said gently. "I will not question you today. I merely came to pay my respects to Signora Montovani. Will you not sit down? I hear you were taken ill when you saw the river. It is most under-standable."

Nell sat next to Angelica. "I am better now. It was just the thought of what happened to my husband that overset me." She sat a little straighter and raised her chin. "And if you must question me, I would rather it be now."

"Is it really necessary to question Nell when you have already had her story from Bernardo?" Angelica said.

Signor Persico leant back in his chair, crossed his legs, and reached into his pocket, withdrawing a note-book and pencil. "I do not wish to cause any unneces-sary upset, but I must. A second-hand account is not always accurate and may miss vital details which might open another avenue of enquiry."

Nell took a deep breath and reiterated her account of that fateful evening, her downcast eyes and the fluc-tuating colour in her cheeks betraying how mortifying it was for her.

"Thank you," Signor Persico said gently when she had finished. "I can imagine how difficult that evening must have been for you."

Nell raised her head, her eyes bleak. "The entirety of the trip was difficult, and that evening was the final straw."

Signor Persico regarded her intently. "Something inside you snapped, perhaps?"

"Yes," she agreed. "In the minutes that followed that horrid conversation, I despised Flint, Count Fringuello and all the men like them. I even despised myself."

His eyes dwelt on her hair for a moment. "Which is why you took the scissors to your lovely locks."

"Yes," she murmured.

"And your husband never came to your room, even for a moment?"

"No," she said dully. "We heard the door to my husband's chamber open and close, but Lady Westcliffe said it must be his lordship's valet because she had seen Flint follow Count Fringuello from the yard."

"Follow?" he said.

"I did not mean to imply that he was following the count, I meant only that he left the yard soon after him."

Signor Persico tapped his pencil against the notebook. "Bernardo did not mention that."

Nell looked at him blankly, not understanding his interest in this small detail. "I do not recall if I mentioned it." She grimaced. "I was afraid that Renn would check on me; he was ever my husband's spy, and sometimes my jailor."

"Lord Flint's valet kept you a prisoner?"

Nell sighed. "When we were first in Italy, I would sometimes go out alone to visit a church or ancient monument. My husband would lock me in my room to punish me and give the key to Renn. He liked to know exactly where I was at all times and who I came into contact with."

"He was a jealous husband, then?" Her interrogator's glance was apologetic. "Forgive me, Lady Flint, but I must ask these difficult questions. Did you give your husband reason to be jealous?"

She laughed bitterly. "If you mean did I have a lover who murdered my husband and threw him in the river, no. Neither did I ever give my husband cause to think me unfaithful."

The mayor nodded. "But you were not locked in your room the night he was murdered."

"No," she agreed. "I had learned to be a submissive wife and had not gone against his wishes for some time."

"Did he ever strike you?"

Nell flushed. "Yes, but rarely, and only when he had been drinking."

"And you say Lady Westcliffe came upon you only minutes after Lord Flint's conversation with the count?"

"Yes."

"Her intervention was most timely. What would you have done if she had not come to your aid?"

Nell shivered. "I do not know, but you may be sure I would not have offered my husband violence, nor would I have simply waited for the count's visit." She stifled a sob. "I did consider throwing myself in the river, but my father is a vicar, and I could not commit such a terrible sin."

"I am glad of it," he said softly. "That would have been a tragedy, indeed."

Nell's eyes flew from her hands to his. "You believe my story?"

He smiled. "I am so inclined, Lady Flint, although I must wait for Lady Westcliffe's letter to confirm it. I had the pleasure of dining with her and her husband and admired her greatly. I am not at all surprised she helped you, and if her account of the events of that evening matches yours, you could hardly have had the opportunity to murder him. Also, as a maid at the Due

Torri confirmed that you were ill and to the best of her knowledge never left your room during your brief stay, you could hardly have arranged for someone else to carry out the wicked deed."

A relieved sigh escaped her.

"Has Nell's version of events opened up any new lines of enquiry?" Angelica asked.

"Perhaps," Signor Persico said, rising to his feet. "We shall see."

A firm tread was heard in the hall and Alexander came into the room, his expression haughty and his eyes hard. They went first to Nell and then to the mayor.

"Alexander," Angelica said. "This is Signor Persico—"

He responded to the man's bow with a slight inclination of his head. "Was it really necessary to question Lady Flint so soon, sir?"

"Alexander!" Angelica protested.

"I am surprised that you allowed this intrusion, ma'am," he said coolly. "Has Nell not been upset enough for one day?"

"Signor Persico did not come to question me," Nell said, rising to her feet.

His eyes went questioningly to the mayor.

"It is true, Lord Eagleton. I came only to pay my respects to Signora Montovani. My father and your grandfather were friends, and your grandmother knew me when I was a child. It was Lady Flint who wished to be questioned immediately."

He glanced at Nell. "You really are a glutton for punishment, aren't you?"

In truth, she was feeling drained, but she did not

regret her decision. "I preferred not to put off the inevitable merely because it was unpleasant."

"Even so, you would have done better to wait until I was with you."

"What difference would it have made?" Nell said, her brow wrinkling. "Your presence would not have altered the truth, and you already know what happened."

His eyes narrowed as they turned on the mayor. "I could have made sure you weren't led into saying anything unwise."

Signor Persico smiled, an amused glint in his eyes. "I think it was better that you were not present, my lord. Lady Flint spoke with an openness that was most enlightening. She did not try to conceal or deny anything, neither did she attempt to make the things that had happened to her seem better or worse than they were."

Alexander's eyes held a challenge. "And what, sir, do you conclude from these facts?"

"That Lady Flint most certainly had reason for wishing to be rid of her husband, but it is unlikely she had the means or opportunity to do so, nor would it have benefited her unless… never mind. Now, I have an appointment, but you are welcome to walk with me, Lord Eagleton, if you wish to discuss this further."

"Thank you," he said grimly. "I do."

Nell watched them leave, confused and a little annoyed at Alexander's high-handedness.

"He was only concerned for you, Nell," Angelica said.

"I think it more likely he was offended that we

dared proceed without the Marquess of Eagleton's lofty presence," she said dryly.

Angelica chuckled. "You wished for his help, Nell, and did he not promise to be as top-lofty and arrogant as his rank allowed in order to help you?"

"Yes," she admitted. "But there was no need for him to speak so rudely to you and Signor Persico."

CHAPTER 19

A lthough it irked him, Alexander matched his pace to the mayor's unhurried gait. "Now, Signor Persico, you may finish the sentence you left unfinished in front of the ladies. Or should I do it for you?"

"Be my guest," he said.

"You said it was unlikely that Nell had the means or opportunity to murder Flint; you did not say it was impossible. Bernardo mentioned you had some half-baked theory that someone, a lover perhaps, might have been induced to do it for her. As she had only been in Verona for two days, this lover must have followed her from Venice."

"Not necessarily," Signor Persico said, his glance enigmatic. "A man may fall in love in an hour, a minute, or even a second when confronted with someone as breathtakingly beautiful as Lady Flint."

Alexander's jaw clenched. "She would not thank you for saying so."

"Then she is unique amongst women."

"Yes," Alexander murmured. "She is. What you almost but did not quite say, is that Flint's death would only have benefited Lady Flint if this lover could provide for her."

"It was a logical conclusion," he said, unruffled. "Otherwise Lady Flint would have been left alone in a foreign country without money or protection."

Alexander came to an abrupt halt. "If you have spent half an hour in Nell's company and not realised that she is quite incapable of such duplicity, so immoral an act——"

Signor Persico held up his hand. "I never thought that theory worthy of serious consideration."

"Then why did you present it to such a young, foolish, and impressionable young man as Bernardo as a possibility?" Alexander said, exasperated. "For that matter, why did you discuss the case with him at all?"

"I discussed the case with Bernardo because I hoped I might gain a fresh perspective. My investigation had grown stale and needed fresh eyes. Captain Flint, quite understandably, wishes for answers, and I have none to offer him. The lover accomplice was Bernardo's theory, not mine. There were no rumours of a lover, on the contrary, Lady Flint's reputation was that of a cold, aloof woman."

"Of course she was aloof. She must have been stretching every sinew not to reveal what a sham her marriage was, to conceal her unhappiness, the fear she must have felt."

"I agree," the mayor said, his expression grave. "She suffered a great deal, I think."

"She is still suffering," Alexander said harshly. "And will continue to suffer if we cannot find the real murderer. She is as much a victim as Flint. It will not be enough that you acquit her of the deed; without solid proof that someone else was responsible, malicious whispers will always abound."

"We?" Signor Persico said. "You wish to help?"

"Of course. Did you not say you needed a fresh perspective? I would like to see all the reports on the case. Murder is usually motivated by money, love, or revenge. I am inclined to believe that Flint's death was connected to his debts. How watertight was this Count Fringuello's alibi?" Alexander's emerald eyes glittered. "He can have no honour if he was prepared to rape another man's wife."

They began to walk slowly on.

"The count enjoyed a short but distinguished military career and was renowned for his bravery and honour. He is originally from Piedmont and was severely injured at the battle of Mondovi in 1796. He was a handsome, dashing soldier, and after his disfigurement, his betrothed broke their engagement."

"Is this potted history meant to make me feel sorry for the man?"

"Not at all. I am merely pointing out that he is not without honour."

"That he was not without honour twenty years ago does not mean he possesses it now."

"The count has business interests in Venice and keeps an apartment there, but his main residence is here in Verona, yet apart from him apparently being prepared to pay to bed Lady Flint, I have heard nothing that would suggest otherwise."

"What do you mean apparently? I thought Bernardo said he admitted it."

Signor Persico sighed. "He admits that he made the bargain but claims that bedding her was not his intention."

Alexander gave a derisive laugh. "Perhaps he was prepared to pay an extortionate price to take tea with her."

"It sounds incredible, I know," Signor Persico said ruefully. "He would not tell me what he intended, but when he said he would not have touched a hair on her head, I believed him."

Conversation was suspended as they crossed a busy street. They entered a square, a faded sign on the corner of a building informing Alexander that it was the Piazza dei Signori, and came to a halt before a red-brick palace, its grand entrance surrounded by white marble and topped by a winged lion.

"This is the Palazzo del Podestà. I have offices and an apartment here. As I said, I have an appointment, but it should not take long. If you wish to come in, I will find the file you requested and you may read it whilst I am engaged."

After following him through a grand entrance hall and down several corridors, he was left in an ante-room, and a few minutes later a bespectacled clerk hurried in with the promised folder. Alexander was relieved to see he carried a candelabra, for the room possessed high, narrow windows which hardly pene-trated the gloom.

The man addressed Alexander in halting English as he placed both items on a table, a relieved smile creasing his face as he replied in Italian.

"No, thank you. I require no refreshment." He opened the folder and glanced at the uppermost paper, his eyes scanning the neat handwriting. "Nor do I need help translating these documents."

He hardly noticed the man scurry away, already absorbed in the information before him. The recorded investigation was not extensive. Various servants at the hotel had been interviewed, a maid confirming that Nell's room had been left in disarray with strands of her hair littering the floor and dressing table, spots of blood also on these items. He frowned. If a maid was privy to this information, it was likely that whatever Signor Persico's wishes, it had become common knowledge in Verona, the facts no doubt becoming exaggerated with each telling. It was true that this corner of Italy was not as popular with English travellers as Florence and Rome, and it was only recently that they had begun to travel again in numbers to the continent, but it was only a matter of time before they reached England's shores.

A series of interviews conducted in Venice confirmed that the five men Flint owed money to there had all been attending events in that city on the evening of Flint's death. That left only Count Fringuello. In Alexander's opinion, his explanation that he had gone straight from the Due Torri to his home on the Via Pigna was weak. His manservant confirmed that he had returned home late that evening, but he could not be specific about the time. No wonder Signor Persico had not answered when he had asked him how watertight his alibi was; it was as leaky as a sieve. A stable hand had heard voices in the yard and had seen the count with Lord Flint. Their conversation had been brief, and when the count left, the stable hand had returned to his bed.

It was thought that Flint had been thrown from the Ponte Pietra. Alexander knew from his visit to the Due Torri and brief exploration of the area surrounding it earlier that day, that it was the bridge nearest to the hotel. Drops of blood had been found on the ground and stone parapet of the bridge, but no one had apparently witnessed any altercation that evening in its vicinity. That was hardly surprising at so late an hour.

He looked up as a discreet cough sounded. The clerk had returned.

"If you will come this way, Signor Persico is ready for you now."

Alexander gathered up the documents and placed them neatly in the folder, before following the man. He was shown into a large, high-ceilinged office. Signor Persico dismissed the clerk, offered Alexander a seat, and poured two glasses of wine. He brought them over, passed Alexander his and took the seat opposite him.

"Did you discover anything interesting?" he asked.

"Only that the count should not have been ruled out of your enquiry. You only have his word that he went straight back to his house."

Signor Persico put his glass down, sat back, and steepled his fingers. "At the time, I had no reason to doubt his word. He was seen leaving the courtyard of the hotel alone and at that time Lord Flint was unharmed."

Alexander was quick to grasp the import of his opening words. "At the time? Do I take it that you are having second thoughts?"

"I discovered something from Lady Flint that

Bernardo had failed to mention to me. It is a small point but perhaps an important one. Lord Flint left the courtyard of the hotel only moments after the count." He frowned. "It could mean nothing, on the other hand, it might."

"You think he went after him?"

"It is possible. Perhaps Lord Flint regretted offering his wife to him, perhaps he had thought of a way whereby he might relieve himself of his debt without forcing such a humiliation on her."

Alexander looked thoughtful. "You think Flint may have tried to murder him, but the count defended himself and, in the process, killed Flint?"

"It is a possibility, you must admit, and would better fit the facts. What reason did the count have to murder the baron? His death only ensured the count would receive no payment of any kind."

"That is true," Alexander said frowning. "But Flint was also counting on an additional payment from the count to keep him afloat."

"Perhaps he meant also to rob him. From all I have heard, Lord Flint had not an ounce of honour."

"Very little," Alexander agreed. "But I think you said Count Fringuello was severely injured. Is it likely he could have fought off an attack?"

The mayor smiled wryly. "He has a bad limp and is blind in one eye, but he has a reputation for being able to defend himself. Apart from that, Lady Flint intimated that her husband sounded drunk. In such a state he might make unwise decisions and be less diffi-cult to overcome."

Alexander pushed a hand through his hair. "If he killed him in self-defence, why not admit it?"

"I have also asked myself that question. My theory is all conjecture; there is no proof either way. The count would have been aware of that. How could he prove that it had been self-defence? Why should he risk his name being associated with such a scandal if he did not need to?" He sighed. "If it were not for Captain Flint's insistence that I do not drop the investigation, I would be sorely tempted to. If it happened as I have posited, we should rejoice that the world is rid of a contemptible man."

"If it were not for the mud that will cling stubbornly to Lady Flint, I would agree with you. But for that, I would shake the man's hand *if* it happened as you said."

He thought it interesting that Flint's successor had not yet taken the title, but a few moments' reflection gave him the reason and explained his desire to find Nell. He must wait until he knew for certain that she had not borne a child.

"It seems we are no further forward than we were before," he said. "But I would very much like to meet the count."

"He does not attend social events. He has no wish to see the shocked and disgusted glances of the ladies when they see his disfigurement, but he often visits one of the coffee houses on the Piazza Bra, especially if there is a musical recital in the Roman amphitheatre. He can then enjoy the music without exposing himself to the crowds. There is such a recital tomorrow. It will be the last performance there until the spring. I was of a mind to invite you all to join me in my box. If Lady Flint is seen in my company at a social event, it may help her cause. She and your grandmother may even receive other invitations. The Montovani name is respected here, after all, and curiosity will be rife."

Alexander sipped his wine as he considered this proposal. "Nell will not like it. She will feel exposed and vulnerable, but I think it a good idea." He rose to his feet. "We are delighted to accept your kind invitation. Might I suggest you join us for dinner first? Shall we say seven o'clock?"

The mayor stood and bowed. "Thank you. I would be delighted."

As Alexander had expected, Nell was far from pleased when he broached the subject at dinner. She laid down her fork and stared at him incredulously.

"First you do your best to alienate the mayor and now you wish me to flaunt myself in front of Veronese society as if I don't have a care in the world? This is the help you offer me?"

"Signor Persico is not at all alienated," he replied coolly. "We parted on very good terms, and he will dine with us tomorrow. What is more, it was his idea that we attend the amphitheatre as his guests, not mine."

"But you accepted on our behalf when you must have known that I would shrink from so public a display."

"I did know it," he said, unabashed. "Which is precisely why I accepted on your behalf."

Nell flushed, her eyes sparkling with indignation. "Of all the high-handed, arrogant—"

"Enough!" he snapped. "I may be both of those things, in fact I know I am, but I am also far wiser than you. You are flinging these insults in my face because you are afraid of what people will think of you. That is a mistake. You do not hide from malicious gossip, you face it. If word has not already got out that you are in the city, it will soon. As is the case in London, if nobody sees you or gets to know you, they will feel free to interpret your character as they will.

"Signor Persico knew within half an hour that you were not an adulteress, that you would never murder your husband or conspire to have him murdered. You need others to know that. If you cower behind these four walls, it will suggest that you are ashamed, that you are guilty in some way. English visitors to this city will hear the rumours surrounding you and take them back with them. Is that what you want?"

He watched the flush of anger fade as she paled but did not allow himself to weaken. "Is that what you want, Nell?"

Her eyes fell. "No," she whispered.

"Very well," he said. "I am not suggesting that you flaunt yourself or that you act as if you do not have a care in the world; I do not ask you to play a part but merely to be yourself."

Her eyes rose at that. "How can I act naturally when I do not know what people will be thinking, what they know or don't know, when I cannot express myself well in the Italian tongue, and when I feel so... so mortified."

He sensed the battle had been won and his expression gentled. "You know the truth and that must sustain you. You have nothing to be ashamed of. And if those who wish to speak with you do not speak English, they will most likely speak French. Do you, Nell?"

She nodded. "Yes. My mother was French."

His eyes brightened with interest. "Precisely how old are you, Nell?"

"Four and twenty," she murmured.

She looked younger. The ramifications of her mother's being French hit him. "Then you were born in 1792. Is it possible, Nell, that your mama was an émigré who fled France before the atrocities of the revolution were in full swing?"

"Yes," she affirmed. "My grandfather, the Comte de Bourdon, was a widower and my mother was his only child. He took her to a seminary near Bath in 1788. There had been a series of bad harvests and a particularly bad winter that year. He knew there was trouble brewing. He visited my mother several times but as the summer of 1789 approached, he did not come. She was invited to the home of a friend, Jane Horton. It was there that she heard of the storming of the Bastille and other riots. Peasants had broken into manor houses and châteaux in order to find and burn the documents granting the landowners their feudal privileges." She looked grave. "Sometimes the buildings burned too."

"Your grandfather was killed?"

She nodded. "Miss Horton married Sir James Larraby at the end of that summer, and she took my mother to live with them."

His eyebrow rose at that. "Sir James was a very benevolent gentleman."

A fond smile briefly touched her lips. "He is a dear. It was not meant to be a permanent arrangement, and then a Bath solicitor tracked down my mother. He confirmed her father's death and also revealed that he had been transferring his wealth to England for some time. Her inheritance was safe."

"And then she met your father," Angelica said.

Nell smiled. "Yes. He helped her to grieve, and they fell in love."

The thought that an impoverished clergyman had taken advantage of a vulnerable young woman's grief to ensure his future comfort crossed Alexander's mind. According to Nell, he had not touched a penny of her mother's money, however, she only had his word for that. He had also not informed her of her inheritance until her marriage. He was not sure he believed this story of him wishing for a well-born gentleman to ride up on his charger and whisk her off into the sunset when he had kept her buried in the depths of north Devon. What were the chances?

"How did Flint stumble upon you?" he asked.

She sighed. "Lady Larraby was unwell and asked if I would accompany her middle daughter, Emily, to an assembly in Barnstaple. Lord Brackton has a house near Umberleigh, a village about ten miles from the town. He rarely visits it. He has been trying to sell it for years, but it is in such a state of disrepair that it is hardly surprising no one has offered to buy it. When he strolled into the assembly with Lord Flint, it caused quite a stir."

"I bet it did," he murmured.

What the hell was Brackton doing with Flint? He was a jovial idiot who wouldn't harm a fly and certainly not a member of Flint's usual circle. Enlightenment dawned. Brackton was also dim-witted enough to believe Flint was interested in purchasing a mouldering house in Devon. Flint had most likely used

the need to view it as an excuse to rusticate somewhere he might not be found for a few days, and he
had probably hoped to fleece poor Brackton at the
same time. If the house was in as bad a state as Nell
intimated, it was no wonder they had ended up at a
provincial assembly. Spending evenings in a no-doubt
cold and draughty house with a man of mean intelligence would not have suited Flint at all.

CHAPTER 20

Nell stepped out of the carriage in Piazza Bra, her eyes sweeping around the square. All was bustle and noise. Carriages queued to drop off their passengers, people strolled arm in arm, and others sat outside coffee houses, something that surprised her at this time of year. She pulled her cloak closer about her, her shiver not due to the chill alone.

Before her lay the amphitheatre, flickering flambeaux illuminating two tiers of vast arches, the time-worn stone tinged with pink. Below them artisans and tradesmen plied their trades by candlelight, the old and the modern strangely united.

"Reserve your judgement until you step inside."

She turned her head and found Signor Persico standing beside her.

"You will not find a greater example outside Rome." He offered her his arm. "Come, Lady Flint. I wish everyone to see that I, the Podestà of Verona, find you worthy of my company."

"You are very kind," she murmured.

He patted her hand. "You look like you fear you are about to be thrown to the lions. Put your chin up, signora. It is true that some ladies have claws just as sharp, but you need not be afraid…" He smiled, his eyes moving past her. "You have a gladiator to fend them off, after all."

She followed his gaze, and her heart missed a beat. Alexander cut an imposing figure, his well-cut, black cloak falling from his broad shoulders in elegant folds. It was lined with green silk, the colour echoed in the emerald he wore on his finger, another nestling amongst the folds of his neckcloth. His expression was haughty, and his eyes moved with deliberation around the square as if he were searching for something or someone. He looked elegant, formidable, almost sinister, Nell thought, which perhaps explained her reaction. As his eyes alighted on her a faint smile touched his lips and he inclined his head, before turning to help his grandmother from the carriage.

"Come," Signor Persico said. "Bolster yourself with the thought that as many eyes will be on the marquess as you."

That was true, she reflected, falling into step with the mayor. She doubted any woman between the ages of seventeen and seventy would be immune to his dark, good looks.

They stepped into a huge oval arena. A wooden stage was lit by a series of lanterns, and in front of it, rows of chairs were filled with wealthy Veronese. There were only two boxes, one on either side of the space, both brightly illuminated. Nell looked up and saw the stars glittering in the sky far above. Stone wooden benches rose to meet them, however all but the occupants on the first few rows remained cloaked in shadow although their chattering voices filled the air. Nell could not see the scale of this architectural marvel, but she could feel it.

"You must come back in daylight, of course," the mayor said, opening the door into the box he had reserved for them.

"You may be sure I will," Nell said.

A blanket was placed on every chair and beneath them a hot brick to warm their feet. On a table at the back of the booth, two bottles of champagne sat in a large bucket of ice. Nell was touched by such consideration for their comfort but was not so happy with the string of lanterns that illuminated the box. She would have preferred the anonymity of darkness.

"As you are not fluent in the Italian tongue, Lady Flint, I will give you a brief explanation of the opera you are about to enjoy. It is called *La pietra del paragone*, which means touchstone, and was written by Rossini. It is quite comical in places and very entertaining. Count Asdrubale is surrounded by fawning admirers who bore him dreadfully."

She glanced at Alexander. He should feel some affinity with the opera then.

"He holds a house party at his villa, and amongst his guests are three widows who are pursuing him. This is no bad thing for he wishes very much to marry, but he desires to be loved for himself rather than just his money."

Again, her gaze flickered to Alexander. There the marquess and the count differed. His head was bent to hear something his grandmother was saying, an affectionate smile on his lips. To be loved by him would be something indeed. She shook her head slightly as if to dislodge the thought.

"He decides to test the ladies' affections by devising a ruse. He pretends he has lost all his money. Two of the ladies think they have had a lucky escape and prepare to leave, only Marchesa Clarice is sympathetic and his friend Giocondo."

"And so his ruse works and they all live happily ever after," Nell murmured.

"Eventually, but that would be too simple. The count becomes jealous because Giocondo flirts with the marchesa and he is now unsure of her. This annoys the marchesa, and it is now her turn to test the count's love. She pretends to be her twin brother who has come to take her away, and it is then, with the threat of her imminent departure, that the count realises his feelings, and all is well."

"If only real life resembled fiction," Nell murmured. If only she had tested Flint instead of taking him at face value.

At the first pull of a bow across a string, the buzz of conversation in the auditorium stopped abruptly, and Nell soon became lost in the performance. The music, acting and singing were so in accord, so well done, that even without Signor Persico's synopsis, she would have understood the bare bones of the plot. It was a farrago of nonsense, of course, but she found herself mesmerised nonetheless.

When the curtain came down after the first act, she found herself joining in the thunderous applause, and it was not until she turned to smile at Angelica that she realised Alexander had gone.

Alexander had been far more interested in the expressions flitting across Nell's face as she leant forwards, her hands on the edge of the box, than he had been in the opera. Although the orchestra and performers were skilled, he thought the plot ridiculous, and he forgave Rossini only because he had undoubtedly brought Nell pleasure. To see her eyes sparkling with appreciation at what he guessed was her first introduction to opera, and to hear the tinkle of genuine laughter on her lips, pleased him greatly. He felt sure he was glimpsing the girl she had been before Flint got his grubby hands on her.

That thought made his hands curl into fists, and as the curtain closed on the first act to a round of enthusiastic applause, he slipped from the box and strode swiftly out of the amphitheatre. His eyes scanned the tables outside the nearest coffee shop, and he smiled grimly as he spotted his quarry. The man sat very straight in his chair, against which a walking stick was propped. One leg was thrust out straight before him and he kneaded it absently with one hand. As Alexander neared, he raised his head and watched him approach as if alerted by some sixth sense that it was he Alexander was seeking.

His appearance was certainly enough to give ladies with too much sensibility nightmares. One eyelid drooped over a milky-hued eye, and an ugly scar ran from it to a thin-lipped mouth that curled cynically as Alexander came to a halt in front of him. Deep grooves were etched into his forehead and the side of his mouth, no doubt from suffering years of pain.

The count spoke softly. "Good evening, Lord Eagleton. Forgive me if I don't get up. My leg is paining me today."

"Count Fringuello," Alexander said nodding and sitting down. "I had not expected the whispers of our arrival to begin so soon. Was it the maids gossiping in the market or my cousin, Bernardo Montovani, who trumpeted our presence?"

"Neither. Signor Persico mentioned that I might expect a visit from you."

Alexander's brows rose at this. "Did he, though? Now, why would he do that?"

The count raised his glass towards a passing waiter and held up two fingers. "I am known for liking my own company, and perhaps he thought it in your best interests that I be warned of the forthcoming interview." He picked up his stick and twisted the silver-clawed top, revealing an inch or two of steel. "I have been known to lose my temper on occasion."

Alexander's eyes grew keen. "Are you threatening me?" he said softly. "I wouldn't if I were you."

The count's eyes held Alexander's for a moment, and then he laughed, twisting the top again and replacing the cane. "I was merely offering you an explanation as to why the mayor might prepare me for this encounter."

The waiter returned with two glasses of brandy.

"I saw Lady Flint earlier," the count murmured. "She is still as beautiful as ever. Once upon a time, beautiful women would look at me as she looked at you."

"And now you seek to rape them," Alexander said, his voice low but hard.

The count's hand again went to his cane, but although his hand tightened on it, he did not pick it up. "It is not wise to provoke me," he said through gritted teeth.

"Is that what Flint did when he followed you from the hotel? Did you use that sword of yours to run him through before throwing him in the river? You mustn't think I object to your ridding the world of so contemptible a fellow; it is your insults to Lady Flint and the malicious rumours that she might have had a hand in his death that appal me."

The count lurched forwards so that his face was only inches from Alexander's. He did not retreat, but stared into the count's good eye, seeing anger blazing there.

"What I said to Flint was not for her ears, I meant to insult him not his wife. I am not like that piece of filth, a coward and a worm. It would have given me great pleasure to run him through with my sword, but I would not do it unless in a fair fight. If he had a shred of decency in him, he would have challenged me to a duel, but he did not."

Despite the anger coursing through his veins, Alexander sensed the truth in his words. "You would have been at a severe disadvantage in a duel. He was younger and fitter than you, or do you have a death wish?"

The count sat back, reached for his glass, and downed the brandy. "There have been days when I have prayed that I would not wake up, but that was not one of them."

Alexander felt a stirring of pity for the man. "If

you did not mean to rape Lady Flint, what did you mean to do with her?"

He did not think the stony-faced count would answer him, but when the tense silence between them reached breaking point, he leant his arms on the table and began to speak.

"I wanted two things. Her company for a few hours—"

Alexander smiled cynically and the count broke off, a dark flush staining his cheeks.

"You think that so incredible?" His lips twisted in a bitter smile. "Of course you do. You can probably have the company of whomever you want with the lift of a finger, as I could once. Tell me, how old are you?"

Alexander blinked, the unexpected question throwing him off his stride. "Eight and thirty, not that I see what that has to do with anything."

"Then we are almost of an age. I was an idealistic nineteen-year-old when I suffered my injury."

Alexander was shocked, he looked much older.

"Yes, I am fully aware I look at least ten years older. Years of physical suffering will do that to a man. Now, try putting your righteous anger aside for a moment and listen. If I want merely to bed a woman, I pay for the privilege, but what a harlot cannot give me is the gentle manners and conversation of a breathtakingly beautiful woman of genteel birth. In Lady Flint's case, I was prepared to pay for that."

Whilst Alexander could understand the count's wish, he doubted very much his encounter with Nell would have turned out quite as he had envisaged. "Do you really think you would have enjoyed a mutually satisfying conversation when the woman was acquired on such terms? Lady Flint would have been frightened out of her wits."

"Not for long, I hope," the count said. "Because the second thing I wanted was to offer her my help. On the evening they left Venice, I saw Lady Flint come out of a hotel with her husband. She looked vulnerable, forlorn, and frightened, and when Flint offered her to me, I knew she had cause. Once the idea that he could use her in such a way had entered that cur's head, it was only a matter of time before he would do it again. I wished to offer her my protection."

"And what form would that protection have taken?" Alexander asked, his jaw tightening.

The count smiled grimly. "Do not judge me by your own standards, Eagleton. I would not have asked her to be my mistress but would have helped her return to England. I own a ship-building business in Venice and have three merchant ships. One of them makes regular trips to Lisbon and London. I would have secured her a safe passage on it." The count got to his feet. "I have only told you this because I don't want you to continue to badger me. Good evening."

Alexander watched him limp away for a moment and then stood swiftly and went to him.

The count turned. "Well?"

Alexander held out his hand. "Thank you for being so frank, Count Fringuello. I believe you and commend you for your good intentions."

The count's stern countenance relaxed, and he shook the hand offered him. "I understand your wish to find Flint's murderer, but if I could not, I do not think you will be able to."

"You searched for his killer?" Alexander said, surprised.

The count nodded. "I did not wish to have a stain on my honour. It is all that remains to me." The dark flush again entered his cheeks, and this time Alexander recognised it for what it was; embarrassment. "I would ask that you explain to Lady Flint my motivations and apologise for causing her distress."

"Certainly. It will perhaps restore her faith in our sex a little."

The count turned to go, but paused, looking over his shoulder. "A word of advice. Watch that cousin of yours. I see and hear many things, and I know that Bernardo Montovani is secretly courting a young woman from a powerful family. They intend her for someone else. There is a long-running feud between her family and his, and if he does not take care, it is his body that will be found floating in the river."

Alexander would have liked to ask him more, but the opening strains of the second act were already drifting across the piazza. As he stepped into the circular corridor that led into the amphitheatre, he sensed he was not alone. He stepped into the shadows by an archway and heard low voices coming from his right. He edged along the wall until he could hear them.

"Bernardo, I must go. Rosa is waiting for me in the dark and she will be frightened. Besides, the second act is about to begin."

"Promise me that you will refuse his offer, Sofia, and I will let you go."

A stifled sob sounded. "I cannot, you know I

cannot. We must think of another way... but now I must go."

"Meet me on Thursday at eleven o'clock at Juliet's tomb. Only gullible tourists will be there and so we need not fear discovery."

"I will try," she said.

Alexander stayed still until he heard light footsteps flee past him and a heavier tread going in the other direction, then entered the arena and slipped back into the box. Angelica passed him a glass of champagne and smiled.

"Is the opera not to your taste?"

He dipped a shoulder and leant towards his grandmother. "I wished to explore the square," he murmured.

"Well, that is a shame, because we received introductions to several ladies, who although very polite, looked a little disappointed that you had absented yourself."

He grinned. "Then you will no doubt see them again very soon."

Angelica chuckled. "Arrogant boy."

He glanced at Nell, who was again absorbed in the performance. "How did Nell cope?"

"Charmingly. She was so animated about the performance that she completely forgot to feel awkward."

His eyes went to the box opposite and he saw two young ladies enter it, one dark and one fair.

"Do you know who is in the other box?"

"Signor Persico tells me that it is the Lonardi family. I do not think we may expect an invitation from them as apparently, Bernardo's father and Signor

Lonardi fought a duel when they were young and remained enemies from that day on."

Alexander raised an eyebrow. "The duel usually ends the argument. What was it about?"

"It remains a mystery. Nobody witnessed their initial argument and neither of them ever spoke of the reason."

"How intriguing. I would be inclined to believe that the reason for their silence was that the argument concerned a lady but for the fact that it remained a secret."

Angelica sent him an exasperated glance. "Are you suggesting that the female sex cannot keep a secret?"

"Not in my experience, and certainly not when two men are fighting over her favours."

"You, my grandson, have spent too much time with the wrong type of female."

He laughed softly. "You have me there."

On the way home in the carriage, Nell said, "Your support this evening was markedly absent at the very moment I might have needed it."

He grinned in the darkness. There was a blend of curiosity and pique in her voice. "But I have it on good authority that you did not require it. Besides, I needed to stretch my legs and rest my ears."

"Oh, how can you say that?" Nell protested. "The performance was marvellous."

"Yes, so you have said... several times."

He expected her to bristle but after a mute few moments, she chuckled.

"I suppose I deserved that. I apologise, it is a dead bore when people go on and on about something one has no interest in. It is just that I had not experienced anything like that before."

"No, it is I who should apologise," he said, a smile in his voice. "I was baiting you. Let us agree that it was a wonderful performance. I will tell you where I went and why when we are sitting next to a warm fire."

CHAPTER 21

A smile touched Nell's lips. Perhaps her stay in Verona would not be so trying, after all. She had enjoyed a wonderful evening and she had only been disappointed when she had discovered Alexander's absence because she had wished to discuss the performance with him.

Whilst she had been talking to Angelica, Signor Persico had wandered into the arena and it was not until he re-entered the box with three ladies in tow, that she had experienced a moment of anxiety. They had been perfectly amiable, however, and the opera had provided them with an easy source of conversation. Alexander had been quite right about their speaking French, and when she did not have the fluency to express her feelings about the opera in Italian, she had switched to that language.

She felt both foolish and guilty for creating such a fuss about showing herself in public. It had been over a year since the dreadful events of that fateful night had occurred and perhaps they no longer held a place in the memories of the Veronese populace. Why should they? Few of them could have been acquainted with her husband, after all, and the fate of an unknown gentleman and his wife had most likely only generated a fleeting interest soon overtaken by a scandal concerning someone of more import to them.

When they entered the entrance hall of the house, Savio relieved them of their cloaks and assured them that a fire had been lit in the library and he would send Timothy up with the tea tray immediately. Nell realised that it had been tacitly agreed that they would avoid the drawing room for the present and felt touched by such consideration.

Alexander left them at the door of the library but promised to return in a few minutes. He was going to check on his daughter, of course. It was the first thing he did whenever he returned home.

"Lady Francesca is a lucky girl," she murmured, watching him take the stairs two at a time.

"Perhaps," Angelica said, taking Nell's arm and walking into the library. She closed the door behind them.

"Perhaps?" Nell said.

Angelica settled herself in a chair by the fire, gazing into it for a few moments before answering Nell's query.

"There is no doubt that Alexander loves his daughter, but love is a gift and a burden. For Alexander, the gift is that he has opened his heart and learned to put someone else's needs before his own, but his burden is heavy indeed." Her eyes became distant, and a bittersweet smile curved her lips. "My darling Eduardo was a strong man, a proud man, and

I never wished to envisage a life without him. The loss of our daughter diminished us both before and after her death, but we still had each other. As you know, Eduardo suffered a stroke, but I always believed he would recover. After his second, I knew that he would not. I had to live with the fear that he might be taken from me at any moment."

Nell's heart constricted. "And Alexander lives with that fear every day."

Angelica's eyes grew moist. "Yes. Not because Francesca is ill, but because all those closely connected to him seem to suffer that fate. That one who had never known love could instinctively love another is extraordinary, but his love knows no moderation. It is too fierce, it consumes him, and it will devour him unless he finds someone… no, not just someone, but the right person to share it with, to temper and dilute it."

"Dilute it?"

"He needs a wife who will love his daughter and help prevent him from becoming an overprotective tyrant."

Nell smiled wryly. "The first of those tasks is easily done; Lady Francesca is extremely lovable, but the second will be a difficult if not impossible challenge. Do you really think the Marquess of Eagleton's future wife will hold any sway over him?"

"Not if he marries for convenience," Angelica said.

Nell's throat suddenly felt dry. "Is that his plan?" she asked, doing her best to sound nonchalant.

"Yes." Angelica sighed. "A good obedient wife, who will shower his daughter with affection and gentleness and never cause him a moment's worry or trouble, may sound ideal in theory, but it would never do in practice. Such a mouse would let him ride roughshod over her and bore him within a week."

"And he would no doubt find his amusements elsewhere," Nell said, not quite able to keep the bitterness from her words. "And she would count herself fortunate and look the other way."

"It is a depressing scenario, is it not?" Angelica said. "Of course, what he needs is to fall so much in love that his wife's happiness is of paramount importance to him, then he would listen to her counsel and perhaps she would chase the ghosts from the corridors of Eagleton Priory." She shook her head. "Of course, he will never allow himself to fall in love."

Nell wound one of her curls about her finger as the tea tray was brought in, a contemplative distance in her eyes as she considered that last sentence.

"Thank you, Timothy. That will be all."

Angelica's voice barely registered, but as the door clicked gently shut behind the footman, Nell managed to coalesce her thoughts into one simple question.

"Surely love seeks no permission, but is involuntary?"

"That is true, but what the heart might acknowledge, the mind can deny. Alexander has a very strong mind, Nell, as do you, I think. You have both been deeply wounded by past events and for either of you to trust another with your happiness will be difficult."

"Yes," Nell acknowledged softly. "Perhaps as impossible as taming your grandson."

Angelica chuckled. "Then it is just as well that I intend to return to England with him."

Nell blinked. "You do? But what about the vineyard?"

"It will do very well without me. I discussed it with Signor Batiste. He is training his son to take over when it becomes too much for him, and I intend to set up a trust. It was Alexander's idea. He is impressed by Luca's son's intelligence and suggested that some of the profits from the vineyard go to setting up and maintaining a school for those who wish to be educated more formally and to a higher standard than is currently available in Malcesine, and I think it a splendid idea."

"So do I," Nell said. "But, Angelica, such a journey will be extremely arduous."

"No doubt, but I believe I can bear being jolted about in a carriage for a few weeks. I wish to visit my daughter, and to be buried next to her when my time comes." She smiled a little sadly. "Eduardo would understand."

Alexander came into the room, a proud smile on his face. "My daughter is apparently making progress; she has learned to crawl forwards."

So had they all, Nell mused. She busied herself making the tea, feeling embarrassed that they had nearly been caught discussing the most personal aspects of his life. He accepted a cup from her, sat next to his grandmother, and stretched his long legs before him, crossing them at the ankles. Nell felt his eyes upon her and glancing up saw that he was no longer smiling.

"I do not wish to alarm you, Nell, but the reason I left you for a short while this evening, is that I wished to have a conversation with Count Fringuello."

Her cup rattled in its saucer, and she hastily put it down.

"It seems we have misjudged him."

The colour leached from her face and angry disbelief sparked in her eyes. "You forget that I heard every disgusting word he uttered. There was no room for misunderstanding."

Alexander's lips twisted. "There is always room for misunderstanding."

She shot to her feet, her legs trembling beneath her. "I see your protection is no better than my husband's. One conversation with a fellow rake, and you take his side."

The sudden anger that glittered in his eyes dwarfed hers, and she took a step backwards, her legs hitting the chair behind her, making her crumple into it. Before she could straighten, he was looming over her. He bent, his hands resting on the armrests, his face so close to hers that strands of his long, raven hair tickled her cheek. She would have brushed it away, but his piercing eyes pinned her in place.

"If having had mistresses in the past makes me a rake, then yes, I am one, but by that calculation so are the large majority of men who have the means to indulge themselves in such a way. If by rake you mean that I have seduced or forced myself on an unwilling lady of any description, then I most certainly am not. Do you understand me, Nell?"

Her chest heaved as if she had run some distance, and she couldn't find the breath to answer him.

"Do you understand me?"

She nodded, suddenly feeling wretched.

"Alexander," Angelica said, "leave the poor girl alone. You must make allowances."

He straightened, spinning on his heel. "And I have, on more occasions than I care to remember. Perhaps it is time Nell made some concessions in this direction." He pushed the hair back from his face and sighed. "Forgive me, both of you. My damnable temper got the better of me."

Nell sat up, her heart giving a thump as realisation dawned on her. He was angry and upset because he thought she had an unfair, biased opinion of him. They had lived cheek by jowl for some weeks and what she thought of his character mattered to him.

"No, it is I who should apologise," she said quietly. "I did not mean it. I was angry and confused, but I should at least have heard you out." Her fingers twined together. "I know that you are not like Flint, and I do not really think you are the sort of man who…" She gulped. "Who would force himself on someone."

Alexander dropped back into his chair, his jaw relaxing.

"But I do not understand how I can have miscon-strued the words I overheard."

"If the count had known you were there, he would never have uttered them. He asked me to offer you his apologies for any distress he caused you and to explain his motivations. You may find what I am about to say difficult to believe, but I know when a man is lying, and I do not believe the count lied to me this evening. One of his admissions, at least, caused him some humiliation, which is no doubt why he did not confide in Signor Persico, although he did tell the mayor that his intentions were not what they appeared to be. The mayor was also inclined to believe him."

Nell suddenly felt parched. She reached for her tea and gulped it down, not caring that the hot brew scalded her throat. "Very well. I will do my best to listen with an open mind."

Alexander spoke calmly and persuasively, and by the time he had relayed the count's background and his conversation with him, her understanding of what had happened that evening had been turned on its head and her mind was reeling.

"That poor man," Angelica said. "What sort of woman abandons a heroic man merely because he has been wounded in battle? He should not hide from genteel society merely because he fears seeing the revulsion on the faces of frivolous women. They would get used to him in time."

Nell recalled the count's scarred visage and her reaction to it. It had, no doubt, added to the horror of that evening. Based on the knowledge she had had at that time, it was understandable, and yet she felt a little ashamed. She had thought of him as a depraved monster for over a year, but he was not a monster, he had wished to help her.

"Nell?"

She met Alexander's enquiring gaze.

"What are you thinking?"

She drew in a deep breath. "I think we should grant Count Fringuello his wish to spend an evening in genteel company. We should invite him to dinner."

A slow smile stretched Alexander's lips. "I think that an excellent idea. My compliments, Nell."

She shook her head. "I do not deserve them. Whether for good or ill, I judge people too quickly."

"You were quite justified in your judgement of the count," he said gently.

Her eyes dropped from his. "Perhaps, but I am not justified in throwing your past in your face merely because you have angered me, or of assuming the worst merely because another abused my trust. I won't do it again."

When he did not answer her, she glanced at him from under her lashes. His smile was crooked and his expression enigmatic.

"Thank you, Nell." Amusement crept into his eyes. "And do you also promise never to try and correct what you perceive to be my other faults?"

She knew he was trying to lighten the moment, and she appreciated the gesture.

"No," she said, her lips twitching. "I do not make promises that I cannot keep."

He and Angelica both laughed, and the harmony of the evening was restored.

Angelica rose to her feet, and Nell was pleased to note how easily she did so.

"Well, I don't know about you, Nell, but I have had quite enough excitement for one evening and shall retire."

Alexander began to rise but she waved him back. "Nell will see me delivered into Beatrice's hands."

He watched them leave, a smile still tugging at his lips. It gradually faded as he recalled the startled expression in Nell's eyes as he had leant over her. He should not have treated her so harshly, had not meant to frighten her, but that she had compared him to Flint, that she still doubted him had made him blazingly angry. That troubled him. Rumours about him both true and false were nothing new and had only ever caused him consternation on one occasion.

When Miss Cressida Harrington had fled Bath to escape his attentions, the rumour that he had deflowered her, and she had gone into hiding because she was with child had begun to circulate. When he had heard this rumour, he had called the man who had dared utter such malicious gossip out. It was not his own honour he had been protecting but hers.

He stood, walked to a sideboard, and poured himself a glass of wine. He wished to protect Nell's reputation too, and not just because it would please his grandmother, but because it was not right that she be denied the standing in society she deserved when she could be its brightest ornament and because he liked her. Flint had hurt her enough when he was alive and that he should continue to do so after his death was unpalatable. Nell's good opinion should not matter to him, but it did. It was why, although he had decided to give her reason to dislike him, he had not been able to execute that plan.

He raised the glass to his lips and downed the contents as his inner demon taunted him.

Be honest with yourself for once. It is not just her reputation you wish to protect; it is her. She has you wrapped about her thumb. One droop of that delectable mouth, one anxious glance from those expressive eyes, one wince of pain from an unpleasant memory has you wishing to gather her up in your arms to kiss away all her troubles, and it is not just because you desire her, it is because you care for her. You are a fool. Miss Harrington did not want you and neither will she. She might not have known that Flint was a profligate, but she knows you are.

Alexander put down the decanter he had just raised to refill his glass. *Was a profligate.*

It does not matter what you were, are, or will be, even if she returns your regard, she will never completely trust you and sooner or later you will grow tired of trying to prove yourself and fail her.

He put his empty glass next to the decanter and went quickly from the room. He had barely put his foot on the first stair when he heard his name spoken. He turned and saw Bernardo striding towards him.

"Cousin, I know it is the ladies' habit to retire early, and I thought to bear you company for a short while."

Bernardo's smile of greeting faded as he observed Alexander's bleak expression. "Have I called at a bad time? Has something happened to my great-aunt?"

"No," Alexander said. "She is well. Come into the library."

He had not informed Angelica of Bernardo's plight because he did not wish to cause her worry and because he was not a talebearer. He had committed any number of follies when he had been a young man and hoped his cousin might be guided by him. He poured Bernardo a glass of wine and joined him by the fire.

"How was the opera?" Bernardo asked.

Alexander met his cousin's enquiring gaze. "Why don't you tell me?"

Bernardo's blue eyes widened.

"You were there, weren't you? You must have wished to see the performance very much to have suffered sitting on one of the cold, stone benches."

Bernardo swiftly regained his composure and waved an airy hand. "Yes, I did. *La pietra del paragone* was a great success when it first came out, and I have long wished to see it."

"Of course," Alexander said. "But you must have seen us in Signor Persico's box; it was lit very brightly, no doubt so that everyone might see who occupied it. Why did you not join us?"

Bernardo shrugged, his eyes wary. "Signor Persico did not invite me. Besides, I did not look at his box."

"I quite understand," Alexander said gently. "You were far more interested in one of the occupants in the other box, and by sitting in one of the darkened tiers, you could gaze upon her to your heart's content. Tell me, is Sofia Lonardi the fair or the dark one?"

Bernardo's jaw dropped. "Mio Dio! How do you know this?"

"That is not important. What is important is that I have it on good authority that Sofia is meant for someone else."

Bernardo's mouth twisted in disgust. "Bah! The Marchese di Tarasoni is old enough to be her grandfather, and for one so pure, chaste, and sweet as Sofia to be sacrificed on the altar of mammon is a despicable sacrilege. He will take her to Rome, and I will never see her again."

Alexander put his finger to his lips and rose to his feet. He felt sure he had heard something brush against the door. Four swift strides brought him to it, and he pulled it swiftly open. A maid stumbled into the room. He put out a hand to prevent her falling.

"I have come to remove the tea things," she said, colour flaming in her cheeks.

"By all means, go ahead," Alexander said softly. "But do not come upstairs again tonight, or I will box your inquisitive ears."

The maid curtsied, muttered an apology, grabbed the tea tray and fled, not once glancing in Bernardo's direction.

Alexander returned to his chair. "I would not keep any servant in my house who behaved in such a way."

Bernardo frowned. "Larissa is a good girl. She came to us a year ago and has never caused me a moment's concern. I would not have sent her here otherwise. Perhaps she was just wondering whether to interrupt us or not."

"Perhaps," Alexander agreed. "But we digress. Are you sure Sofia sees things quite as you do?" Alexander asked, recalling that Sofia had said she could not refuse the marriage proposal. Had she meant it, or had she been letting Bernardo down gently? After all, if the marchese was so old, she might see the advantages of becoming a marchesa in the hope that she would be widowed whilst she was still young enough to make another match.

Bernardo jumped to his feet and began to pace the room. "She is repulsed by him, but her family will not listen to her. They tell her it is her duty to help restore the fortunes of the House of Lonardi and that if she refuses to do her duty, she will be sent back to the convent where she was schooled for the rest of her days."

A satirical smile curled Alexander's lips. "A harsh fate, indeed, but you can hardly believe they would carry out such a draconian decree. As they need Sofia to marry money, it would make no sense. They might put her in a nunnery for a time to protect their investment, if you will, but surely only until they found another likely prospect."

Bernardo continued to stride from one end of the room to the other. "It does not matter what you or I believe; it is what Sofia believes that matters. Besides, that outcome would not help us. A stupid feud between my family and theirs has set them against me, and how can I try to reason with Signor Lonardi, to try and make amends when I don't even know what caused it?" He pushed both hands into his hair, tearing at it in a dramatic fashion. "The last time I tried to see him, I was thrown down the steps of his palazzo on his orders and told never to darken them again. It was a cowardly insult. The House of Montovani is as noble as that of Lonardi, but I could not have the satisfaction of calling him out because at five and fifty he is an old man, and——"

"And it would not have helped your cause at all," Alexander finished for him. "Now sit down and calm yourself. This show of thwarted passion leaves me unmoved and is damned unrestful."

Bernardo dropped into a chair. "I offend your English reserve. I apologise, but you must understand that Sofia and I are very much in love. We have loved each other for over a year. Sofia has been constant, even though my father sent me away on business so much."

Alexander had thought it odd that Bernardo's

father had reduced his son to the status of a salesman, but now he thought he understood why. The man had liked the match no more than Signor Lonardi.

"I am surprised you agreed to go," he said softly.

Bernardo sighed. "I would have done anything to make the business more successful and I did. But it is not enough. I can support a wife, but I cannot yet enrich another's coffers for the privilege."

A few more pieces of the puzzle that was Bernardo fell into place.

"Which is why you made yourself known to your great-aunt. You hoped she might make you her heir, and that before too long you would become wealthy enough to change Signor Lonardi's mind."

Bernardo's face reddened. "I had wanted to meet my great-aunt for some time. I think these feuds positively archaic, but my father was an intractable man and would not hear of it. I will admit the thought occurred to me when I saw my great-aunt's estate, but the *prospect* of inheriting was enough. I did not wish her to die. My mother is a cold, bitter woman, and my great-aunt welcomed me with open arms. I felt drawn to her, she has a quality… I cannot put it into words."

"You do not need to," Alexander said, softly. "I know precisely what you mean. Does your mother know of your attachment?"

Bernardo hunched a shoulder. "No. She hates the Lonardi family, and I could not bear to hear Sofia slandered."

"How you must have resented me," Alexander murmured.

Bernardo denied it vehemently. "No! My hopes may have been dashed down, but I believe family is important. I hope to have a large, happy one. I was delighted to know I had an English cousin."

Alexander's eyes narrowed. "But you were not delighted to find Nell on such good terms with my grandmother. You tried to scare her into leaving."

Bernardo took a swig of his wine. "It is only right that you should inherit, but the thought that someone who was not of our blood might do so was unpalatable, and then I heard the scandal—"

"The scandal was not of her making."

Bernardo gulped at the steel in his words. "No, I know that now, and am a little ashamed."

"I believe you," Alexander said more gently. "And I would help you if I could, but I do not see what is to be done. Even were I to offer Signor Lonardi some money on your behalf, there is still the problem of the feud."

Bernardo leant forward, resting his arms on his legs, his expression eager. "You are very generous, my cousin, but I think you underestimate yourself. There is something very formidable about you. Perhaps you could try to make him see that whatever happened between him and my father has nothing at all to do with me."

Alexander looked thoughtful, his fingers tapping the arm of his chair. "I will do as you ask on one condition."

"Anything," Bernardo said. "Name it."

Alexander smiled wryly. "Let me give you a piece of advice. Think with your head, not your heart. You should never agree to any deal before you hear the terms."

"But you are my cousin," Bernardo said. "You are to be trusted."

"My word is to be trusted," Alexander confirmed, "but it does not mean you will like my terms. You have already informed me that you were offered violence at the request of Signor Lonardi, and I believe if you are caught conducting clandestine meetings with his daughter, he will offer you some more. I will seek him out, but only if you give me your word not to meet Sofia at Juliet's tomb." An ironic smile curved his lips. "You may wish to be her Romeo and I can, of course, see the poetry in the chosen venue, but I would not wish for such a tragic outcome. You will neither meet Sofia there nor anywhere else until I have had the opportunity to meet with Signor Lonardi."

Bernardo looked at him in amazement. "I said you were formidable, but how you know so much I cannot imagine."

Alexander did not enlighten him but stood and offered him his hand. "Well? Do I have your word?"

"Yes," Bernardo said, taking it in a firm hold.

CHAPTER 22

I t was many hours until Nell fell asleep. With her realisation that Alexander cared what she thought of him, had come another. She had been afraid when he had cornered her in her chair and berated her, but not of him. She had feared that she had pushed him too far and may have lost his good opinion forever. Unable to take her anger out on Flint, and confused by her contradictory feelings about Alexander, she had taken it out on him almost from the moment they had met. But her outburst tonight had been fuelled by an extra ingredient. Fear that the man who had crept into her heart and mind inch by inch so that she had hardly noticed it, whose very presence made her feel protected, safe, and alive, was as much a figment of her imagination as Flint had been.

She knew it wasn't true. Her husband had never cared for anyone but himself or taken responsibility for the welfare of any of his dependents. She could not imagine why Flint's valet had remained so loyal to him for she was sure he had paid Renn infrequently, if at all, and he had accorded him little courtesy.

Alexander was as genuine as Flint had been false. He did not try to hide his past, nor did he try to make excuses or apologise for it. He did not sweeten his words or flatter her, and he did not make her false promises. Apart from his assurance that he would not try and seduce a guest in his grandmother's house, he had made her no promises of any kind. Did she want him to? When Angelica had said he was looking for a wife and a mother for Francesca, her heart had missed a beat.

Some part of her had thrilled at the thought of being his wife, not as the meek, submissive creature Angelica had described, she would never be that again, but as the recipient of his love. The sort of love that was not moderate, that was fierce and passionate and would have him taking the stairs two at a time in his eagerness to be with her.

She knew that Alexander was attracted to her – the dance they had shared at the harvest celebration haunted her dreams – but could he love her? Could he bear to carry the burden of another life he felt he must protect at all costs, and could she love him with an open heart that held no fear of betrayal?

She had meant it when she had said she would never again throw his past in his face and that she would not assume the worst merely because Flint had abused her trust, but it was one thing to still her tongue and another to still her mind. For there to be any future between her and Alexander, they must be able to trust both themselves and each other, and she doubted that was possible.

She fell asleep on the thought that it was likely they would only have a few more weeks together at best; by then Lady Westcliffe's letter would have arrived, proving beyond doubt her story. She would enjoy whatever this city had to offer and his company. If all she had to remember Alexander by was memories, they would be good ones, and so she would live in the present and worry about her future afterwards.

She went down to breakfast the following morning to find Angelica and Alexander were before her.

"Good morning," she said, smiling brightly at them.

Alexander stared at her for a moment and then stood to pull out a chair. "What has put you in such a good mood?"

"The realisation that I am fortunate enough to be amongst friends in such an interesting and ancient city. I intend to enjoy it and explore it."

Angelica smiled. "It is indeed a fine city, and I am happy to take a drive with you this morning and show you the principal streets and squares."

"That would be a wonderful start."

"However, if you wish to explore the many fine examples of medieval architecture, I suggest you visit the churches, although I fear you must ask Alexander to indulge you in that. I feel sure I would find it fatiguing."

"And I would find it a dead bore," Alexander said bluntly.

Nell's smile did not slip, and she sent him a look of innocent enquiry. "Exploring the city or doing it in my company?"

He had been looking stern since she entered the

room, but at that, his lips twitched. "Nell, are you inviting me to be uncivil?"

She chuckled. "That bull is already out of the gate."

His laugh transformed him, she reflected. He did not do it enough.

"Very true," he acknowledged. "How unlike you not to haul me over the coals for my rudeness."

She assumed an angelic expression. "I am making a concession. I do not believe it is unusual for a man to be ill-tempered over the breakfast cups."

She thought his grin even more infectious than his laugh and found one curling her lips.

"As you have been so magnanimous, I will admit that it is neither your company nor exploring the city that would bore me."

"Oh, then is it the architecture or the churches?"

"The latter," he said in an expressionless voice.

She thought she understood him. "Ah, you are reluctant to enter a Catholic church, but—"

He cut her short. "I am reluctant to set foot in any church."

This shocked her, but then she remembered that his uncle had been fanatical in his religion and had used it as a weapon. She had made a misstep but saw a way to correct it.

"Then, of course, we shall not do so. As it was not until 313 AD that Emperor Constantine recognised Christianity in the Edict of Milan, and not until 380 AD that it became the official religion of the Roman Empire, I think there can be no difficulty in inspecting the amphitheatre in daylight, and perhaps the Roman theatre that Signor Persico mentioned to me last evening. Both were constructed somewhere in the first century AD. Would that be acceptable to you?"

His lip curled. "Who am I to cast aspersions on a civilisation that worshipped Bacchus?"

She felt he was challenging her to remember his excesses, but she did not rise to the fly. "Who indeed? And as Angelica owns a vineyard, it seems appropriate that he is the Roman god you should think of." She looked rueful. "And as Signora Fratelli made such an intoxicating punch this year, I would not be at all surprised if she still worships him."

Amusement chased away Alexander's sneer. "Most likely. I have something I wish to do this morning, but I would be happy to escort you this afternoon. How on earth do you know all these dates and facts?"

"Did I not tell you that my father educated me? As a vicar, he was interested in when Christianity was adopted in various civilisations, and as a scholar, he is interested in many things."

The thought of her father caused a pang of sadness, but she pushed it away. He had not understood; even she had not known the full extent of her husband's perfidy when she had written to him.

"Well, then," Angelica said, amusement glimmering in her eyes at this exchange, "everything is settled."

Alexander rose to his feet. "I shall be on my way, and I will send a note to my coachman to bring the carriage in half an hour."

∾

Alexander had not thought to ask Bernardo Signor Lonardi's direction, but as he descended to the hall, he saw the maid who had been eavesdropping crossing towards the door that led to the kitchen, a covered basket in her hand. At sight of him she scurried away, but he called her back.

"Larissa, isn't it?"

She nodded and dipped into a curtsy.

"Do you know where I might find Signor Lonardi?"

Her eyes widened and he thought he saw fear there. He frowned. He may have threatened to box her ears, but he would never have executed it. He had never struck a woman in his life.

"Larissa, there is no need to be alarmed. Last night you overstepped the mark, but I am sure you will not do it again."

"No, Lord Eagleton. He lives on Piazza Bra. Ask anyone, they will show you."

"Thank you."

As he had not yet formulated what he would say and knew the general direction of Piazza Bra, he allowed himself to be lured into narrow side streets, interested to see what lay behind the public façade of grandeur that lined the main thoroughfares. He was not disappointed. He had always had an eye for detail and found himself charmed by the faded frescoes that decorated some of the three-storey buildings, their trifoliated windows, and their stone balconies sculpted into delicate designs and liberally laden with plants and flowers. He could understand why Shakespeare had chosen a balcony scene for a pivotal point in his play. A line came to him. *Call me but love, and I'll be new baptised.*

Laughter sounded in his head, followed by the voice he was beginning to hate. *You have been called love many times, but it has made no noticeable difference.*

He strode on, his mouth grim. It was true enough, but not by anyone who mattered or had meant it. He came to a halt as he found himself before the last house in the lane. Its green paint was cracked and peeling, but the bronze knocker wedged between the jaws of a lion, the symbol of Venice's dominion over Verona for hundreds of years, was polished to a high sheen, perhaps indicating that whoever lived there held fast to their old loyalties.

He had had a fascination with old doors since a small child. Eagleton Priory had several of them which had been locked in his youth. This had both scared him and given him hope, for the idea that if he could just open the right one, he would find his mother and father not dead but held prisoner or find himself transported to a different time and place had taken possession of his mind. Of course, the truth had been far more mundane; they led to disused cellars, dilapidated towers, and the gun room. His thoughts had been the wild imaginings of a miserable, power-less boy.

He turned the corner and began to make his way out of the maze of twisting, narrow streets that suddenly seemed suffocating. He was no longer powerless, and perhaps happiness was within his reach.

Another fairy tale.

Shut up! Just shut up! I will no longer listen to you. The future is what I make it and if I want a damn fairy tale, I shall have it!

He groaned as he saw a street urchin regarding him. He must have spoken aloud. No wonder the boy was looking at him as if he were mad. Perhaps he was. Thank God he thought in English. He smiled ruefully, flicked him a coin, and hurried away.

A few minutes later he reached Piazza Bra. A waiter outside one of the coffee houses directed him to the Lonardi palazzo. It stood a stone's throw from the arena in a corner of the piazza and extended some way down an adjacent street. The majority of its numerous windows were hidden behind faded blue shutters, giving it a deserted air. Huge double doors were set between two chipped marble pillars and topped by a pediment that must at one time have held a relief of a winged lion similar to the one that hung above the door of the palazzo del podestà. However, although the marble slab remained, it was pitted and scarred where the lion had been torn from it, only the tip of a wing remaining. He wondered if the French had committed the vandalism when they had forever ended the Venetian Republic in 1797, or if the Lonardis had removed it themselves to show allegiance to the new order in the hope that their assets would not be seized. If so, as the family were apparently in dire need of funds, it did not seem they had been successful.

He somehow doubted *he* would be. He was prepared to offer them a monetary incentive, but the Marchese di Tarasoni had already done that. His only hope was to appeal to Signor Lonardi's better nature and political ambition. To point out that if he could only overcome his prejudice, he might ensure the happiness of his daughter and keep her close, that Bernardo was well on the way to repairing his family's fortunes, and that an alliance between the House of Lonardi and the House of Montovani could only strengthen the power and influence of both.

The steps up to the door were shallow and dipped in the middle, the stone worn from the tread of thousands of feet. Alexander reached for a doorknocker, which seemed designed to discourage visitors, its bronze loop set between the leering mouth of a gargoyle. A footman must have been hovering nearby for it was soon opened. Alexander handed him his card, requested an interview with the master of the house, and was left to wait in a cold, gloomy entrance hall.

The servant soon returned carrying a small silver platter, upon which lay a gilt-edged invitation card.

"Signor Lonardi is very busy today and regrets that he cannot see you, but he asked me to give you this."

Alexander took the card and glanced at it. He, Nell, and his grandmother were invited to a ball that was to take place that evening at the palazzo. His mobile eyebrow flew up. That any of Bernardo's family should be invited was surprising, but perhaps a good omen. It was not the ideal opportunity to plead Bernardo's case, but perhaps he might be granted a few moments alone at some point during the evening or at the very least make an appointment for another day.

He was surprised to discover his grandmother and Nell were at home upon his return, and even more so when he discovered them in the drawing room. His eyes went straight to Nell, and he was pleased to note no signs of anxiety on her face. On the contrary, her eyes lit with amusement at sight of him. He was too enchanted by the curve of her lips, the delicate colour in her cheeks, and the glow in her eyes to take affront, and found himself returning her smile.

"Do you care to let me in on the joke?"

It was Angelica who answered him. "We were on the point of setting out when we received a visit from two of the ladies we met last evening. They were most disappointed that you were not at home."

Nell chuckled. "We thought they would never go. Their eyes went hopefully to the door every time Savio entered the room. What a shame you did not come home five minutes earlier."

"Is it though?" he said ruminatively. "That depends on the two ladies. Describe them to me."

Another gurgle of laughter escaped Nell. He thought he would never tire of hearing that sound.

"Signora Rossi has coal black eyes and hair, her lips are full, her expression animated—"

He eyed her suspiciously. "And her figure?"

"Voluptuous," Nell said.

"You mean, of course, that she is as wide as she is tall," he said dryly.

"Perhaps," Nell concurred. "But she is very amiable."

"And her companion?"

"Signora Ferrari is a widow. She dresses in the first style of elegance, is very striking, and not at all fat."

His lips twitched. "Let me guess. She is as thin as a broom, has a cast in one eye, and a receding chin."

"Not at all. She has thick black eyebrows that meet in the middle, a square chin, and a hint of a moustache, but is also very amiable."

"Baggage," he said, sitting next to Angelica. "I am pleased that you feel comfortable enough to come into this room, Nell."

"We could hardly receive our guests in the library," she said lightly. "Besides, my turn was the effect of an overwrought imagination. It won't happen again. As I told you this morning, I intend to enjoy my time in Verona."

"Then I hope you won't be too displeased at yet another example of my high-handedness." He took Angelica's hand and raised it briefly to his lips. "Tell me, grandmother, do you feel up to attending a grand ball this evening, or have your visitors worn you out?"

"If I have a rest this afternoon, I am sure I will manage," she said, surprise and amusement mingling in her green eyes. "But whose ball and how did you inveigle an invitation from them on such short notice?"

"Signor Lonardi and his wife are holding a ball at their palazzo this evening."

"Then we must certainly attend. It is in Bernardo's interest that we do so."

Alexander's lips twisted. "More so than you realise. I had not meant to tell you, but it has occurred to me that you or Nell might be able to soften Signora Lonardi a little to his cause, whilst I try to do the same with her husband."

Angelica's eyes brightened with quick intelligence. "You are not just speaking of the feud, are you?"

"No, although it is at the heart of everything."

As he came to the end of a short but succinct recital of Bernardo's woes, Angelica drew in a deep breath. "You should have come to me straight away. I would also like to help Bernardo, and I would like to meet this girl to discover if she truly loves him."

"Poor Sofia," Nell said quietly. "To be sold off to the highest bidder and to a man old enough to be her grandfather is a horrible fate. We must certainly go to this ball. If all we can achieve tonight is to become on good terms with the Lonardi family, that will be something, and perhaps they will be more willing to listen to you, Alexander."

His pulse beat a little faster as he saw the glow of admiration in her eyes.

"You were very right to accept the invitation on our behalf," she continued, "and I think it admirable that you wish to help a cousin with whom you are so little acquainted."

"I did not have much choice," he said dryly. "Bernardo is young, and I feared he would do something impetuous and put himself in serious danger if I did not offer to do something."

"Even so, it was very good of you."

Alexander put a hand to his brow and groaned. "I had forgotten that we had invited Count Fringuello to dinner this evening."

Angelica smiled. "You need not worry; he refused dinner but has asked if he might visit us this afternoon at three o'clock. I think we should give him a few moments alone with Nell when he first arrives, and she has agreed."

Alexander frowned, his eyes going to Nell. "Are you sure?"

"Yes," she said. "Just five minutes so that I may thank him for what he wished to do for me and give him the opportunity to apologise if he wishes without an audience."

Alexander's lips curved into a gentle smile. "That is very brave, thoughtful, and kind of you, Nell."

"It is the right thing to do," she said. "But I am afraid that we must put off exploring the Roman ruins until tomorrow morning."

"As you wish. But you may be too tired after the ball."

"I won't be," she said firmly. "Because Angelica and I will not stay late."

Alexander glanced at the door as it opened, his brow wrinkling when no one came into the room. Then he heard Mrs Farley say gently, "Go on. Your papa is in there."

His eyes dropped to the floor, and he saw his daughter crawl into the room. When she saw him, she smiled, allowing him a glimpse of her two tiny bottom teeth.

"Good afternoon, my lady," he said, beginning to rise.

"No, stay seated, my lord, and let her come to you," Mrs Farley said. "She needs the exercise."

"And she has a new trick to teach you," Timothy said, stepping into the room. Against all convention, a wide, proud smile lit the footman's face.

He was suddenly pushed to one side, and Maria appeared beside him.

"Out of the way. Me, I wish to see also."

Alexander's eyes dropped again to his daughter who moved with surprising swiftness to his chair. Her little chubby hands tried but failed to gain purchase on his gleaming boots. He offered her his hands, and Lady Francesca wrapped her fingers around his thumbs, pulled herself to her feet, and said one little word that stopped his heart.

"Papa."

"Clever, clever, girl," he said softly, picking her up as her legs started to wobble.

CHAPTER 23

Nell swallowed the lump in her throat, unable to tear her gaze away from Alexander's face as he spoke softly to his daughter. His expression was so gentle, his eyes glowing with such adoration that it made her heart ache. In Lady Francesca's presence, he was at his most open, his feelings exposed for the scrutiny of any who happened to be present.

Soft whispers from the doorway made her look up. Maria stood on tiptoe whispering something in Timothy's ear. Nell rose to her feet and went quickly across the room.

"Maria, I am attending a ball this evening. You may prepare my white satin gown with the white net and pearl roses." She glanced at the footman. "Timothy, we are expecting a visitor, Count Fringuello, at three o'clock, and in the meantime, I am sure Savio will find something for you to do."

She looked back at the sofa as they hurried away, saw Alexander and Angelica's heads close together, the baby between them, and followed her maid from the room. Tears suddenly blurred her eyes, and she crossed the hall to the library, going in and shutting the door behind her. She was happy that Angelica and Alexander had found each other, touched that the bond between them and Francesca was so strong. It was nonsensical that she should suddenly feel so miserable, such an outsider, and so unnecessary to their comfort. She had witnessed such a scene many times before, so why should it affect her so now?

She wiped at the tears on her cheeks and gave a shaky laugh.

You are an idiot, Ellen Marsdon! What happened to your determination to enjoy every day in Verona? You are in love and feeling vulnerable, but that is no excuse to behave like an irrational schoolgirl who feels jealous pangs every time the object of her affections bestows his attentions elsewhere, especially when it is directed at his close relations! Alexander has made no declaration of his feelings and may never do so, you are not even sure what you would reply if he did, so make the most of every moment in his company, bask in his every smile, and allow yourself to be happy, even if only for a short while. Now, go back to the drawing room and behave like the sensible woman you are.

She did so and was rewarded with a gummy grin and a clap from Francesca. When Nell held out her arms, the babe reached for her and started to babble.

"Papapapapapa."

Nell hid a smile as Alexander looked crestfallen.

"Indiscriminate babe," he said, passing her over.

"She knows full well you are her papa," Nell said, settling the child on her lap. "It is just that her vocabulary is limited, and certain sounds are easier for her to utter than others." She smiled tenderly at the little bundle in her arms. "Is that not so?"

Lady Francesca gurgled, dribbled, and then as if trying to prove Nell wrong, added some variety to her babbling. "Mamamama."

Nell blinked back the tears that again threatened. For heaven's sake, she was turning into a watering pot. Seemingly exhausted by her linguistic endeavours, the babe snuggled into Nell and closed her eyes.

Mrs Farley came quickly forwards, saying softly, "I'll take her now, my lady, and put her down for her sleep."

Nell stood, cradling the babe in her arms. "It would be a shame to wake her. I'll carry her up."

Alexander watched her leave, an arrested expression in his eyes.

"She will make a wonderful mother one day," Angelica said casually. "She was cruelly treated by Flint, and yet she has not an ounce of cruelty in her."

"No," Alexander said softly. "She has not."

"And yet she has spirit enough. There is nothing milky about her."

He smiled wryly. "As I have reason to know."

Angelica sighed. "I shall miss her when we return to England."

"She will accompany us, surely?"

"Oh, yes," his grandmother said. "She will accompany us on the journey. I feel it my duty to see her home safely, but whilst it was perfectly accept-able to have Mrs Marsdon as my companion, it would not be fitting to have Lady Flint take on that role."

He frowned. "What do you think she will do?"

"I'm not sure," Angelica said. "Perhaps she will return to her father, or perhaps to the dower house on Flint's estate. I am not sure how things stand, but we must hope that the new Lord Flint will be able to salvage something from the wreck his brother left him and provide for her."

"I don't know what sort of a man Captain Flint is," Alexander said pensively. "As he is some ten years younger than I and joined the army, he has never come in my way."

Angelica glanced at the clock. "Good gracious, it is half past two already! I must go and freshen up before the count arrives."

Count Fringuello arrived five minutes early, and leaving Nell to greet him, Angelica and Alexander waited in the library. He paced the carpet, his eyes repeatedly going to the ormolu clock on the mantlepiece.

Angelica watched him in some amusement. "Alexander, the time will not go faster merely because you wish it so. I am sure Nell is perfectly all right."

"But what if she is not? What if seeing the man again has alarmed her?"

She chuckled. "Have you forgotten that you instructed Timothy to leave the door ajar and stand guard so that he would hear if she called?"

"Nell feels sorry for the count," he said irritably. "She will put on a brave face even if she feels repulsed by his disfigurement or sick at the memories he evokes."

His eyes snapped back to the clock, and he held out his hand to his grandmother. "Come. His five minutes alone with her are up."

Angelica ignored his hand, saying in a voice that brooked no argument, "We shall give him five more unless Nell sends for us. That poor man was so desperate for a few hours in her company that he was prepared to pay an exorbitant sum for it, and then rescue Nell from her sorry excuse for a husband. The least we can do is grant him ten minutes of her time." She grasped his hand and tugged it. "Now, sit down! Your pacing is extremely unrestful."

He stared at her and then laughed ruefully. Her words echoed his to Bernardo's the evening before, and he was being just as needlessly dramatic. He dropped down beside her.

"Forgive me, grandmother. It is just that I feel very protective of Nell."

"I quite understand," Angelica said. "I do myself. But you should have more faith in her. I do not believe she will be either repulsed or made to feel sick by the count. She is not so shallow that a few battle scars will strike terror into her bosom, and in coming to Verona she has faced and overcome her fears of that night."

He smiled. "You are right. I should not underestimate her."

"No, you should not. Or yourself. We shall return to Eagleton Priory, and we will make it a home that you are proud of."

"Very well," he said. "But I warn you, the moors are a far cry from the beauty of Lake Garda."

She reached up and touched his face. "You need to look upon it with fresh eyes, my grandson. Look for ugliness and you will find it, but by the same token, if you look for beauty you will find that also. Now, you have not looked at the clock once, and the ten minutes are already up."

They stepped into the drawing room as Nell stood on her tiptoes and placed one hand on the count's shoulder. He stiffened for a moment and then bent to receive a kiss on his scarred cheek.

"Count Fringuello," Angelica said, going forward, a warm smile on her lips. "I am delighted to make your acquaintance."

He coloured and offered her a jerky bow, saying in a rough voice, "As I am yours, Signora Montovani. You must forgive me, I cannot stay."

He rushed from the room as fast as his limping gait would allow, and as he passed Alexander, he saw a sheen of tears in the man's eyes.

"Oh dear," Nell said, dismayed. "I did not mean to offend or upset him."

A lopsided grin tugged at Alexander's lips. "Do not concern yourself. He was not at all offended but on the contrary, touched so deeply that he was on the point of tears. He will no doubt treasure that memory until the day he dies."

"I sincerely hope you are wrong," Nell said with some asperity. "I meant only to show him that I was not at all repulsed by him because after speaking with him, I was not. If only he will allow himself to believe it, there is no reason why he should not find a good woman with whom he can share his life.

"Loneliness is a state of being, but it can also become a sort of illness. It erodes your self-esteem and makes you so anxious and miserable that to do even the simplest of tasks is a struggle. It takes such deep root that even when you are given the opportunity to engage with people on a meaningful level you avoid them, because it is easier not to, and because if you do they will see your pain…" She broke off, her chest rising and falling rapidly. "I am sorry. It is just that I feel so very sorry for the count. I don't understand where that all came from."

Alexander understood all too well. The count's visit had evoked painful memories, but not the ones he had expected. Nell was not just describing the count's loneliness, but her own whilst she had been with Flint, and although it had not been her intention, she had described his own experience, and judging by the expression on his grandmother's face, hers also.

"How right you are, my love," Angelica said gently. "And I would not be surprised if your actions do have a positive effect on the count. Now, I think you are a little overwrought and should lie down and rest, as I intend to do. We must be bright and fresh for the ball, after all."

"Yes, I think I will," Nell said.

Alexander wanted to put out a hand to stop her leaving; to tell her that if she would just put her trust in him, she would never be lonely again. That he had thought their pasts made them incompatible, but he had been mistaken. That although their experiences differed, a shared understanding of how they had each been affected by them could forge a bond so strong between them that it would never be broken.

Instead, he watched her leave. Now was not the time. Not only was his grandmother still in the room, but he did not want Nell to come to him merely because she never wished to be lonely again, but because she loved him. She had baldly admitted when under the influence of Signora Fratelli's punch that she was attracted to him, but she had also stated in that burst of honesty, that she did not wish to marry him.

It was entirely possible that her feelings had changed as much as his since then, but although he had forgiven her for flinging his past in his face last evening, he had not forgotten. She needed more time, more evidence that he was worthy of her, and he intended to give it to her whenever an opportunity presented itself.

When she came down the stairs later that evening in a white satin dress, pearls at her throat and in her lustrous red hair, this reasoning deserted him, and he knew the mad impulse to try his luck there and then. Not only because she took his breath away, but because he knew that she would draw the eyes of every gentleman present at the ball, and he wanted them all to know that she was his, would only ever be his.

He bowed gracefully over her hand, raising it to his lips and dropping a light kiss upon it. "You look exquisite, Nell."

Delicate colour infused her cheeks, and her hand trembled a little in his light clasp.

"As do you," she said, a shy smile curving her lips.

He pulled her gently towards him. "Then we complement each other perfectly."

He bent his head, his nostrils flaring as the sweet, heady scent of jasmine engulfed him. She raised her face, her softly luminous eyes seeming to invite his kiss.

"Nell," he murmured as his lips hovered above hers, "I—"

"I hope I haven't kept you waiting. Oh, am I interrupting you?"

Alexander sighed and straightened. "Not at all, grandmother."

Nell's eyes had closed in anticipation of Alexander's kiss, but they snapped open as Angelica spoke. She was grateful that although Alexander had turned towards his grandmother, he remained in front of her, his broad shoulders shielding her, so she had a moment to compose herself. She felt light-headed, her pulse was erratic, and the abrupt and anticlimactic end to their brief encounter left her frustrated and disappointed. Pinning a smile on her face she stepped out from behind him, but both her greeting to Angelica and her acceptance of that lady's compliment on her appearance were automatically done, her mind otherwise.

Her distraction continued for the short duration of their carriage ride to Piazza Bra, and although she was aware of a muted conversation between her companions, she neither listened nor contributed to it. She was more focused on the warmth and happiness that was gradually spreading through her veins and the reason for it.

Her toes curled in her satin slippers as she recalled the naked longing in Alexander's eyes, but it was not the evidence of his desire that thrilled her the most, but the look of adoration that had preceded it. For a moment she had seen into his heart and knew his feelings ran as deep as hers. He could have just taken the kiss she would have freely given, but he had not. He had wanted to say something first. She did not know if it would have been a declaration of love or a proposal of marriage, but she felt certain it was one of those two things, and her heart had soared. She had suddenly known with complete and utter certainty that this was the man she wished to spend her life with, that he needed her as much as she needed him, and that it would be madness to do anything else.

"Nell?"

She had not noticed that the carriage had come to a halt or that Alexander was waiting to hand her down from it, a small frown of concern wrinkling his brow. A radiant smile of pure happiness lit up her face, and the frown was gone. As she stepped down from the vehicle, he bent and whispered in her ear.

"We will continue where we left off later, and in the meantime make sure you reserve that smile only for me or I will be too busy fighting off an army of admirers to speak with Signor Lonardi."

This reminder of the serious nature of their purpose that evening sobered her. She had been so busy dwelling on her happiness that she had completely forgotten that Bernardo was relying on Alexander, perhaps them all, to secure his.

"I shall not encourage any admirers," she said. "I shall reserve my attentions for Signora Lonardi."

Alexander laughed softly. "Nell, they will need no encouragement. When I am not with you, stay close to my grandmother, and if she tires, take the carriage and go home. I am quite happy to walk."

They joined the steady stream of visitors entering the palazzo. The entrance hall that had been so gloomy earlier was now lit up with candles and adorned with greenery and flowers as were the several corridors they had to traverse in order to reach a large reception room, at the end of which two double doors were thrown open, affording a glimpse of the ball-room. A little to one side of them the Lonardi family stood in a line to receive their guests.

Nell covertly observed them as they approached. Signor Lonardi's dark hair was streaked with grey, but his back was ramrod straight and his expression aloof. He evinced a haughty pride which was echoed in his two sons whose resemblance to him was marked. His wife was a faded beauty, her black hair greying at the temples and lines of care permanently etched on her forehead and about her mouth.

One of her daughters was the embodiment of what she must have been in her youth. Glossy black ringlets framed a heart-shaped face dominated by a pair of huge, sparkling black eyes. Her nose was small and straight, and her smile held a hint of mischief. Her sister was also pretty and yet somewhat thrown into the shade, her golden curls and blue eyes seeming insipid in comparison, or perhaps it was because she had none of her sister's vivacity. Her face lacked the roses that bloomed in her sibling's cheeks, her eyes seemed dull, and her smile forced. And no wonder, Nell thought, her heart going out to the girl. She must be Sofia, and unlike her sibling could not look forward to an evening of unalloyed enjoyment with the prospect of an unwanted marriage hanging over her head.

They were greeted by the family with cool civility, the encounter by necessity brief due to the press of people behind them, but Nell caught a swift look of appeal in Sofia's eyes as she greeted Alexander. It brightened them, the look strangely familiar. Then they were in the ballroom, surrounded by dozens of strangers who sent them glances both curious and admiring but who did not approach them. An orchestra played on a raised podium at one end of the room, their music all but drowned out by the buzz of conversation.

"I wonder if Signor Persico is here," Nell said, her eyes scanning the room. "He could introduce us to some of our fellow guests."

Alexander led them to a cluster of vacant chairs so that his grandmother could sit down. "I felt sure he would be," he said. "But when I asked Signor Lonardi if he had arrived, he said that the mayor had sent him a note not an hour ago, excusing himself due to some unexpected business arising. And whilst it might make things a little awkward, we have, at least, been intro- duced to those we need to speak to." He signalled to a footman who carried a tray laden with glasses of champagne. "Whatever Signor Lonardi's circum- stances may be, he must have spent a small fortune on his refreshments."

He passed them each a glass but did not take one himself. "I am going to hover by the door. I wish to speak with our host at the earliest opportunity. Sofia Lonardi looks ill, and so I assume she is close to crum- bling under the pressure being brought to bear on her to marry the Marchese di Tarasoni."

Nell's eyes followed him, smiling at the effortless

ease with which he cut through the crowd, his lack of acquaintance making it unnecessary for him to waste any time on civilities. She stifled a giggle as his purposeful stride was rudely interrupted as two ladies blocked his path, one fat and one thin. Already twice denied an introduction, it seemed Signoras Rossi and Ferrari were determined not to be disappointed a third time.

"Oh dear," she said. "I should not laugh; the ball-room is almost full, and he will miss his opportunity to speak with Signor Lonardi."

But even as the words left her mouth, he bowed gracefully, said something which made both ladies blush and titter, pointed in her and Angelica's general direction, and carried on his way, the crowd closing behind him.

"I wonder what he said to them?" Nell mused.

Angelica chuckled. "I wouldn't enquire if I were you."

"No," Nell said. "You may be sure I won't. Whatever it was it did the trick, and that is the main thing."

The ladies soon emerged from the hubbub, their arms linked and their smiles broad.

"Signora Montovani, Lady Flint, how delightful it is to see you again," Signora Rossi said. "It is amazing, is it not, that with so little notice, the Lonardis can fill their ballroom?"

"Oh," Nell said. "I thought it was only us who received our invitation today."

"Ah, that is because you are so newly arrived in our fair city," Signora Ferrari said. "The majority of us received our invitations a week ago, but still, it is very short notice. Signora Bianci is most put out because she had to cancel her conversazione after she received so many cancellations."

"I sympathise with her," Signora Rossi said. "But it is many years since the Lonardis held a ball and it was only to be expected that everyone would flock to it." She smiled at Angelica. "I did not expect to see either of you here. The Lonardis are very proud, and what with you being related to Bernardo, and Lady Flint—"

Her companion poked her with her bony elbow.

Nell felt a prickle of unease. Suddenly the curious glances she had received took on another meaning. "Please, Signora Rossi, finish your sentence."

"It does not matter," she said. "I spoke without thinking, and now that Signor Persico has been seen in your company, many of the wagging tongues have been stilled."

"But not all," Nell said, a little stiffly. "I see that I am honoured indeed that you have acknowledged me."

Signora Rossi threw up her hands, making her ample bosom wobble. "I knew as soon as I spoke with you that nothing I had heard was true. It is why it is so wonderful that you have been invited tonight even though Signor Lonardi does not like scandal. If you will permit us, we will introduce you to many others who will soon know it also. It is what Signor Persico would want."

Nell marvelled at her own simplicity. The rumours concerning herself and her husband had not faded into obscurity, it was merely that the mayor had hand-picked who she had been introduced to at the opera so that she would not be alarmed. A soft sigh escaped her. It was a reminder that without concrete proof of who had killed her husband, they would always abound. Feeling the need for reassurance, she stood, her eyes scanning the crowd for Alexander. She saw him striding rapidly towards them, a thunderous expression on his face.

CHAPTER 24

Nell went to meet him and put a hand on his arm. "Alexander, what has happened to put you all on end?"

He looked down at her and the furious expression gradually left his face. Even so, his tone was clipped as he said, "Signor Lonardi has no time to talk with me, but even if he did, I could not have anything to say that he wished to hear."

Nell sensed that it was not only that his purpose had been thwarted that had riled him, but also that he had been treated with so little respect.

"That is unfortunate, but—"

"I did not, of course, merely accept this. I stood in his path and told him that if money was the problem, both I and my grandmother could come to some arrangement with him, that it made far more sense to make a close alliance with a local family than to send his daughter so far from him, and that Barnardo should not be made to pay for his father's sins whatever they had been."

"All very good arguments," Nell said. "And perhaps when he has had time to——"

"At which point," Alexander continued, the fire back in his eyes, "he nodded to his sons and they stepped to either side of me and physically removed me from his path. Did he invite me here merely to insult me? If so, he will learn soon enough that I am not to be used in such a manner."

"Oh dear," Nell said, her hand squeezing his arm. "It was very bad of him, but Alexander, all is not lost. I have not yet had the opportunity to speak with Signora Lonardi, and perhaps she will——"

It seemed Nell was not destined to complete a sentence, for at that moment, Signor Lonardi, his wife and Sofia ascended onto the dais at the end of the room and a hush fell. Sofia was almost cowering, her shoulders slumped, but then her mother bent and whispered something in her ear, and she straightened.

"Welcome one and all," Signor Lonardi said in a deep booming voice. "I must thank you for attending our ball when you were given so little notice." The hint of a smile touched the corners of his lips. "It is good to know that the Lonardi family still commands the respect of so many."

A polite round of applause greeted this statement.

A muscle twitched in Alexander's square jaw. "The self-satisfied, pompous——"

"You are no doubt wondering why this event was arranged so hastily, and I will now satisfy your curiosity."

Alexander's eyes narrowed, as excited murmurings whispered in the stultifying air.

"But first, I would like to introduce you to my

honoured guest. Many of you will not have met the Marchese di Tarasoni, who I had the pleasure of meeting last year when I and my sons visited Rome. He offered us such generous hospitality at his estate, which I think must be one of the finest in any of the Italian states, that it gives me great pleasure to be able to return it." He gestured towards someone to the right of the dais. "Come, do not be shy. I am sure the citizens of Verona will greet you with all the respect you deserve."

By now, everyone was hanging on his words, necks craning in an effort to see who he was addressing. An old man with a walking stick hobbled onto the stage. Tufts of grey hair sprouted at irregular intervals on his balding pate, and his smile revealed the blackened stumps of his teeth.

Nell gasped. "No, surely he cannot give away his daughter to such a decrepit gentleman."

"That is precisely what he intends to do," Alexander bit out.

"Good news is always worth sharing," Signor Lonardi continued. "And it is with great pleasure that I can announce that my beautiful daughter, Sofia, has this day been contracted to marry the marchese."

That gentleman nearly overbalanced as he bowed, and Sofia Lonardi fainted clean away. Gasps and sudden exclamations, many of them echoing Nell's feelings, filled the air like a swarm of bees and almost but did not quite cover the sound of breaking glass. Nell glanced in the direction from whence it came and saw a footman bent over as he simultaneously tried to mop up the champagne and collect the shards of fine glass with a handkerchief.

"Come," Alexander said abruptly. "We will no longer play any part in this tragicomedy."

They found Angelica beside them.

"I quite agree. Signor Lonardi is a monster to wish such a fate upon his daughter."

"He is greedy, conscienceless, and has the manners of a goat," Alexander said between gritted teeth, as they weaved their way towards the door. "And it would not have mattered what I offered him, because he is also malicious. He arranged this hasty ball to put an end to Bernardo's pretensions to his daughter's hand, and he invited us only to be his messengers."

The journey home was made in silence, each of the occupants of the carriage dwelling on what had occurred and what could be done about it. Only when they were ensconced in the library, the tea tray between them, did they voice their thoughts.

"I wish I knew what had caused this feud between our families," Angelica said pensively. "It must have been something terrible for Signor Lonardi to still bear so bitter a grudge."

Alexander smiled cynically. "Need it? Some people need no excuse to behave with cold, calculating cruelty."

"I feel for Bernardo," Nell said, "but my heart bleeds for that girl. Can nothing be done?"

"The announcement has been made and the contracts signed," Angelica said sadly. "It is too late."

"What would you do in Bernardo's position?" Nell asked Alexander.

"Elope," he said unhesitatingly. "And I've half a mind to help him do it."

The thought had also occurred to Nell. "Only half a mind?"

"Count Fringuello warned me that if Bernardo was not careful, he would be found…" He paused. "Never mind."

Her eyes widened. "Murdered?"

Alexander nodded. "And even if he did manage to marry Sofia, I fear it would not protect him from such a revenge." He grimaced. "As a matter of fact, I think it would guarantee it."

"Then you must ensure he does not make the attempt," Angelica said firmly. "If the girl marries the marchese, it is likely she will be a widow within a few years, and then she can make her own choice."

"It is a sound argument," Alexander said. "But I doubt Bernardo will be appeased by it."

Nell shivered. "And in the meantime, Sofia would be forced to share that man's bed."

Angelica sighed. "We must put Bernardo's interests ahead of hers." She rose. "I am tired. It has been a busy day." She accepted Alexander's arm. "I shall send a note in the morning, inviting him to join us for luncheon. We shall break the news to him together. If you set out early, you shall then have time to accompany Nell on her Roman excursion."

Nell had followed them to the door, and said, "That is not important—"

"I beg to differ," Alexander murmured softly as Angelica left the room. "I am prepared to put Bernardo's interests ahead of Sofia's, but not before my own. I had hoped to finish what we started earlier, but I must consider how best to handle my cousin." He smiled wryly. "I also think it best that I choose a time and a place where there is little chance of us being interrupted."

Nell's pulse fluttered. "Then I will bid you goodnight."

It was still dark when Maria shook her awake.

"You must get up, signora. Lord Eagleton is waiting for you downstairs."

Nell sat up, rubbing the sleep from her eyes. "What time is it?"

"It is fifteen less than seven," Maria said, a dimple peeping in her cheek. "He says we must hurry or you will miss the sunrise. That one, he is romantic."

A slow smile spread across Nell's face. It was certainly a romantic gesture, and who was she to discourage so charming a trait? She suddenly scrambled from the bed and hurried over to her washstand.

"Pick me something long-sleeved and warm," she said.

Maria pulled a face. "That is not at all romantic."

Nell laughed. "Neither is my teeth chattering. Besides, my dress will hardly be on show. I shall wear my Pomona green velvet pelisse over it with the cream satin trimming."

Maria smiled. "Si, that is a good choice, and matched with the straw bonnet with the green satin ribbons, will make a delightful ensemble."

It seemed Alexander agreed, for the warmth in his eyes when he greeted her was unmistakable.

"You look charming, my dear," he said. "Let us go at once."

She laughed as he took her hand and ran with her down the stairs to the entrance hall. His curricle was awaiting them, and as he handed her into it, Timothy ran out of the house carrying a basket.

"Ah, our breakfast," Alexander said, laying it on the floor between their feet.

The smell of hot baked rolls made Nell's stomach rumble. "You have thought of everything," she said softly.

Alexander smiled ruefully. "Not quite. I am still undecided where to take you. I have been told that the Roman theatre you wish to visit is an excellent spot to view a sunrise, but I am afraid we will have to cross the river to get there."

Nell's heart melted at this display of concern. "Then we shall cross it."

He raised her hand to his lips. "Good girl. Just concentrate on the architecture of the structure. The Ponte di Pietro is also of Roman origin."

The sky was beginning to lighten as they approached the bridge. Nell gazed at the white stone arches, marvelling that something built such a long time ago was still so robust and fulfilled its purpose as efficiently as it had then.

"Are you sure you are all right?"

She glanced up at Alexander. "Perfectly sure." She smiled shyly. "When you are with me, I feel I can face anything."

She watched in fascination as colour winged along his high cheekbones, his eyes going back to the road as they turned onto the bridge. "I am honoured by your confidence."

She wrapped her arms about herself, hugging to herself the knowledge that her words had touched him in some way, that her trust mattered to him, that she mattered to him. At that moment the golden orb of the sun peeped above the horizon, the sky about it a mixture of red and orange, and Nell realised how absolutely perfect it was that he should choose dawn for whatever declaration he wished to make. Whether he told her he loved her or asked her to be his wife that morning, it would mark a new beginning for them both.

He slowed the horses to an idling walk and glanced down at her. "Nell, my beautiful darling——"

She did not look up, could not look up, for she was frozen in horror, her eyes wide and staring, for not far in front of them stood three gentlemen, and one of them was her husband.

"It is impossible," she whispered.

Alexander came to a halt. "Nell?"

She pointed a shaking finger. "It is Flint."

Alexander cursed himself for listening to her. He should never have brought her this way. He wrapped an arm about her and pulled her against his side. She sat ramrod straight, her eyes unblinking. "Nell, you are mistaken. Perhaps the sun blinded you——"

"Look," she said.

He looked. He had been so caught up in formulating what he would say to her that he had not noticed Signor Persico, a man who had the look of a valet, and one other, who bore a striking resemblance to Flint, standing by the wall.

"Nell, it is not your husband. Look again. He is

younger, thinner, and taller than Flint. If I am not much mistaken, he is your brother-in-law."

She sagged against him. "Yes, I see it now. But that is Renn with him, my husband's valet, and my mind played tricks on me. What are they doing here?"

"There is only one way to find out. Stay here——"

She sat up. "No, I will come with you."

He saw the determined set to her chin and the colour begin to seep back into her cheeks. "Very well."

The men were deep in conversation and did not look up until they were almost upon them. Signor Persico looked surprised, Captain Flint irritated, and the valet shocked. He was tall and slender, and his face cast in so delicate a mould it was almost pretty. His gaze was fixed on Nell, and a tick began to pulse in his cheek as his eyes suddenly narrowed, anger chasing out the shock. His face twisted as if he were in pain.

"It is her fault. All her fault. She never loved him, but I did. I would have done anything for him."

Alexander stepped forward but Signor Persico put a restraining hand on his arm.

"Not now," he murmured. "He is about to crack."

Captain Flint regarded Nell in some surprise, gave her a slight smile and a nod, and said in a low, persuasive voice, "Look at me, Renn. I don't doubt your loyalty to my brother, or your grief at his death, but why do you blame Lady Flint?"

The valet looked at him and some of the fury left his face. He gave a sob. "Because she deserted him, and if she hadn't, none of it would have happened."

"None of what, Renn?" the captain said, his voice firm but gentle. "Start from the beginning. You will feel better for telling me, and I will think more of you for doing so no matter what happened."

The valet sucked in a deep breath and nodded. "I heard my lord's voice in the courtyard and went downstairs in case he needed my help. He had a nasty temper when he was drunk, and who could blame him with all the bad luck he had suffered? I hovered in the shadows until the man he was talking to left the yard, and then begged him to let me take him upstairs." Another sob broke from him, and he started to shake.

Captain Flint dropped a hand on the man's shoulder. "Calm yourself. I take it my brother was not amenable to that suggestion?"

Renn shook his head. "If only he had listened, but he said he needed to clear his head and he was going to take a walk by the river. He told me to lock Lady Flint's doors and go to bed."

Alexander's jaw clenched, and it took all his willpower not to punch the valet's retrousse nose. Instead, he took Nell's hand and gave it a reassuring squeeze.

"I went back upstairs, but it took me a while to find the keys." He darted a resentful look at Nell. "I knocked on her door to tell her what I was about to do and that it was for her own safety…"

Like hell, Alexander inwardly fumed. You wanted to gloat.

"…and discovered she had packed her bags and gone. I went to find my master to tell him and found him here. He fell into a rage, blamed me for not stopping her, s-said he would be taken back to Venice and most likely killed." His voice started to rise. "He went purple, and his eyes started to bulge in his head, and then he had a knife in his hand. I begged him to calm down, we struggled, and I managed to wrench it from him, but I fell back onto the road."

He covered his eyes with his hands and wailed. "I don't know exactly how it happened, perhaps he tripped or lost his balance, but he was suddenly on top of me, and the knife was in his belly. I pushed him off to see what could be done – I'll never forget the look on his face – all the rage had gone. He looked surprised and then tired.

"He said I'd killed him, but it was not my fault and that I was to obey his last orders to the letter. That after he died, I was to throw him in the river and in the morning make a grand fuss. He said he did not want any blame to be attached to me because I had been more loyal than he deserved."

He dropped to his knees and began to sob uncontrollably. "It was a horrible accident, and I'll never forgive myself."

Captain Flint stepped past him and bowed to Nell. "Lady Flint, I am sorry that we meet in such distressing circumstances. If you will await me in my private parlour at the Due Torri, I will come to you shortly." He held out his hand to Alexander. "I must thank you and your grandmother, my lord, for taking such good care of my sister."

Alexander led her back to the curricle and gently lifted her into it. Nell said nothing but smiled wanly. He backed his horses off the bridge, turned, and drove the short distance to the hotel. He sat her by the fire in the parlour they were shown to and ordered coffee and tea, and then knelt before her and took her cold hands in his.

"Nell, Flint only had himself to blame."

She nodded. "I know, and it is some comfort that it was a terrible accident rather than cold-blooded murder."

"There is more comfort to be had in the knowledge that the world will know that you had no part to play in Flint's demise."

He rose swiftly to his feet as a serving girl carrying a tray came into the room. He took it from her and made Nell a cup of hot, sweet tea. He had no sooner handed it to her than Captain Flint came into the room. Like his brother, he was tall and broad-shouldered, but his hair was a darker brown, his eyes a deeper blue, and his chin more decided.

"Please do not get up, Lady Flint," he said as Nell began to rise.

She sank back into her chair with a grateful smile. "As you have acknowledged me as your sister, would you very much mind calling me Nell?"

He gestured for Alexander to sit opposite her and seated himself between them. "Not at all. I have many times wished to disassociate myself from my name, but alas cannot."

"You have my sympathy," Alexander murmured.

Captain Flint smiled wryly. "We cannot change our destiny, however much we may wish to. I had hoped mine would be to retire to my little estate in the Cotswolds and become a gentleman farmer."

"Is that why you have not yet taken the title?" Nell asked.

"No," he said gently. "I always knew there was a strong chance that I would one day be forced to step into my brother's shoes although I did not expect it to be so soon. I would not take the title until I was sure that your unfortunate marriage had not borne fruit."

Nell blushed and shook her head. "It did not. Is that what you came to find out? I heard that you had recently written to Signor Persico about my whereabouts, and thought, perhaps, you suspected——"

He held up a hand. "I never suspected you of anything other than being a gullible pawn in my brother's selfish games. He should never have married. I had reason to think he would not. I should have foreseen, however, that he would run himself so far into the ground it would become a necessity."

"But why did you think he would never m——?" Nell broke off in some confusion, remembering Renn's impassioned declaration that he had loved her husband and that Flint's last act on this earth had been to protect him.

"Precisely," he murmured.

"But his mistresses…"

"A smokescreen."

"Oh," Nell said. "I see. Is that why you fell out with Flint?"

The captain shook his head. "As long as it is consensual, what people do behind closed doors does not concern me. I fell out with my brother because he was destroying everything our parents had worked so hard to create, and because he did not care a fig for any of his dependents." He sighed. "But we have strayed quite far from the point. I did indeed write to Signor Persico, but soon afterwards I had a very interesting interview with Lady Westcliffe when I went to Ashwick Hall to procure some of her apprentice servants. As you may imagine, economy is a consideration for me and will be for some time to come."

"I have so much to thank her for," Nell said quietly.

"Yes," he said, frowning. "I may not have seen eye to eye with my brother, but I never dreamed that he would do something so... so base as to sell you... well, you know what I am referring to. Suffice it to say that I was shocked to the core. I had always thought it my duty to find you but did not know where to start. Armed with your likely route, I decided I would try and find you myself, brandishing your description in every town the diligence might have stopped."

"Thus making her infamous throughout Europe," Alexander muttered.

"I did not use her name," the captain said. "It was unnecessary, for if Nell was half as beautiful as Lady Westcliffe described, I knew it would be unnecessary." He smiled. "She did not exaggerate. By the time I reached Torbole I was quite disheartened, as you might imagine, but the story of the beautiful, red-haired young woman who survived being thrown into the lake, was washed up on a beach at Malcesine, and had now been whisked off to Verona by a handsome marchese, soon reached my ears."

Alexander looked at Nell and smiled gently.

"It sounded like a fairy tale," he said. "But it was my only lead and so I followed it. I arrived in Verona last evening and visited Signor Persico."

"And where does Renn come into all this?" Alexander asked.

"I wrote to Signor Persico and asked him to make arrangements for my brother's body and his valet to be shipped to England. As my batman did not wish for civilian life, I employed Renn." His lips twisted. "I look very like my brother, and he needed no encouragement to take me up on my offer. I have never been comfortable with him as my valet, but I decided to keep him close because I sensed that he held the key to what had happened.

"He has made frequent visits to the mausoleum and always returns looking quite ill. He also suffers nightmares. When he did not wish to accompany me on this trip, pleaded to be allowed to stay behind, I felt certain that he knew something. Signor Persico and I hatched a plan. We felt sure that making him return to the place where my brother met his end might shake the truth out of him."

He glanced at Nell. "I did not recognise you, at first, and will admit that when I saw you both, I knew a moment's consternation. Renn was close to breaking, and I thought the distraction would give him time to regroup." He smiled ruefully. "But it proved otherwise. Your presence, Nell, made him lose the last vestiges of his self-control."

"What will happen to him?" she said, her hands twisting in her lap.

The captain looked grave. "As well as his self-control, I fear he may also have lost his wits. I left him in the charge of one of my servants as he is rambling quite wildly. I have seen it before although in very different circumstances. A man's mind can suddenly snap when he has been exposed to constant stress and guilt. I will take him back to England with me and find a safe place for him."

Nell nodded. "Yes, that would be for the best. I

never liked him, and I believe he hated me, but it was an accident, and he has suffered enough."

Alexander was amazed at her capacity for forgiveness. He didn't care what state the valet was in. He had been cruel to her and acted as her jailor, he would have stood back and allowed Flint to abuse her as he would, and by hiding the truth, Renn had made Nell a suspect in Flint's murder. Alexander would like to rend him limb from limb and throw his body to the crows.

Nell rose to her feet and held out her hand. "Thank you, Captain Flint, for all your efforts on my behalf."

He bowed, clasping her hand. "Do not thank me but accept my apologies for all that you have been through. I will make only a short stay in Verona; I wish to return before the snow makes the mountain passes impossible to navigate. You are very welcome to return with me, Nell. I understand that Flint Hall may be distasteful to you, but the dower house is a very pretty cottage and may suit you. I will also, of course, make sure you receive any stipend you are due."

"I have been reliably informed that the snow will not fall in any great amount for another month," Alexander said brusquely. "And Nell will return with me and my grandmother."

The captain, unimpressed with this decree, regarded Alexander coolly. "Until I am told otherwise, Nell is now my concern, not yours. I will visit my sister later this afternoon when she has had time to come to terms with all that she has learned and see what her wishes are."

CHAPTER 25

By tacit agreement they returned home, the groom up behind them so he could return the curricle to the hotel. Now was not the moment for declarations of any kind, and Nell's mind was too busy trying to digest all that she had learned. No wonder Flint had been so expert at deception; he had had to live a lie for years. Had it been that circumstance that had driven him to his excesses? Had he been angry, bitter, perhaps even ashamed? The thought saddened her but did not alter facts. He had been a cruel, selfish shell of a man, unlike his brother, who was good, honourable, and had spent years serving his country. It was a shame they looked so alike, for however much she respected the captain, Nell did not think she would ever be able to be in his company without thinking of Flint.

She could hardly believe it still wanted a few minutes to nine when they entered the house; so much had happened that day. It seemed a long time ago that she and Alexander had run hand in hand down the stairs with laughter on their lips. They now ascended them in pensive silence.

Voices from the dining room suggested that Angelica was at breakfast, probably having a conversation with Savio, who she treated more as one of the family than a servant.

Alexander turned to her saying gently, "Go in and join my grandmother. You may not believe it, but you will feel better when you have eaten something. I will join you when—"

"You have said good morning to Lady Francesca," she finished for him.

"Oh dear," he said. "Am I so predictable?"

"Only in that habit," she said. "I will have something to eat. It was not a pleasant scene, but perhaps a necessary one, and it is a relief to know precisely what happened."

He reached out a hand and wound one of her curls about his finger. "You are not only beautiful inside and out, but you have uncommon good sense." He dropped a kiss on the top of her head. "Do not exhaust yourself further by explaining all to my grandmother. I will do so when I come down."

Angelica glanced up as she came into the room. "Nell! I did not expect you back so soon." A mischievous glint brightened her eyes. "Is there something you wish to tell me?"

A rueful smile curved Nell's lips as she took a seat next to her friend. "There is much to tell you, but not, perhaps, what you were expecting to hear. Alexander will explain everything—"

She broke off as what could only be described as an anguished roar reverberated through the house.

They looked at each other in astonishment, and then both rose to their feet. Nell rushed into the hall, Angelica following as fast as she was able with Savio's help. Timothy appeared and raced towards the stairs but before he reached them Alexander bounded down them, his eyes wild, and his lips compressed so tightly they were but a thin slash in his alabaster face.

"Get all the servants here now!" he barked at the footman. His eyes swung to Savio. "Who has stepped foot inside this house today?"

"Not a soul, my lord."

Nell stepped towards him and laid a hand on his arm, but he threw it off, saying from between gritted teeth, "Do not touch me. I am not safe."

"Alexander," Angelica said imperatively, "Calm yourself and tell us what has happened."

By now all the servants from kitchen to attic were crowded into the hall and he turned in a circle, his eyes raking them all.

"My daughter is not in her room, and her nurse has been drugged. You have precisely ten minutes to search every nook and cranny of this house, and then you will gather again here. Now, go!" His eyes went to Timothy. "Stand guard by the front door. If whoever took her is still in the house, they will not escape."

Nell and Angelica clung to each other as the servants scattered, and Alexander began to race from room to room as if he did not trust them to do their work. Nell pushed away the pain of Alexander's rejection and the mounting fear that made her heart tremble and led Angelica to a chair by the wall. The old woman's face was ashen, and she suddenly looked every one of her four and seventy years.

She sat beside her and took her hand. "It will be all right," she said, her words lacking conviction. "She will be found." Her voice dropped to a whisper. "She must be found."

Alexander came again into the hall, staggering as if his legs were unsteady. His eyes fell on Nell, and she began to rise, wishing to go to him and offer him some comfort, but at the cold, almost maniacal look in his glittering green eyes her courage failed her, and she sank back down.

"You said checking on my daughter was my only predictable habit, but I did not check on her this morning in my eagerness to catch the sunset." He put his clenched fists to his temples, his words becoming increasingly incoherent. "I should never have allowed myself to become distracted... but for you... I will never again..."

He had not said it was her fault, but Nell knew it is what he meant. If he had not been with her, he believed Francesca would never have been taken. And he was probably right. If no one had entered the house, then someone within it must have taken the child, and she doubted they would have dared to do so unless they had known he was absent.

The servants were returning to the hall, Timothy included. Alexander drew in a deep breath as if to calm himself.

"I told you to stay by the door," he said in a steely voice.

Timothy held up a note. "This was pushed under it. I thought it might be important."

Alexander tore it from his grasp, scanned the lines,

and then his long fingers curled about it. Angelica went to him and wrapped her hands about his fist.

"Do not keep us all in suspense, my grandson. We all love Francesca and will do whatever we can to help find her." Her hands trembled on his. "She is not… not…"

"No," he said bleakly. "She is alive and will be returned to us unharmed the moment Sofia Lonardi is returned to her father." His eyes were chips of ice, but he had regained his composure. "Bernardo eloped with her last night." His eyes scanned the waiting servants. "One of you must know something."

Nell had also been regarding the servants, and she now stepped forward and looked at the cook-house-keeper. "Where is Larissa?"

The woman looked startled. "She went out very early in order to get the freshest produce from the market and has not come back. She had a closed basket, but if she had the babe in it, I would have heard."

"Not if my daughter had also been dosed with laudanum," Alexander bit out. "I only hope the treacherous maid did not give her too much." He glanced at Timothy. "Go to the Due Torri and order my groom to bring my curricle, and to ensure that my pistols are primed and loaded."

The footman nodded and hurried away.

Nell blanched "What do you intend to do?"

"I intend to pay Signor Lonardi a visit," he said, his voice dripping with malice. "I have no intention of scouring the countryside for Bernardo. He may go to the devil for all I care, but I do intend to get my daughter back immediately, and God help anybody who gets in my way."

"Let me come with you," Nell said urgently, afraid that he would do something terrible or be hurt himself. "You will need some help with Lady Fr—"

"I neither desire nor need your help," he said, his tone as cold as his eyes. "Timothy shall accompany me." His gaze again swept over the servants. "You may go back to your duties."

Nell stumbled backwards, desolation sweeping over her. She sank onto a chair, her head drooping and the ache in her chest so fierce she put a hand to it, the image of her and Alexander spending a future together lying tattered and shredded at her feet. His heart had opened to her for a short while, but it had now clammed shut and she doubted it would ever be prised open again. He would never have come to Verona if it were not for her. She and Bernardo would forever be the ones who had put his daughter at risk, an unforgivable sin in his eyes.

A commotion in the hall downstairs brought her head up in time to see Timothy returning.

"Why the devil are you still—"

Nell gasped as she saw what had stopped Alexander's words. Following Timothy were the last three people she had expected to see. Sofia Lonardi, her head bowed, and Bernardo, his hands tied behind his back, and his eye swollen and half closed stepped into the hall. Count Fringuello limped behind them.

Bernardo, completely unaware of the drama of the last few minutes, immediately made a heartfelt appeal to Alexander. "Cousin, tell this interfering fool that what I choose to do is none of his business and send him on his way, will you? And for heaven's sake untie me."

Alexander stepped towards him, and Bernardo turned around so that he had access to the thin cord that bound his wrists. Alexander made no attempt to untie it, however, but put his arm about his cousin's neck and hauled him against his chest. He spoke low in his ear, but his crisply enunciated words reached everyone who remained in the hall. "Unlike you, the count is no fool, and I shall be forever grateful to him, for now, I can deliver you into the hands of Signor Lonardi and let him do with you what he will."

His grip on Bernardo's neck was so tight that his face turned tomato red, and he began to choke.

"Let him go," Angelica said imperatively. "You will do no such thing. Bernardo could not know the consequences his actions would bring down on you." She glanced at the servants who still lingered in the hall, openly fascinated by the drama unfolding before them. "I believe my grandson told you to return to your duties. Savio, bring refreshments to the library, Timothy, wait here for further instructions, everyone else follow me."

Nell did not expect Alexander to bow to her commands, but to her surprise he released Bernardo and did as he was bid, his clenched jaw betraying how much it cost him to do so. Bernardo doubled over coughing, and when Sofia raised her hands to her mouth in obvious distress, the count pulled a sword from his walking cane and cut the cord that bound him.

He glanced at Sofia, saying roughly as he took

Bernardo's arm, "I am truly sorry for your distress, but believe me when I say that I had no choice."

The girl raised unflinching eyes to his countenance and nodded. "You were right to bring us back. When you told us that my father would hunt him down and kill him, I realised it was true." Her blue eyes turned to Bernardo and filled with tears. "I can bear anything but that, even if it means marrying the marchese."

"No!" Bernardo choked out as the count marched him towards the library. "Let me go, damn you!"

Nell took the girl's arm, gave her a sympathetic smile, and followed them.

Alexander stood before the fireplace, one arm on the mantel, his fingers drumming so relentlessly on the marble they had gone numb. The blinding rage and crushing fear that had gripped him since the moment he had discovered his daughter missing had eased. He knew who had taken her and why, and thanks to the count, now had the means of getting his daughter back without resorting to bloodshed. It was not that he did not wish to spill Signor Lonardi's blood; nothing would give him greater pleasure, but as his grand-mother had just pointed out, Lonardi had two strapping sons and an army of servants, and he would be no good to Francesca dead or incarcerated for murder.

He did not care how or why the count had acted on his behalf and would rather by far have delivered Sofia immediately to Lonardi than waste time listening to the story of her and Bernardo's failed elopement. But again, his grandmother's words had weighed with him, and if truth be told, their insight and ruthlessness had impressed him.

"Knowledge is power, Alexander, and a man who would snatch an innocent babe cannot be trusted. Signor Lonardi is proud, arrogant, and has a malicious streak as you pointed out last night. I know you would never really give Bernardo into his hands; no one knows better than you that impetuous actions lead to unforeseen consequences, but that will not prevent the family seeking revenge.

"Signor Lonardi's Achilles heel is his fear of scandal, and the more you know of what occurred between Bernardo and Sofia, the more sway you will have over him. For all we know, they may have consummated their love before Count Fringuello came upon them, and that knowledge would be a powerful weapon indeed."

But it was Angelica's physical presence that swayed him more. He had watched her grow stronger every day since his arrival in Malcesine, but now, although her words were forceful, she seemed to have shrunk. The last thing he wished was for her to have a relapse. And so he waited with what patience he could muster as the others trailed into the room.

The frown that etched his brow grew deeper as he saw Nell. She looked pale and ill. It was no wonder; she had witnessed so many unpleasant scenes that day. Her eyes met his for the briefest of moments, but that was all it took for him to see her pain. He knew she would be worried for Francesca and for him, but somehow knew it was more than that. Was she hurt because he had rejected her offer of help? She must know that he would never put her in the middle of so volatile and potentially dangerous a situation.

A prickle of unease raised the hairs on the back of his neck. Had he said or done something else to distress her in the moments after he discovered his daughter's absence? A swift search of his memory proved futile, his mind unable to penetrate the red mist of fury and panic that had overtaken him.

The count deposited Bernardo in a chair and came to Angelica, bowing awkwardly before her.

"Signora Montovani, I was honoured by the invitation to your house, and am fully aware that I was unconscionably rude when I left so precipitously."

She smiled gently at him and patted the space beside her. "Sit down, Count Fringuello, the honour was all ours. We already had so much to thank you for, and now we are forever in your debt."

"Nonsense," Bernardo said resentfully.

She regarded her great-nephew with a peculiar mix of compassion and exasperation. "Bernardo, you are unaware of the service the count wished to offer Nell, as you are blind to the consequences of your flight. Early this morning, Larissa, the maid you put in this house, took my great-granddaughter, a babe of only seven months. Signor Lonardi now has her and will not return her unless Sofia is restored to him."

Bernardo's eyes flew to Alexander. "Mio Dio! No wonder you wished to strangle me. But how could I know? It is medieval! Monstrous! As for Larissa, I took her in when she was cast out from the Lonardi household without a reference because she was caught with a letter in her possession."

"Let me guess," Alexander said dryly. "A letter from Sofia to you."

"Yes," Bernardo admitted. "It was Larissa's loyalty to Sofia that persuaded me she was trustworthy." He groaned as enlightenment dawned. "But she was playing a double game, and once planted in my household, she would know when I was at home or away on business, and so Signor Lonardi would know when to guard Sofia more closely. In short, she could spy on me."

Alexander regarded his cousin, his eyes smouldering with anger. "And you put this spy in my grandmother's household, and she took my daughter. You also broke your word by eloping with Sofia before I had spoken with you."

Sofia, who sat on a chair next to Nell at the back of the room, suddenly surged to her feet, tears running down her face. "I must go home at once. It is my disobedience, my failure of my duty to my family that has caused this. That an innocent baby should suffer for my sins is more than I can bear."

Only seconds before, Alexander had been quite prepared to sacrifice Sofia on any altar offered him in order to retrieve his daughter; he still was, but now reluctantly. It suddenly occurred to him, that he might use the scandal her father was so afraid of to her advantage. He might even be able to persuade Signor Lonardi to consent to her and Bernardo's marriage.

"Sit down, Sofia," he said gently. "You will be returned soon enough." His gaze swivelled to Bernardo.

"Now, cousin, without any unnecessary embellishments, you will tell me precisely what occurred between you and Sofia from the time you spirited her away until the present."

Bernardo was granted a few minutes to collect his thoughts as Savio just then entered the room. Despite the early hour, his tray held a decanter of brandy, which he placed on the sideboard next to the wine. A maid and the housekeeper followed him, with tea, coffee, and a variety of cakes. Bernardo was the only one to accept the brandy. It seemed to fortify him, and when the servants left the room, he began to speak.

"I did not break my word to you, cousin. I promised only that I would not approach Sofia until you had spoken to her father."

"How did you know that I had done so?"

"I went to the ball; not to speak with Sofia but to reassure myself that she was all right and had not yet succumbed to the pressure being brought to bear on her. I was only a few feet from you when you spoke with her father."

"Nonsense," Alexander snapped. "I would have seen you."

"You did not see me because I wore the wig and livery of a footman. It was the perfect disguise because whilst the guests might take the refreshments they offer, no one really looks at them." A small smile tilted his lips. "You did not when I brought you champagne."

"No, I did not," Alexander murmured.

Bernardo took a sip of the brandy, his hand trembling a little. "I did not expect to hear the announcement of the engagement and I dropped my tray." He grimaced. "Fortunately, the guests were too busy commenting on the grotesque farce unfolding before them to pay me any heed. By the time I had mopped up the mess, I had formulated a plan. I hid in one of the many unused rooms in the palazzo until all was quiet, and then went to Sofia's chamber. She dressed and we left.

"My coach was waiting at a nearby inn, and so we made our escape. We went first to my estate so I could pack my things and borrow a few of my mother's for Sofia, as she had not dared venture into her dressing room in case she woke her maid. We then made our way towards Vicenza."

"Why Vicenza?" Alexander asked.

Bernardo sighed. "When my father died, I discovered that he had bought a small villa not far from the town where he housed his long-term mistress. As no one knew of the existence of either, I thought we would be safe there until I had decided what we should do. We were halfway there when we damaged a wheel." He glared resentfully at the count and tossed off the rest of his brandy. "He can tell you the rest."

CHAPTER 26

Count Fringuello, quite unused to such close scrutiny, reddened as all eyes turned towards him. Angelica patted his hand encouragingly.

"There is no need for you to feel uncomfortable. You are amongst friends, and we are all interested in what you have to say."

"He's no friend of mine," Bernardo muttered.

Ignoring him, the count fixed his gaze on Alexander. "I was on my way to Venice when I saw the carriage drawn up on the side of the road. They were standing beside it. I offered to take them to their destination, but instead ordered my coachman to return to Verona." His lips twisted. "When your cousin realised what I had done he became enraged, and I was forced to restrain him."

Alexander frowned. "Do not misunderstand me, I am very grateful that you brought Bernardo and Sofia back, but why did you? You could not have known that my daughter had been taken."

"No, I did not, but I was grateful for the kindness I have received in this household." His gaze strayed to Nell and Angelica before returning to Alexander. "I wished to repay it in some way. I warned you that Bernardo's interest in Signorina Lonardi had put him in danger, and if I had allowed him to elope with her, I feared it would not just be his body that was in peril, but his soul."

"What nonsense——"

"Be quiet," Alexander snapped. "You will let the count finish."

He had no opportunity to do so, however, for low urgent voices sounded in the hall and then the door opened and a woman, the hood of her cloak drawn up so that her face remained in shadow, came into the room, a baby cradled in her arms.

For a moment, Alexander was frozen into immobility, but then a strangled sob issued from his mouth, and he strode to her, snatching Francesca from her arms. When the rough movement did not wake her, he stroked her cheek and called her name, and then bent his head to her face, feeling weak with relief when he felt her soft breath on his cheek.

"Do not be alarmed," the woman said. "She is unharmed, the doctor assured me of it, but said she will sleep deeply for a few hours yet."

"The doctor?" he said quickly, his eyes going to her.

She pushed back her hood, revealing ebony hair streaked with grey.

"Mama!" Sofia gasped, rushing to her and throwing herself into her arms. "I am sorry. I did not wish to do it, but I could not marry that man!"

Signora Lonardi stroked her hair. "Hush, my darling, you will not need to."

Sofia was not so easily placated. "Papa will make me," she sobbed. "He loves Rosa, and I know it is a wicked thing to say, but I th-think he hates me." She glanced up at her, tears blinding her eyes. "It is true, isn't it? That is why Rosa had a governess, but I had to go to the Sisters of Mercy."

Signora Lonardi closed her eyes and sighed. "He cannot make you, my child, for the Marchese di Tarisoni died early this morning."

Sofia's lips trembled. "W-was it the news that I had gone that killed him? A-am I a m-murderess?"

"No, my love," Signora Lonardi said gently, pushing Sofia's hair from her brow. "He died from overexertion when he took one of the maids to his bed."

Sofia gasped.

"Precisely," Signora Lonardi said. "You have had a lucky escape."

"This is all very interesting," Alexander said tightly, "but I believe you mentioned a doctor."

"Yes. I am so sorry you have suffered such anxiety," she said. "It was none of my doing. The maid's screams roused the household, and it was then that Sofia's maid discovered that she had gone. My husband immediately sent my sons out to find her and Bernardo, but for added insurance, he sent a message to Larissa telling her to take the babe. Her room has a window, and she knows that if three knocks sound upon it, my husband has orders for her." She put a trembling hand to her brow. "I do not disobey my husband, and so when he bade me take the child and go to a villa we have on Lago di Garda, he had no reason to believe I would not do so. I waited only until he left the house, and then I ordered the carriage and went to a doctor because Larissa told me she had administered a small amount of laudanum to the child. He is confident that no harm has been done."

"No harm done?" Alexander said, his jaw tight.

"At least not to the child," Signora Lonardi said. "I understand how difficult it must have been for you… how extreme my husband's actions—"

"He is a madman!" Alexander bit out.

He saw Timothy hovering by the door and went to him, passing him his daughter. "Take her up to her room and stay with her and Jane. If you have any reason to suppose either of them is in trouble, send for a doctor and alert me immediately."

He saw tears shimmering in the footman's eyes and put his hand on his arm for a moment. "I know, but everything will be all right now."

"Yes," Timothy said softly, looking adoringly at the bundle in his arms. "Because I'll guard her with my life."

"I know you will. Now go."

When he turned, he saw Bernardo next to Sofia, pleading with Signora Lonardi. His eyes narrowed.

"Good God!" he murmured.

"But why?" Bernardo said. "Why can I never marry her? We have loved each other almost from the moment that we saw each other. There was an instant connection… it is hard to explain, but it was as if we were extensions of each other."

Signora Lonardi's hand covered her mouth, and she choked back a sob. Alexander poured her a glass of wine and guided her to a chair, pressing her to drink it. When Bernardo started to speak again, he shook his head.

"Bernardo, sit down," he said gently. "And you too, Sofia. Your mother is about to explain why the two of you can never be married."

Signora Lonardi met his eyes and nodded. She put down her glass, clasped her hands before her, and stared at the floor for a few moments as if gathering her thoughts. When her eyes rose, they went to Bernardo.

"The reason you feel such a strong connection to Sofia is that there is one. My marriage was arranged and has never been a love match. After I had given my husband two sons, he lost interest in me."

As she paused, Alexander went to stand behind Bernardo.

"I had known your father for years, and he, feeling sorry for me, became my friend and confidant." She swallowed. "And then we became more than friends."

As Bernardo's shoulders hunched, Alexander dropped a hand on one and gave it a squeeze.

"That is why they duelled," Bernardo murmured, his voice hoarse.

"Yes," Signora Lonardi said. "We were discreet, but when my husband discovered I was with child, he knew it could not be his and forced me to name the father. You can never marry Sofia because it would be a grave sin. She is your half-sister."

〰

When Sofia returned to the chair beside her, Nell took her hand. She knew what was coming. It was not until she had seen Bernardo and Sofia standing side by side that she noticed the similarities between the two. It was not just that their colouring was similar, it was their expressions. The look in their blue eyes as they had pleaded with Signora Lonardi had been identical, as was the droop to their mouths when she unequivocally told them that they could never be together. No wonder Signor Lonardi had gone to such great lengths to retrieve Sofia.

And then the blow fell, and Sofia slumped sideways into her lap as she fainted. Nell stroked the girl's head, her heart bleeding for her. She wondered bleakly which torment was worse, knowing that you could never be with someone because they were too closely related to you, or knowing that there was no such impediment, but that the person you loved so desperately had rejected you because of his deeply rooted fears of losing his daughter, and that even if that person forgave you this time, there might come another when he would not. It would be impossible to live with such a sword of Damocles hovering above your head.

She was roused from such depressing thoughts by Signora Lonardi, who was suddenly by her side.

"Lay her down and leave her to me. Sofia was reared very strictly at a nunnery, and she will not easily recover from the knowledge of what might have happened if… well, it does not bear thinking about."

Supporting Sofia's head in her hands, Nell eased out from under her and helped Signora Lonardi arrange her along the chairs.

"She is a very special young woman."

They both glanced up to see Count Fringuello standing a few feet away.

"She never once flinched at my appearance."

Signora Lonardi gave a sad smile. "She would not. The nunnery she grew up in had a hospital wing, and she learned to care of the sick and injured." She went to him and laid a hand on his sleeve. "I was warned that my daughter was here by the butler, and he also informed me that it is you I have to thank for bringing her back to Verona. You will have my eternal gratitude."

He nodded. "I often take the less frequented alleys in order to avoid the stares of the curious or frightening stray children, and I have twice seen them together. I suspected the truth but could not be entirely sure. My suspicions would have been enough to persuade me to act even if I had not had the added incentive of wishing to repay the kindness of Lady Flint and Signora Montovani."

He bowed and left the room. Nell glanced at Alexander who stood over Bernardo frowning. Even the knowledge that Francesca was safe, and his cousin had forever lost his love had apparently not softened his heart towards him. At least Bernardo could escape to his estate to lick his wounds, but Nell would have weeks in which she must endure Alexander's company before she could do the same. She could not do it. She had borne the strain of being with Flint because it had been her duty, and because she had not loved him, she had endured it. To be in Alexander's company knowing what might have been was more than she could bear. Her heart was splintering into pieces now, just looking at him. She dragged her eyes from him and followed the count from the room.

Alexander frowned down at Bernardo. His cousin's countenance was green, and he was fairly certain he was going to cast up his accounts at any moment.

"Here," Angelica said, holding out a brass coal scuttle. "The count obligingly emptied its contents onto the fire."

As Bernardo groaned, Alexander placed it on the floor in front of him and thrust his head between his knees. He felt as if he were at the centre of a Greek Tragedy, but now his daughter was safe, he felt some sympathy for the young man. Damn secrets and lies! They had marred his own life and had nearly destroyed his cousin's. Thank God providence, in the form of Count Fringuello, had intervened before the unthinkable had happened.

Bernardo was young, however, and perhaps in time, he would realise that the love he felt for Sofia was not as unnatural as he now imagined. It was possible that he had mistaken brotherly love for romantic love. The more Alexander considered it, the more he was certain of it. If Bernardo had loved Sofia with passion, he would never have acquiesced to being separated from her for months at a time. If, however, he had never known lust, the connection he had felt to Sofia coupled with a wish to rescue her from an unhappy situation, might easily have made him mistake his feelings.

His eyes searched for Nell. A wry smile twisted his

lips when he did not find her. He did not blame her for leaving such a scene. He was glad she had had the good sense to. She had been through the wringer that day and needed to rest. As soon as he could rid himself of their guests, he would seek her out and ask her to explain the unhappiness he had seen in her eyes earlier, and if he was responsible for it, he would beg her forgiveness.

A discreet cough at his elbow drew him from his ruminations. Savio regarded him apologetically.

"First of all, my lord, I beg leave to tell you how happy I am that Lady Francesca has been returned to you unharmed."

"Thank you, Savio," he murmured, wincing as Bernardo retched again into the coal scuttle.

The butler glanced at the still unconscious Sofia and then at Bernardo. "I realise that this is a most inopportune moment for further visitors, but as it is a Captain Flint who has come to call, I felt I must admit him. I have put him in the drawing room. As he said he had come to see his sister, I had meant to inform Lady Flint, but as she is not here, thought it best to tell you."

"You were very right to do so," Alexander said. "Lady Flint is not to be disturbed. She has had a very trying day."

"Ah," Angelica said. "Do I take it that you made his acquaintance this morning?"

Alexander sighed. "Yes. I will tell you all about it later. Suffice it to say that the mystery of Flint's death has been solved and Nell acquitted."

"I am very glad to hear it. Go to him, my dear," Angelica said. "I will oversee things here."

"You should also be resting."

She smiled and held out a handkerchief to Bernardo. "I think myself far better equipped to deal with fainting women and sick young men than you, Alexander."

He smiled wryly. "I concede your point. I will get rid of our guest as soon as possible, however."

But the interview with the captain took longer than he would have liked. The man apologised for coming much earlier than he had intended but explained that Renn had deteriorated to such an extent that they had been asked to leave the hotel.

"I think it best that I get him back to England as soon as possible, and it is going to be a damned uncomfortable journey. However, I offered to take Nell with me, and am quite prepared to hire another coach so she need not hear his demented ravings."

"That is an extravagance you can ill afford," Alexander pointed out to him. "And is wholly unnecessary. I told you that she will travel with us."

"I would like to hear that is her wish from her own lips," the captain said. "As I told you, she is my responsibility, not yours."

"Not for much longer," Alexander said with what patience he could muster. "If we had not come upon you on the bridge, we would now be betrothed."

By the time he had persuaded the captain that Nell wished for the union as much as he but that she was too overwrought to tell him herself, that he would have the opportunity to see Nell before the wedding to confirm it, and that he had Alexander's word as a gentleman that he would take very good care of her, half an hour had passed. Even then, it took Angelica coming into the room and adding her assurances before he would take his leave.

Alexander then felt as if he needed to lie down himself and advised his grandmother to do the same.

"Yes," she said wearily, "I intend to. Signora Lonardi has taken that poor girl home, and I have had a bed made up for Bernardo; he is in no state to travel home or be by himself."

Alexander paused at the top of the landing, tempted to go to Nell, but feeling they would neither of them be thinking straight at that moment, went instead to his daughter's room. He found Mrs Farley sitting up in bed, a dazed expression on her face.

"I'm that sorry, my lord," she said. "I don't know how I came to oversleep."

"You are not well," Alexander said gently. "Go back to sleep. Timothy is with Francesca."

As if recognising her name, the babe gave a little cry. Alexander exchanged a grin with the footman and went to her cot. His daughter regarded him with sleepy eyes, burbled, and then went back to sleep.

"Go and get some rest yourself, my lord," the footman said softly. "You look quite haggard."

He needed no further encouragement. He did not intend to propose to Nell looking anything but his best. It was mid-afternoon before he awoke, and after washing and changing his crumpled clothes, he glanced into his daughter's room. Mrs Farley was up and dressed, and Francesca was sitting at her feet playing with a ball of string.

The nursemaid flushed. "I was mortified when Timothy told me what happened, my lord. I always have a glass of water by my bed, and that good-for-nothing maid must have slipped something in it."

"It was not your fault, Jane," he said. "None of us could have foreseen what happened." He glanced at Timothy, who had not yet left his post.

"You may stand down. I cannot imagine that any further drama awaits us."

He went downstairs determined to clear up any misunderstanding between him and Nell, but both the drawing room and library were empty. Coming back into the hall, he glanced at Timothy, who stood at the bottom of the stairs.

"Do you know where Maria is?" he asked. "I thought Lady Flint would be down by now."

"I'll see what I can discover, my lord," he said.

Having found that a faint but unpleasant aroma still lingered in the library, he waited in the drawing room. There was a connecting door to Angelica's bedchamber, and before Timothy returned, it opened.

"I thought I heard your voice," Angelica said. "Now, are you ready to tell me what happened this morning?"

He did so, swiftly and succinctly.

"No wonder Nell looked so worn earlier," she said. "What a shock it must have been for her." A mischievous twinkle came into her eye. "I feel for you. I think that is the second time your proposal has been left unsaid."

He smiled wryly. "You are quite correct."

Angelica chuckled. "There is nothing I would like more than for you to marry Nell, and I promise that the moment she comes downstairs, I will make myself scarce."

"Thank you," he said. "I would appreciate it."

Timothy came into the room looking quite distracted. "Lady Flint is gone, my lord. And she has taken my Maria with her."

For the second time that day, Alexander's world turned upside down.

CHAPTER 27

January 1817, Ashwick Hall, Somerset

J Nell stared out of the parlour window watching the children play in the snow. She had been at Ashwick Hall for three weeks. Her first two she had spent recovering from a six-week sea journey in one of Count Fringuello's merchant ships. He had warned her of the possibility of storms and rough seas, but it had not deterred her. Travelling back to England with Captain Flint and Renn had appealed to her as little as travelling with Alexander, and although the prospect of another sea journey had dismayed her, she had comforted herself with the thought that at least she would not be overtaken on the journey. She had been vilely ill, however, and had had reason to be grateful that Maria had insisted on accompanying her.

She jumped and gave a shaky laugh as a snowball hit the window. She had been teaching a few of the orphans to read and write for the last few days. It was a satisfying task that kept her occupied and stopped her dwelling on what might have been. Her thoughts on the journey home had nearly always started with two words: if only. If only they had not gone to the bridge that day, if only Francesca had not been taken, and if only she had not responded to Alexander's reaction so precipitously.

The last thought disturbed her the most, for it had occurred to her that her fears and insecurities might have been as much responsible for her present predicament as Alexander's. Flint had made her feel worthless and although she had felt for a few fleeting moments as if she was precious to Alexander, she had not had enough evidence to feel confident in that assertion. All it had taken was an implied accusation and a few coldly spoken words to convince herself that their fledgling relationship was doomed. She had frequently flared up at Alexander on the slightest provocation, and yet when he had done the same in a moment of extreme stress, she had given him no chance to explain or apologise.

She glanced at the group of ladies who were huddled around the fire. They ranged in age from eighteen to eighty, and all owed the roof over their heads and the food in their stomachs to the kind benevolence of Lady Westcliffe, who not only provided a home for the indigent poor but also took in penurious women of gentle birth who found them-selves in difficulty. She set no time limit on their stay at Ashwick Hall, but when she felt they were ready to move on, helped them find suitable positions else-where. In the interim, it was up to them how much or how little they contributed to the running of the orphanage in the west wing. It had its own staff, but most of the ladies helped in some way, whether it be mending clothes or bedlinen, supervising the girls as they learned household tasks, or giving extra tuition to those who were struggling with their lessons in the schoolroom.

Unlike most of her fellow residents, Nell had other options. She had written to her father, Lord Flint, and Angelica only a week ago to inform them she was safe, although she hadn't given her direction. She knew they would all put a roof over her head, but to return to Flint's estate would be to rake up a past she wished to forget, and she was a very different person to the girl who had left her father's household. She certainly did not want to go to her father whilst she was feeling so broken; he would want to know things she was not ready to tell him and she could not yet speak of Alexander, nor could she possibly live with him.

Lady Westcliffe understood that. She had visited Nell soon after her arrival, and both reassured and warned her that although all the genteel ladies in the house had a painful past, they did not speak of it until they were ready, and some not at all.

"It is necessary that I am aware of all the circumstances surrounding my ladies. That knowledge allows me to help them as best I can, particularly when it comes to placing them in a suitable post if they wish to leave. Each of you must come to terms with what has happened to you in your own way. Not only is it painful to talk about the past, but it can also be dangerous. A slip of the tongue or an unguarded comment beyond these walls about one of the residents here could have serious consequences."

It was why none of them went by their true names. Nell had reverted to Mrs Marsden for the benefit of the servants and children and was Nell to her companions.

She sighed. When Lady Westcliffe had first told her that at Ashwick Hall she would have time to heal, she had been referring to the invisible wounds her husband had inflicted. Those wounds may have left scars, but they faded into insignificance when compared to the gaping hole in her heart caused by Alexander's absence.

"Come to the fire, Nell, you will get cold, and you have only just thrown off that nasty chill you arrived with."

Nell slipped from the window seat and went to sit with the young woman who had spoken.

"I am quite recovered, Emma."

That lady briefly laid her hand on Nell's, saying softly, "No, not yet, but you will be soon, I think."

Nell blinked away tears and was grateful when the oldest occupant of the room, a white-haired old lady, who was hard of hearing, said loudly, "Her ladyship shouldn't have come until the snow cleared. She should take better care of herself."

"I hear the roads are passable now, Flora," Emma said. "The post was brought up this morning."

"I didn't realise Lady Westcliffe was expected," Nell said, surprised.

Flora frowned at her. "What's that you say? Speak up, girl."

Nell obliged her.

The old woman snorted. "She's never expected. Turns up as the fancy takes her, and it shouldn't have taken her today. But she's got a soft heart, and I expect that young man I saw her taking into her bookroom is her latest charity case."

Nell would not be at all surprised. Although only children were accommodated in the west wing, there were several barns and cottages on the property that housed young men who were trained as gardeners, grooms, or household servants.

The subject of their discussion entered the room and they all rose to their feet and curtsied, apart from Flora whose knees wouldn't allow it. She inclined her head.

"Good morning, ladies. I hope I find you well."

As the others murmured a quiet assent, Flora made her feelings known.

"Never mind us, my lady. You've got windmills in your head to come in all this snow, and so I told everyone."

Lady Westcliffe smiled. "I am sure you did, Flora."

"I expect it's all on account of that young man I saw you with. My eyes aren't what they once were and I'll admit he looked miserable, but not starving or ill. Emma will tell you the same, for she saw him too. There was no need for you to risk being caught in the snow and catching your death for him."

"Flora," she said gently, "Westcliffe Park is only five miles from here, and as you know I like to greet any new arrivals. Besides, this one is a special case and required my immediate attention."

"Dangerous, is he?" Flora asked. "If so, put Jim on to watch him; he'll sort him out."

"I doubt that will be necessary." She glanced at Nell. "Could you spare me a moment of your time, my dear?"

"Yes, of course," Nell said.

She led her to her bookroom but paused outside the door, her grey eyes serious.

"I hope you will believe me, Nell, when I tell you that all my actions concerning any person at Ashwick Hall are guided by what I believe to be in their best interests."

"Yes, I do," Nell said, her brow wrinkling. "Is this concerning the new arrival?"

Lady Westcliffe smiled. "Yes, my dear. He is very much in need of our help, and I think you might be the one to put him at his ease."

She opened the door and signalled for Nell to precede her into the room. The curtains were drawn, and the room dimly lit. The small fire glowing in the grate and the candelabrum set on the mantel above it only illuminated a few feet. Both wingchairs were unoccupied, and Nell's eyes scanned the room for the visitor. As her eyes adjusted to the gloom, she saw the silhouette of a tall man standing behind the desk. She glanced over her shoulder as the door clicked softly shut behind her and realised that Lady Westcliffe had left her alone with the stranger.

Prickles of awareness made the hairs stand up on her arms as she slowly approached the desk. The way the man held himself was familiar. She shook her head. Her mind was playing cruel tricks on her. She began to retreat as he moved around the desk and then froze as he spoke.

"Don't go, Nell."

Three simple words that were not simple at all, because each one held a depth of emotion that stopped her breath. And then he was standing before her, his eyes drinking her in as if she were a mirage he feared would disappear if he blinked. He had changed. His face was thinner, the fine lines about his mouth and between his brows deeper, and his green eyes solemn.

"No," she whispered. "I won't go."

He took a step closer and reached out a hand, tentatively curling his fingers around hers, his grasp so light the merest movement of her hand would break it.

"My grandmother said I may have given you the impression that I blamed you when Francesca was taken, but I didn't know what I was saying, Nell. I didn't mean it, and I would have explained that to you if you had not…" he briefly closed his eyes, "… had not left me."

"It was not just that," Nell said quietly. "When I asked to accompany you to the Lonardi Palazzo, you spoke so coldly to me, telling me that you neither desired nor needed my help." Her lips trembled. "Those words seemed so final, seemed to suggest that you would never desire or need my help again, that you would never forgive me." She blinked back tears. "I couldn't bear it. I couldn't bear to have you look at me in the cold way Flint used to look at me."

His fingers tightened on her hand. "Nell, I did not want you to come with me because I would not put you in danger, and if I spoke coldly, it was because I was desperately trying to control the maelstrom of emotions that were threatening to tear me apart."

He raised his other hand to her cheek and traced a line from her brow to her chin.

"Nell, my foolish darling, do you not know that you have become as necessary to me as breathing, eating, or sleeping? Have you any idea what you have put me through?"

"I can only speak of my own experience," she murmured, nuzzling her cheek into his palm. "Every day since we parted I have felt as though a part of me is missing, that the sky is grey even when the sun is shining, and sometimes my heart hurts and at other times it feels utterly empty. But perhaps it has been different for you because you have Francesca and Angelica."

"It is precisely how it has been for me," he growled, pulling her into his arms. "I love them, but it is an entirely different kind of love."

His green eyes suddenly glowed with a fierce light, and Nell felt her legs tremble.

"Is it?" she murmured. "Perhaps you had better show me how it differs."

He kissed her long and hard until her breath was coming in short gasps, her body was on fire, and her knees buckled. Then he picked her up and went to one of the chairs, settling her in his lap. She gazed up at him, her expression dazed.

"I didn't know that kisses could be like that."

He looked ruefully down at her. "Our first proper kiss should not have been like that."

"No? Then how should it have been?"

He showed her. This time kissing her slowly and gently, almost reverently. She sighed her disappointment when he raised his head.

"Is it always like that when you kiss someone you love?"

"Explain *that*," he said softly.

"That you never want it to end, and although it is pleasurable, it is not quite enough."

He smiled crookedly, a tender glow in his eyes. "I hope it is always like that for us, Nell. If you would do me the honour of becoming my wife, we will find out."

"I would very much like to be your wife," she said. "But I am a little afraid. You are so attached to Francesca—"

He laid a finger gently against her lips. "That I have left her at Eagleton Priory without even Timothy to protect her."

Nell's eyes widened. "Why?"

He smiled. "I have brought Timothy with me as he was just as eager to reclaim his love as I was, and he also wished to see his mother."

Nell blinked. "His mother?"

"He grew up at Ashwick Hall with his siblings, and his mother and one of his sisters still work here. Half a dozen of my servants have come to me on Lady West-cliffe's recommendation."

"But I thought you said you had never met Lady Westcliffe."

"I had not before today," he said. "I have corresponded with her, however. Or rather, my secretary has on my behalf. I do not hire my own servants."

Nell had been reclining against his shoulder but at

this, she sat up. "Alexander! Do not try to hoax me. It may have been your secretary who wrote the letters, but it was you who ordered him to. You hired servants from Ashwick Hall because you wish to give people who have had a difficult start in life an opportunity to better themselves."

"Perhaps," he allowed.

"And do not think to distract me. You have explained why you brought Timothy, but not why you left Francesca behind. You haven't been parted from her a night since she was born."

"I did not mean to distract you, Nell, merely to leave the most important answer to your question until last. When you left me, I realised something."

"What?" Nell breathed.

He lifted her hand to his lips and kissed it. "That my fear of losing Francesca had made me lose you, and that I had no one to blame but myself. My instinct to protect those I love will always be strong, but there is a difference between protection and suffocation. I left Francesca at Eagleton Priory to prove to myself and to you that I could. I cannot promise that I will never be an overanxious parent or possessive husband, Nell, but with you by my side to speak reason in my ear, I believe I can do better."

She raised a hand to his face and brushed a dark lock of hair from his brow. "Alexander Wraxall, are you giving me permission to rake you down whenever I deem it necessary?"

"No, minx, only when I am being unreasonable." He bent to kiss her but paused, his lips hovering above hers. "Nell, I love you, I want you, and I need you. I am quite prepared to spend the rest of my life proving it to you. Will you be mine?"

"Yes," she murmured, her lips whispering over his. "I will always be yours."

The next book will start a new series and will feature Emma. You will also hear a little more about some of the characters in this book.

ALSO BY JENNY HAMBLY

Thank you for your support! I do hope you enjoyed
Eagleton. If you would consider leaving a short review on
Amazon, I would be very grateful. I love to hear from my
readers and can be contacted at: jenny@jennyhambly.com

Other books by Jenny Hambly

Belle – Bachelor Brides 0

Rosalind – Bachelor Brides 1

Sophie – Bachelor Brides 2

Katherine – Bachelor Brides 3

Bachelor Brides Collection

Marianne - Miss Wolfraston's Ladies Book 1

Miss Hayes - Miss Wolfraston's Ladies Book2

Georgianna - Miss Wolfraston's Ladies Book 3

Miss Wolfraston's Ladies Collection

Allerdale - Confirmed Bachelors Book 1

Bassington - Confirmed Bachelors Book 2

Carteret - Confirmed Bachelors Book 3

Confirmed Bachelors Books 1-3

Ormsley - Confirmed Bachelors Book 4

Derriford - Confirmed Bachelors Book 5

ABOUT THE AUTHOR

I love history and the Regency period in particular. I grew up on a diet of Jane Austen, Charlotte and Emily Bronte, and Georgette Heyer.

I like to think my characters, though flawed, are likeable, strong and true to the period.

I live by the sea in Plymouth, England, with my partner, Dave. I like reading, sailing, wine, getting up early to watch the sunrise in summer, and long quiet evenings by the wood burner in our cabin on the cliffs in Cornwall in winter.

Printed in Great Britain
by Amazon

44796340R00209